Not Good Enough For You

A Novel
Inspired by a True Story

By: Elizabeth Lyon

Copyright © 2022 Elizabeth Lyon

All rights reserved. No portion of this book may be reproduced, stored in a retrieval system, or transmitted in any form or by any means- electronic, mechanical, photocopy, recording, scanning, or other- except for brief quotations in critical reviews or articles, without the prior written permission of the author.

Cover Copyright © Erica Doiron

To Lorelai. You are my shining beacon in the dark night. Shine bright and keep persevering.

Prologue

I can feel my body being tugged down the table; yet from my chest down, I feel nothing. I know they are working on me as I can feel my arms shake even though they are both laid out straight as if I am Jesus being crucified. I can hear my husband on my left telling me everything is going to be alright even though I am trying not to think the worst.

I hear the movements from some of the doctor's going toward the side of the room but don't hear anything else. My eyes are still closed as I don't want the thoughts invading my brain. I didn't think this would happen and am beating myself up about it. I did not want to have a cesarean. I wanted a vaginal birth for her but it seems like nothing about this pregnancy went the way I wanted it to go.

I finally hear a cry and my heart soars. I am relieved my baby girl is alive! I thought during labor I had made the wrong call and hurt her. I have been trying my hardest to ensure she would be born healthy and we would show those doctors were wrong.

I hear my husband talking to the doctors as they rattle off her measurements. I wish I could hold my baby girl but know that isn't feasible as my arms are still strapped. Now I know why they are as my arms have not stopped shaking since the surgery started.

"Would you like to see your baby girl?" someone asks me.

I turn my head to the left and see my chunky monkey. She is big and quite adorable. She lies on my left chest as I kiss her head and whisper, "Mommy loves you. Stay strong, Sookie."

After my husband takes a picture of us, Sookie is whisked toward the neonatal intensive care unit. My heart sinks as I know it's going to be a long road ahead of us and I know this is just the beginning.

This pregnancy hasn't been the easiest, emotionally or even physically, but I try to stay strong for my girl. If I don't stay strong for this family then we aren't a strong unit and I have to be strong despite not feeling it.

I know my husband left the room with Sookie as I heard his conversation with the doctors at the door. I still can't see anything even though my eyes are open and staring at the light above me.

I really hope the doctor's tightened everything inside me as I really don't want any more complications. That is the last thing I need.

"That looks good. Let's clean everything up and move her off the table."

I am not looking forward to this but I don't feel anything so at least I have that going for me. Before, I felt everything despite the epidural.

Chapter 1

I can tell something isn't right. My period is like clockwork as I take the pill. I haven't had a headache in a few days like I normally do. I don't have cramps today, which is the day my period should begin. I try not to freak out as I pull into the parking lot at work.

I take out my phone and bring up a friend whom I know can help me. I scroll down a few and click on Jackie. We bonded at work roughly two years ago as gym managers in addition to sharing a name. Although, my name is Jacqueline and her's is just Jackie. When she was hired at my previous job, I called myself Jackie One but it didn't stick as we look vastly different.

I am a bit taller than Jackie but not by much, maybe an inch. She has black hair and I have dirty blonde hair. She has a bit more of an athletic build than I do as I am a bit of a lean machine. I've been told I have manly shoulders and love it. It means my hard workouts are paying off. She has brown eyes and I have blue eyes. Dean always says he loves my eyes as they are a clear blue like the sky. I have always gotten compliments on my eyes.

Me: My period hasn't come yet. It normally comes every Wednesday in the morning.

I wait for a response and know it will come soon as she responds quickly. That's why I always go to her.

We would always vent about stuff as we both used to be managers for the same gym just at different locations. She made working there fun for me.

Jackie: Wait a day and see what happens. Has it been late before?

It has been late before. I knew she would make me feel better.

Me: Yes, a few times.

Jackie: Okay, then just wait. If it's still late then buy a test.

Me: Okay, hopefully, it comes while I'm at work.

Jackie: Are you and Dean trying?

Me: Kind of? We want a baby but he keeps saying how he wants to fix the house up more before a baby comes which I get. I just know that people are never truly ready for a baby.

Jackie: That's true. It wouldn't hurt to buy a test but just wait a day.

Me: Thanks! I need to get to work.

I put my phone on the side pouch of my lunchbox and grab that as well as my gallon water bottle. I climb out of my car and walk across the street toward work.

I wonder if I do have a baby inside me. I have always wanted to be a stay-at-home mom. I know it's not feasible as Dean and I can't live off just his salary as he is a high school teacher. Sadly, teachers get paid crap even though we encourage the young to constantly learn and fail forward.

I try not to go down that rabbit hole or I will be in a sour mood the whole day. I greet the leadership team at the door as I make my way to my toddler classroom and get settled. I have been working at a preschool, ages four months to five years old, for a little over a year now and enjoy it. I breathe in and remember when I was a kid.

I never wanted to be a mom. In fact, I never thought I would get married either but here I am married to my best friend and am the happiest I've ever been. I actually thought I would live by myself with at least six dogs and work as a screenwriter. It's crazy how life works.

My day surprisingly goes by fast. Currently, I am driving home and stuck in traffic which is typical. Traffic in Massachusetts is just dandy. I mean who doesn't love traffic? It's where I get all my thinking done. Normally, I would call Dean and talk with him during my ride home but I still can't think straight.

What if I am pregnant? I drank almost a whole bottle of wine last night as Dean surprised me with it. I had a crappy day and he bought it for me to cheer me up. Now, I feel crappy for drinking it if I am potentially pregnant.

I try not to think about it and just press the dial button on the steering wheel. I tell my car to dial Dean's cell.

"Hey honey, how was your day?"

His voice makes me feel better but also kind of nervous. I know I suck at lying so I decided to just say it.

"It was okay. I, um, well. I have something to get off my chest."

I can tell he just wants me to say it so I just blurt it out, "My period never came this morning and I don't know if I should take a test or not."

"It wouldn't hurt to take the test. Do you have one?"

"Yea, you know that ovulation kit I bought? It has a pregnancy test in it."
"Then take the test when you get home. Are you almost home?"

"I'm getting on route two so in about twentyish minutes if it doesn't get backed up due to the construction."

"Okay, how about I start some dinner as it will be almost done when you get home?"

I truly do have an amazing husband as I can hear my stomach rumble. I look at the clock and it reads five thirty-eight. I leave work at five and always get home at random times. It is never the same time which irks me. I like having a consistent schedule.

I sigh and say, "That sounds wonderful."

We say goodbye so he can start dinner and I focus on the road. Route two is always under construction. I doubt I will be home by six but a girl can hope. I try not to speed but it's quite difficult when I know I'm closer to home.

I finally pull into our driveway and grab all my stuff. I open the door and can smell something cooking. It smells like steak which makes my mouth water and my stomach grumble in anticipation.

I open the door to the kitchen and am greeted by Dean cooking steak on the stove. This is a sight I love seeing after a long day of work; especially since I've been an emotional wreck.

He comes over with a small glass of wine and says, "Even if you are pregnant it's okay to have a small glass of wine. If you are pregnant, then that's okay too. Did you want to take the test now or later?"

I look at him as if the answer is obvious, which he gets as he laughs and says, "Silly question, of course you do."
I place my stuff down on the wooden center island that we bought from Ikea years ago when we had our third apartment together. "I'm going to go upstairs."

"Okay, I will be up in a few minutes," he says and he leans in for a kiss. His touch makes me feel better instantly, but I'm still freaking out because, well, babies are expensive. Financially, I feel we aren't ready but I've always wanted to be a mom. I don't get why life has to be so difficult and so costly.

I walk through our dining room and living room to get to the stairs. As I'm taking the stairs, I'm taking deep breaths to calm myself. We both want a baby so at least I know he won't be upset about that. I just can't stop thinking about the finances. How do other families make it work; especially with one income?

I go into the bathroom and take the ovulation test strip out of the package that I got from the hallway linen closet. I read the instructions and grab a cup to pee in. Once everything is done, I place the test strip in the cup and wait.

At this point, Dean is at the top of the stairs waiting for the color to change. It changes. Holy shit. I'm freaking pregnant.

I look at Dean and say, "You want to look at it or shall I tell you the results?"

He comes and hugs me. "We're pregnant!"

I look at him and his face is pure joy. I don't see any worry in his face. I don't see anything other than happiness.

I look at him and say, "We are pregnant. Should I take another test just to confirm though? My friend from work said she took at least four tests because one said no but the others said yes."
"If that will make you feel better, then do it."

Dean is always so supportive. I hug him and breathe him in, I can smell the steak he was just cooking. I look at him and say, "Well, let's eat."

The wineglass remains untouched as it doesn't feel right to me. I want my baby to be healthy.

Chapter 2

My doctor's appointment is today and I am a bit nervous as I have no clue what to expect. How can you be truly ready to be pregnant? I feel okay about when my baby comes as I work with infants at my job but I have never been with a newborn.

I remember after taking my first test, I grabbed a Clearblue package just to make sure and had two more tests telling me I'm expecting so I don't know how the doctor's will determine that I'm pregnant. My friend at work told me it's a blood test and I hate needles. I don't know if it's just the sight of them or the painful prick that just stays with you. Everyone tells me a needle is like a bee sting but I have never gotten stung by a bee and don't plan on it. I don't like pain. I mean, who does?

I left work a little early for this appointment even though I know I should be saving my paid time off for future appointments. I get anxious about getting to places on time, and when I say on time, I mean fifteen minutes early. I hate being exactly on time. If I am on time or even a couple minutes late, I worry so much that my stomach hurts for the whole day. My husband always tells me to calm down because it makes me smell like a pig as I fart.

I listen to navigation even though I have been to this doctor's office once before. I am horrible with directions and remembering how to get to places. Dean is so much better which is why I let him drive everywhere. I also hate driving as I don't trust other drivers and have been hit a few times. Once you have been in a few accidents it makes you paranoid that it's going to happen again. One look away from the road and you smash into someone.

I attempt to stop thinking about accidents and focus on driving. My anxiety made me miss my turn so I circle back where I came from. This is why I give myself extra time because I can't think straight in new locations. I know I can be hard on myself but my navigational skills are not the best; at least I can admit it to myself and other people.

I grab my purse, a mask, and walk toward the building. I use some hand sanitizer per the instructions upon entering the building and check in. It took me an hour and change to get here so my butt hurts from driving but I don't want to be standing and making the other patients feel put off by me; especially with COVID going on.

My name is called and they take my temperature before checking my height and weight. I am proud of my weight as I weigh one hundred and thirty-eight. I used to weigh one seventy-five and was obese according to the doctor's. Once I met Dean, we started working out recreationally. I came to love working out. I try to workout at least six times a week to maintain my weight as I'm happy with my body.

The nurse ushers me into a room and grabs all the basic information and I'm sitting on the table waiting for the doctor. I feel like this is where patients do all the waiting as doctor's are never on time. I get that they have other patient's and then have to record everything but normally during the appointments they are typing most of the time so I still don't understand why they are late. It's quite bothersome as I would like this appointment to not last an hour or more and I bet they don't either.

She finally comes in and says, "Pleased to meet you Mrs. West. Congratulations on being pregnant!"

"Thank you. Will you be testing me to make sure I am pregnant?"

"That won't be necessary as you took three tests and are six weeks late according to your last missed period."

"Oh, okay. So no needles?"

"No needles! Today I will be asking a lot of questions about your health, your family history, and your husband's family history. It should take about a half hour and then you will have another appointment when you are twelve weeks along."

I sigh in relief as I was worried about the needles. She explains she is a midwife and asks about my family history first which I answer as best as I can. My mom always talks about her parent's health but my dad doesn't as much; sadly, we don't talk a lot.

"Those are all my questions. Do you have any questions?"

I try to think and have no clue what kind of questions I should be asking. This is my first pregnancy and none of my friends are pregnant. I have one friend who has kids but we don't talk much. I rack my brain and finally ask, "When will I get my first sonogram done?"

"We do sonograms at twenty weeks as that is when the baby is more developed and we try not to expose you to too much radiation."

I had no clue that sonograms had radiation. "Well, what if I'm having twins? Twins run in my family and I want to know as soon as possible if I'm having twins. Plus, I want to have a sonogram to tell my family and I don't think I can wait that long."

"If you are worried about twins then we can do the sonogram at sixteen weeks along but I wouldn't worry too much about that. Do you have any other questions or anything I should know about?"

I can't believe I'm the first one of my siblings to be pregnant. I'm the youngest in my mom's household and I know I still act like the youngest because I haven't been around my younger siblings enough to feel like a middle child. I remember them as babies and holding them. They were actually quite adorable then but I've never felt like an older sibling. They never come to me about anything but I also don't check in on them. Distance makes people forget about contacting others which is sad. I know I'm not the greatest at communicating and sometimes I just feel awkward contacting old friends or even family if it's been too long because I feel bad. I know communication is a two-way street and it's not just my responsibility but it's half of my responsibility.

As I can't think of anything else to vocalize, we say bye. I walk to my car feeling nothing. I wonder if this is normal.

I sigh as I drive home thinking of everything. I'm excited about being a mom but I am nervous. I'm nervous about being a good mom. I'm nervous I could lose my child. I'm nervous that I won't be able to fully provide for my baby or babies. I don't even know what gender I'm having.

Oh my God. A gender reveal! I definitely want to do a gender reveal party but with stupid COVID I can't do anything with more than ten people. This virus is such a damper. Hopefully, when I learn the gender, I can keep it a surprise at least. I am not the greatest at keeping secrets and Dean knows it. I know a lot of people are saying this but COVID royally sucks.

It's a week away from Christmas and I feel like I am already showing. My stomach is normally a bit flat and since I wear a lot of small shirts, it's showing a slight bump. Dean has been amazing and already bought me a pregnancy pillow that our cat is loving. Lance, our cat, loves it when we roll the pillow up like the poop emoji so he can sit atop it. Lance is such a king.
I'm trying to walk around Lance to get to the couch but he won't move out of the way.

"Lance, I swear to god, I will maul you if you don't move," I growl in frustration.

I must be hungry if I'm wanting to attempt murder on my cat. I sit down with a heavy thud and wish I had a bowl of ice cream.

Dean bought me my favorite Hood ice cream of chocolate ice cream with peanut butter chunks in it and other bits of chocolate in it during my first week of pregnancy. I actually felt sick from eating a bite of it and said no way. If I can't have chocolate throughout this whole pregnancy, I might go crazy. I love chocolate. I'm obsessed with chocolate. I need a little bit of chocolate every day to keep me sane. I'm going insane with not eating chocolate. I feel off balance. I can't remember going this long without chocolate.

Thinking of Dean makes me wonder where he is in this house. I have heard him walking around but I don't see or hear him on the first floor. He must be in the basement thinking of his next move on what to do for one of the renovations he is doing.

He has been working on our downstairs bathroom as our toilet broke a while ago and I decided we should just renovate the whole thing. Our house was built in the 1940s so it needs quite a bit of work but I love the character. Yet, the bathroom Dean is working on was the worst out of all the rooms in the house. I'm glad he is currently working as I'm lounging on the couch.

I'm scrolling through Etsy as I want to give my mom a t-shirt about our pregnancy as well as Tracy, Dean's mom. I know they both will love it. The thing is Tracy is coming over today and I don't want her to suspect anything but I've been feeling crappy. I'm tired and my stomach has been going crazy.
"Dean?!" I make sure I'm loud enough and my voice is crazy enough for him to come running.

I'm on our couch in the living room and I believe he is working on the bathroom which is on the same level just through the dining room that is adjacent to the guest bedroom where the bathroom is located.

"Yea?!" He is definitely downstairs in the basement.

"When are your parents coming over? I don't want your mom suspecting anything and I feel really queasy."

Dean walks into the living room wearing his cargo pants and no shirt. I love it when he wears no shirt. He knows I objectify him. If he didn't weightlift every day and had a gut I may not objectify him, but I do. He works hard at the body he has and I'm just appreciating the view.

He looks at his watch and says, "In about fifteen minutes. Why? Do you need something?"

"I feel like crap and my stomach is just going haywire."

"Okay, let me check to see if we have ginger ale in the basement."

He goes through the kitchen and down toward the basement. I hear him open and close the fridge and come up short handed. Our floors are very thin as I can always hear him walking around upstairs when I'm downstairs, or vice versa. It makes me worried about having sex when our baby is born. I try not to think that way as our sex life is good, at least for me.

"Sorry honey. Do you want me to go out and get some?"

"Would you mind? I really don't want your mom to guess."

"She won't. Trust me. She probably won't think anything of it."

"Are you sure? She is smart and knows you best."

"I promise. I'm going to the store now before she comes and will be back. Do you want anything else? Maybe an ice cream sandwich?"

That does sound good right about now. It's the right amount of chocolate and vanilla. Right now, I have been craving vanilla and wanting those Oreo ice cream sandwiches.

"That sounds amazing. Can you get those Oreo ice cream sandwiches? I saw them in a Christmas movie yesterday and I've been craving it since. Thanks honey!"

Dean gets his shoes on and goes out the front door. I try to find Lance to see if moving helps my stomach. It doesn't. I still want to know where our cat is so I go upstairs as he loves the office where he likes to sit on the hassock or lie on the carpet. I don't see him so I go to the door on my left,

in the hallway, which is where the nursery is going to be. I look in and see the work that Dean is doing here. The office and nursery both have wood paneled walls which we both love but the walls need lots of work. The family before us carved things into the walls and one of them is about Harry Potter. Whoever those kids were, they at least have their heads on straight about Harry
Potter. Dean is currently sanding down the walls to even them out and lighten it up. He is already doing such an amazing job. However, no sign of Lance. I sigh and walk toward our bedroom and still no Lance. Our cat has good hiding skills, but our house has lots of hiding spots.

I walk back downstairs and plop onto the couch. I pick up the book I was reading but my mind isn't into it anymore.

I've been getting a bit moody with my cravings and it throws me off. I also have been extremely tired no matter how much sleep I get. Dean has been great by letting me rest as he does the house renovations. I do pitch in by cleaning and doing laundry as those are the two things I love doing. The rest I leave up to him.

I hear the front door open and a "Hello?!"

Crap. Tracy and Pete are here. We haven't told them about me being pregnant and I'm waiting for a cute t-shirt for Tracy to break the news. Dean does not like this idea and wants to tell them but I want it to be a surprise. He has been amazing throughout this whole experience so far and letting me call most of the shots.

I get up and walk to the kitchen, "Hey Tracy!" I try to sound upbeat and look energetic even though I don't feel either.

I walk back toward the living room and plop back down on the chair this time so Tracy and Pete can have the couch. They trail behind me and I hear Tracy put her purse on one of the dining room chairs.

"How are ya?" Tracy inquires as she sits on the couch as Lance scurries upstairs from wherever he was.

Lance does not like Tracy as she "tortures" him by playing with him. Lance is never entertained with her except when he hisses at her and bats at her hands.

I'm not entirely sure how to respond so I tell her I'm doing okay but have a stomach ache. I cover my stomach with a blanket just in case and hope I'm being inconspicuous. Dean always says I'm an open book but this is something I want to keep a secret as it's so exciting; not just for me but for everyone.

"Oh, I'm sorry to hear that. Where's Dean?"

Pete says very little but when he does talk, he normally adds knowledge to the conversation. I think he just likes to be in his own world and when he is needed he will help...occasionally. I'm the same way so I get it.

"He went out to get ginger ale for my stomach ache."

As I'm saying this, I hear the front door open and the door from the entryway open as well. Our house is a maze and when people come over, they always get confused. I personally love our house. When I saw it for the first time, I fell in love with the crown molding and built-ins. The rooms with the paneled walls were a nice touch. Two of the bedrooms have porthole windows which give off a cool vibe. The nursery has one huge built in with a cupboard that a little kid would love to hide in. I love our house despite all the work it needs.

Tracy gets up to go to the kitchen to greet him and I want to stay but don't want to give anything away so I get up begrudgingly. Everyone knows I'm all about getting my steps in.

"I got the ice cream sandwiches like you said," Dean says proudly.

They are indeed ice cream sandwiches and not the Oreo ones that I thought I requested. I swear I asked for the Oreo ones.

"Did they not have the oreo ones?" I just have to ask.

Dean looks dejected at my question and says, "I thought you wanted ice cream sandwiches. These looked good and were on sale."

I take one as I'm hungry and bite into it. It isn't what I wanted and it tastes too chocolatey for my liking. I really hope this weird craving goes away because I'm going to miss my chocolate flavors.

"How is it?" Dean looks at me and I don't want to hurt his feelings but I'm just not feeling it.

"It's not what I expected." Hopefully that won't hurt his feelings but it does. I always suck at getting my point across with him even though he knows me better than my mother. I feel like Dean lives inside my head sometimes as we say the same thing at the same time. We are oddly similar yet vastly different. It makes us great together.

I walk back to the living room and sit in the chair. Dean comes in and sits on the floor and starts talking about the renovations he is doing in the downstairs bathroom with his dad. I hope he gets it done before the baby is due in August because he always piles too much on his plate.

His mom keeps looking at me but I have nothing to say and am honestly so tired that I look at Dean, even though I'm not invested in his conversation.

"How is work Mrs. Jacqueline?"

Tracy loves to say my full name as I think, she thinks it irks me but I love my name. Jacqueline Marie West. I think it has a nice ring to it and Dean's last name fits perfectly at the end.

I'm hoping I have a girl but since Dean is betting it's a girl, I have to side with a boy. I'm obsessed with Gilmore Girls and Sookie is my favorite character so I want to name my daughter Sookie. I mean, how many Sookie's do you know? It's not a common name which is what I want; an uncommon name.

"It's going well. I got my original pay back."

After being home during the whole stay at home mandate due to COVID, my pay dropped. I wasn't too worried once I started working again because I love working with kids.

Some people aren't cut out for kids but I love them. I was working with the one-and-a-half year olds but once I went back to work after the mandate, management put me with infants as support staff. Since the drive is about an hour and the pay is so so, I wasn't too thrilled but I knew it was temporary. I also figured that someone wouldn't be happy with the job they were assigned. I figured if I just did what I needed to and talked to adorable babies, I would most likely get what I want.

In just a week I was asked if I was okay with full time and I happily obliged. I was working with infants six to twelve months and absolutely loved it. It gave me baby fever and I'm now brimming with happiness to have my own. I was the only teacher with three kids and despite how crazy it could get, I always kept a smile on my face and sang. I would literally sing what I was doing to the kids and they loved it.

Apparently if you sing to your kids and make sure they are happy, well fed, and learning the curriculum you wrote then you get a raise. I also don't complain because working with babies is fun and I don't mind being by myself.

"That's excellent! Good for you. Anything else new?"
I swear she knows because she keeps asking me questions but I just say no.

The men are in the bathroom starting the project. Dean and I had taken the tiles off the floor together. It was a great way to destress by hammering away and tugging at the tiles. Dean had to get the tiles in the corners as those were tricky for me.

"What workout program are you doing?"

I'm an avid workout junkie but workout from home. I wake up at four in the morning, hit TV power, select my workout, and sweat. Despite being a personal trainer, I hate having to come up with workouts; especially short ones.

"I'm in between right now as I'm not sure which one I want to commit to."

I know working out is good during pregnancy but I've gotten lazy and haven't done anything in a while.

Tracy looks at me, making me feel weird. I feel like I have to say more. "I honestly haven't gotten up in time to workout so it's been a while. How are your group classes?"

When I was a gym manager at the local gym in her town, she signed up and fell in love with Zumba. It helped both of us as my gym desperately needed new members. Being a manager was not my thing as I did not like working six to seven days a week, or working overtime and not getting compensated for it. Once Dean and I got engaged it was too much for me. Whenever I hired someone, the person didn't like the pay even though I had no say in their pay rate. I would always talk to my manager about the pay but it was never my decision. Another task I was not fond of as a manager, was constantly cold calling people who weren't interested in a membership even though the company had a five call policy. I felt like a debt collector at times.

"It's going great! Due to the virus, we are doing it through Zoom so I Zumba my way around the house at times."

That must be an entertaining site to see. I'm curious if her two dogs dance with her. I giggle at the thought. "That sounds fun!" I too dance around my house and love it.

I'm getting hungry, again, and a bit bored. I don't know how long they are staying for but Dean doesn't tell me details about visits even though he knows I want them.

I walk toward the bathroom and try to pull him aside into the kitchen which is semi successful since we are in the dining room.

"How long are your parents staying?"

"I don't know. Does there have to be a time limit?" I give him a pointed look. "Well, I need some answers from my dad about the bathroom, so maybe an hour?"

I sigh and say okay. It's going to be a long day.

Chapter 3

I should have gotten myself a shirt that says "I can't keep calm, I'm going to be a mom" because my emotions go from happy to sad to mad to happy in a span of a minute.

I'm just a day away from twenty weeks and will finally get my first ultrasound. I'm at work and can't even think straight. How can I think about getting a four-month-old to touch paint in a Ziploc bag? I want to see my baby!

Just one more day. One more day and I can finally have my ultrasound! I also did the lab tests for Spina bifida as well as Down syndrome for my baby. I sucked it up and did the blood work. I was hoping to have the results by now because the blood test will tell me the gender of the baby. I'm not doing so well with waiting for the gender of my baby or seeing my baby for the first time.

I haven't heard anything from my doctor since I did the blood work but I am excited to see my baby tomorrow. I would be devastated if my little one had Down syndrome like me. In general, it's always been challenging. At school I didn't have the support I needed. School was challenging due to my poor short-term memory.

Not that I'm not as smart as I think I am. However, I had to work extremely hard as my short-term memory is not the best. I like to say my memory is like the girl in the movie Fifty First Dates. Math is the worst for me. If I can't apply something to what I know then I won't remember, so math goes in one ear and out the other.

I at least made it this far in my life and went to college and graduated in Health Education with a minor in English. I've always thought of being a gym teacher as I love working with kids. Their energy and curiosity is what I want my kid to have. The sense of wonder kids have as they view our world is beautiful. Unfortunately, our world is a germ fest right now. I hope our baby stays healthy in this world. I place my hand on my stomach and can't wait to meet our precious infant.

It's been a whirlwind getting to twenty weeks. I switched doctors because Dean went with me to see the baby at fourteen weeks. We both weren't thrilled. Not only did I repeat myself a lot at the doctor's office, but I remembered that I never mentioned I have Mosaic Down syndrome. According to tests my mom had, I have a percentage of cells with Down syndrome. My doctor had never heard of it and had to Google it. That was the red flag for both of us.

Ellie, my sister-in-law, did some research and saw that the hospital in our town is ranked high in the northeast region so I transferred to a practice there. Best decision yet because when I met my doctor, he wasn't thrilled that I never had certain tests done such as the urine test. I never had to undress at the family practice for any matter, yet at the hospital I had to so he could check my cervix. Now I feel like I'm being properly cared for.

When I told my new doctor about my diagnosis of mosaic Down syndrome, he knew exactly what I was talking about and even brought in a genetic doctor to go over any questions I may have, which wasn't many. The genetic doctor explained that my daughter may have a high percentage of having Down syndrome and explained mitosis of all things. I'm happy I looked into the hospital that Ellie referred me to.

If it weren't for Ellie, I wouldn't feel so well cared. Ellie has been a godsend. The best part is that she's pregnant too! I accidentally stole the thunder from her and my brother Matt. They were going to tell my family about their pregnancy during Christmas! She's a month ahead of me and has an ultrasound picture that I'm jealous of. She has been to a few appointments and Matt was able to go to one with her.

I wish Dean could come with me to my appointments but sadly there are many restrictions due to COVID. The hospital I'm at says he can only come to one ultrasound when I'm in my second trimester. Being pregnant during a pandemic royally sucks. There really is no other way to describe it.

Ellie told me that Matt isn't able to go to any more appointments. How can first time parents experience the joy of seeing their baby for the first time and not share that moment?

I look at the babies I'm with now and can't wait for tomorrow morning. It's almost time for me to leave and, as I support two classrooms, I make sure the teachers don't need anything.

I head toward the exit of the school and I hear a chorus of "Bye Jackie, drive safe!"

The leadership team is amazing here. I've never felt so supported at a job before and am glad I work here. I just wish it wasn't so far away. The drive has been getting to me lately as I'm always needing to pee.

I realize I forgot my gallon of water and walk back in. I punch my code into the door and hear, "Back so soon?"

I see the principal and say, "I just can't stay away!"

I walk into the last room I was in and see no kids and my friend picking up. We worked together as co-teachers but then with a mishap on my behalf my friend became the teacher of my old room. To be honest, she's a great teacher with her energy and creativity. She just lacks a bit of confidence and self-esteem.
"Jackie! I thought you left?"

"I did but I forgot this," as I hold my jug up.

"I don't know how you drink all that."

"I've been doing it for a few years. Now I feel sluggish when I don't drink this much water!"

"Well, drive safe! Text me later."

Sasha has been amazing. Sometimes our ages clash as I'm six years older than she is, but I also don't feel thirty. I also don't look thirty years old as some people look at me and think I'm twenty-five.

As I leave, I say bye as I don't think I did before. I think I'm free as someone asks, "You have your first ultrasound tomorrow, right?"

I look and it's the whole leadership crew. "Yes! Bright and early too so I should hopefully be here for ten."

"We have you down for coming in then but let us know if you will be late. We know things happen!"

This is why I love them. They get that life happens.

"I definitely will!"

"Have a good night, Jackie!"

I walk out the doors again and to my car. Looking at my green Kia Soul, I call the guac box. I wonder if I should think of getting a family car. My car is spacious and is safe. It did save me when my car slid on black ice getting onto the highway. I was just an inch away from hitting the median and felt as if I had a mini heart attack. The only thing my car needed was a realignment of the tires.

Dean would say something about my Kia Soul and since he hasn't, I shouldn't worry. He wouldn't put me or the baby in harm's way.

———

Today is the day! I'm not exactly twenty weeks pregnant as that is tomorrow but I get to see my baby for the first time...and know the gender! I honestly think I'm having a girl but don't want Dean to know I'm siding with him. I've always wanted a girl so we can be best friends like Lorelai and Rory from *Gilmore Girls*. I'm so happy that I almost walk into a sign.

As I have no clue where radiology is I'm looking overhead to guide myself. I'm so nervous I keep touching my face and I'm basically running. When I'm nervous I'm in overdrive. I speed everything up which isn't good as when I'm driving my foot just keeps pressing down on the gas. With being pregnant I can't do that. I have to stay calm as my baby feels everything I do.

I take a breath as I finally see radiology. Oh my God, finally! I check myself in and take a seat. I look at everyone coming in and just have an anxious feeling in my stomach. I place my hand on my stomach and hope to feel my baby. I can't wait to feel a movement.

"Jacqueline West?"

Someone is standing next to me and I say "Yes, that's me!" I jump up and follow her into a room.

She tells me to lift my shirt to my bra and pull my pants slightly down. I'm a little embarrassed that I'm wearing pregnancy pants as I'm not really showing. Pregnancy pants are just very comfortable!

I try to relax on the hospital bed but she sticks the gel on the doppler and puts it on my stomach which makes me tense. I look at the screen. I see movement and instantly feel tears fill in my eyes. Why am I crying? I can't have this stranger see me cry! I blink furiously as I look at the screen.

She asks me all sorts of questions - whether it's my first, it is, and what I do for work. She asks if I want to know the gender and I say yes and nod my head.

"It's a girl. Do you have a name?"

I let out a breath I didn't realize I was holding and shed a tear. "Sookie."

"That's a beautiful name. How did you get that name?"

"I'm obsessed with Gilmore Girls and I also wanted a unique name."

"Is your husband okay with that name too?"

"He is. His only objection was no food, flower, month, or season for a name."

The technician laughs and keeps taking pictures. Sookie is moving yet I barely feel a thing. I look from the screen to my stomach just picturing her. She keeps to my right side and is moving her head and feet.

The tech seems to be having issues getting pictures of her head since Sookie has been rolling. She asked me to empty my bladder twice which didn't help and even made Sookie move to the other side. The tech put my head at a decline which also didn't work. Now, I'm on my left side which also doesn't seem to be working to get a clear picture of Sookie's head.

"I'm going to have to get these pictures vaginally, would you mind changing out of your pants and underwear please?"

I'm glad I shaved my legs recently as that would be awkward for me.

I'm in the hospital gown she gave me and I get back on the bed. She puts more gel on the doppler and sticks it up my vagina and takes some pictures. This just feels weird but soon I'm going to have a human come out this way so I have to get used to this.

"All set! I have all the pictures I need. I'm going to print those adorable pictures of Sookie so you can show your husband."

Oh. My. God. I just realized I will know something he doesn't for once and can surprise him with the gender. I have to think of a special way to surprise him! He loves motorcycles but I want it to be a joint thing we love which means hiking, snowboarding, and movies.

Harry Potter! I already told him if it's a boy I wanted that to be our baby shower theme and Gilmore Girls if it's a girl, so I can surprise him by switching it.

I quickly go onto Etsy as I walk toward my doctor's office near the front of the entrance. I check in but they usher me into a room right away. Thankfully, I can sit and look at how I can surprise him. I can't keep secrets for long so this gift has to get here pronto.
The cutest thing I found is a cauldron where I add pink bubbles to the pot and it boils over revealing the gender. Hopefully it's simple so I can surprise him and not have to ask for his help.

I look at the time and it's past nine which means I'm going to be late for work. I'm starting to get nervous as I hate being late, yet my first time here he didn't make me wait.

I decided to wait five minutes and text my friend Jackie. I don't tell her the gender which is extremely hard. How do people keep secrets?! I like to say I can keep secrets but I don't know if I can do this. This is driving me crazy and it's only been a couple of minutes.

He still isn't in here and it's been five minutes. I know if I don't leave now, I definitely will be late. I quickly text work letting them know my doctor is running behind and I will hopefully be thirty minutes late.

The place I love working at is fifty miles away. My mom always tells me how she drove into another state for work when I was younger and you sometimes have to do things you don't like in order to get what you want. I get what she's saying but I don't have to like it.

I groan as I don't know what to do. I'm wanting to leave so I can get to work but I also know I need to stay put. I poke my head out at the door and see my doctor standing at the desk.

"I'll be in, in a few minutes. I'm looking at the ultrasounds," my doctor states. He doesn't look happy and I start to worry.

Chapter 4

"Your baby has Down syndrome."

The doctor came in not too long ago and sat down since I stuck my head out the door asking for him as he was reviewing the pictures.

At first, I feel like I'm being punked but then I look at his face. I'm still. I don't want to show how upset I am because once I do, I know the tears won't stop. Once I cry, the tears will keep coming. I just can't stay strong once I get bad news.

Why?! Why me? I wanted my baby girl to be strong and healthy. I wanted her to live a long life with no health complications or labels. If she has one hundred percent Down syndrome, she could have many health problems throughout her life.

I also don't want doctors labeling. I want her to be treated equally, but now will she? How can she grow up and be a happy, normal child? I remember being young and feeling so different. I felt as if other kids knew what I had and shunned me for it.

Stay calm. Be cool. Breathe in and out. I can't really breathe with this mask on, damn it.

"You seem very calm with the news I just gave you. Do you have any questions?" The doctor asks with concern laced in his voice.

I can't trust my voice as I'm not calm so I shake my head to answer his question.

"I contacted a specialist and will be referring you to UMass Medical in Worcester. They have a Down syndrome clinic and will be able to follow your journey there."
I nod to acknowledge I'm listening. I just can't trust myself to talk but I have to know. "How do you know?"

"Your blood test came back and it was positive for Down syndrome, however that isn't conclusive since you have mosaic Down syndrome. It could be either of you so I would suggest getting an amniocentesis. Another indicator of my prognosis is your sonogram. She has some fluid in the brain which isn't normal. It's quite high at the moment and will need to be closely monitored."

I can't control my emotions anymore and the tears start flowing despite my attempts to stay strong and calm. I hate myself so much right now. I hate myself for crying in public and not being healthy for my baby girl.

My Sookie. If she has Down syndrome hopefully it is mosaic just like me. It's not that I'm against anyone having Down syndrome, but people judge. People stare. Kids will point and will say what's on their minds. None of that is fair to anyone.

As I grew up, I was on an individual education plan, IEP, and had to be in special classrooms for certain subjects. For English, science, and history I was mainstreamed. My childhood was okay growing up but it was more me who couldn't get over being different than everyone else. I hated that I needed extra help. I still hate how it takes me forever to learn a new skill because I can't just pick something new up quickly. I have to do something repetitively to remember it. That's why with math I can never remember anything, except the nine timetables as I do the hand trick.

My body starts to tremble so I don't bawl my eyes out. It seems as if all the bad things I did in my life are throwing it in my face by saying: your daughter will have a complicated life. I feel like such a failure. I should have prevented this.

The doctor hands me a tissue and says, "If you have any questions before UMass contacts you, please reach out to us. You should hear from them today."

I nod my thanks and try to control my emotions. I try to breathe, but my mask is now soaked with snot.

The doctor steps out of the room so I pull my phone out to use the mirror to see how horrible I look. I know I'm an ugly crier. When I cry my face gets all red. It seems as if the mask will cover most of it and if I put my sunglasses on no one will know.

I head out and keep my head down. I can't stop the thoughts running in my head. Fluid in the brain. I don't know much about all the health complications that come with having Down syndrome, but I'm going to learn. I can't just give up on my baby girl.

I can't believe this is happening to us. How can I be such a horrible mom already? How can I have let this happen to my baby? Thinking these thoughts make me choke on a sob as I walk to my car.

As I climb into my car I cry uncontrollably as the tears come down my face and I just can't stop. The tears are coming out like a waterfall. My sister would be proud as she would always say, cry me a river. I'm definitely crying a river now. I can't stop the tears and I rip my mask off and just cry with my head on my steering wheel.

I don't know how I can calm down. I can't help but think how I can be such a terrible mother.

I take my phone out and google the school Dean works at. I dial the number and ask to speak with him. I'm hoping my voice isn't cracking or sounds like I'm crying.

"Hello." I tune the woman's voice out for a moment so I can focus on my breathing. I need to sound strong to a stranger right now. "How may I help you?"

"I'm calling for Dean West." I hope I sound somewhat normal and not like I cried my heart out.

"Hang on, sweetie. Let me page him for you."

"Thank you." My mom would be proud that I'm using my manners when I'm distraught.

"Hello?"

Dean. He is going to be so disappointed in me. Would he leave me because Sookie has Down syndrome? Would he blame me as well?

I choke as I try to breathe while weeping, again.

"Jackie? Hey. What's wrong? Talk to me honey."

I don't know how to tell him. What will he think of me?

"Our baby has Down syndrome." Finally, I said it.

I'm still crying as he tells me that it's okay as we will get through this together. He doesn't mention leaving me or asking me to get rid of our baby. He told me what I wanted to hear.

I'm nodding my head even though he can't see me. My voice comes out small, "Okay. Thanks. They are referring me to UMass in Worcester."

"That's one of the best hospitals so I'm glad our baby will get the attention it needs. This isn't the end of the road. We will get through this together."

He is making me feel somewhat better but I still can't believe this is happening to us.

"Do you need me? Are you going to work? It might help you calm down."

I completely forgot to call work. I know I need to call them but I just can't think of them right now.

"I can't go to work. I'm just going to look at my kids and hope our baby will be just like them. Strong and healthy...and normal."

I hate myself for saying that but I've struggled with not being normal myself. I don't want my girl to have insecurities like me.

"Do you need me to come home?" Dean asks, always being so sweet.

Of course, I want him home with me but I don't want to sound weak. I don't want to sound needy. Tears well up in my eyes again and I blink rapidly to dispel the tears.

"No...you need to work. You hate taking any time off."

It's true. He never calls out and even goes into work when he doesn't feel well. Dean rarely gets sick. When he does get sick he just goes into work and works through it. All of his paid time off and sick time doesn't go into his paycheck at the end of the year and it doesn't roll over, so I think he's nuts.

"I would do anything for you, Jackie. If you need me throughout the day just text me. I will respond and just let my boss know we got some news about the baby and you need me."

Tears spring to my eyes but I blink rapidly so I don't cry anymore. I don't know how I got so lucky to be with him. Even though I walked into a bar and sat next to him didn't mean we would end up marrying each other but it did. I'm glad I walked into that bar. I'm glad he chose me to be with him.

We say goodbye and I look at the time. It's a little after ten in the morning and I'm emotionally drained. I feel like I should go into work but I don't want to be an emotional wreck whenever I look at my kids. I'm a teacher and need to have positive energy which will definitely not be happening today. I hate calling out but I need to take a mental health day.

I try to breathe but to no avail. I dial work still crying like a lunatic in my car.

Maria picks up and I ask to speak with Olive, the assistant principal. Dean made a horrible joke when I told him my boss's name but he always makes dad jokes. He said, "What kind of olives do I like? Olive them."

Thinking of his jokes makes me choke out a cry.

"Hey Jackie, how did your appointment go?"

Breathing does absolutely nothing for me so I try to be audible. "Not so great. I got some news that I'm not dealing well with. I don't like doing this but can I take a personal day?"
Our school is a bit short-staffed due to COVID. Calling out would mean a shift in floating teachers or someone from the leadership team stepping in.

"Oh no. I hope everything is okay. Take the time you need. Will you need tomorrow off too?"

"No. I just need to accept my baby's diagnosis and I'm expecting a few calls as I'm getting referred to another hospital."

"If you need anything, let us know. Thank you for calling."

I can't tell if she's disappointed I'm not coming in or not, but I'm relieved to go home and get into comfortable clothes.

I pull into our driveway and think that I will miss being able to drive just a couple minutes to my appointments.

As I walk into our house, the tears come again. I hate myself for not being strong enough. How could I have let myself do this to our child? My vision is blurry as I almost trip up the stairs.

I am wondering where Lance is. I could definitely use some cuddles right now. Thankfully, he is lying on our bed and his eyes look at me. Lance doesn't even lift his head, just watches me with his yellow eyes.

I pick him up. "Oh Lance. I really need some love so please don't scratch me."

Lance will only take forced cuddles for a millisecond and then will make an annoyed meow and bite you. He is a feisty cat and hates most people. He hisses at everyone and then walks away. He thinks it scares other people but it makes me chuckle. Lance thinks he owns this house.
I've never had a cat before but Dean wanted one when we lived in our last apartment. It took me a while to relent and I'm glad I did. Lance cuddles with me and plays with Dean; it's a good combination.

Lance purrs in my arms. I give him a kiss as I set him back on the bed, not wanting to force it longer. Dean left his pjs on the bed so I decide to put those on.

Dean told me to call my mom as she went through the same experience just thirty years ago. He has a point but I hate crying in front of my mom. The only person I'm comfortable crying in front of is Dean.

My mom has seen me cry. However, she's a strong woman that I feel I have to be as well. She took care of my older siblings and me most of our lives. She rarely showed me anything but happiness. I always knew she was sad at times but growing up I knew nothing about stress and anxiety.

I learned about stress and anxiety when we lived in our last apartment and my last job. I was twenty-eight when I learned about stress and anxiety.

I've known about sadness my whole life though. I've known about feeling alone my whole life. I know I'm not alone but I feel it right now.

I didn't expect my pregnancy to be flawless but I wasn't expecting this. I know I have to stay positive for Sookie since she can feel my emotions but it's difficult.

I look into the body length mirror in our bedroom and place my right hand on my belly. I try to connect with Sookie.

"I will do anything I can for you to be happy and healthy."

I grab my phone that I threw onto the bed and head downstairs. I don't know what to do but I know Dean is right.

I call my mom not knowing what to expect. My mom picks up and instantly asks how my appointment went.

With a shaky breath I say, "Our baby was diagnosed with Down syndrome."

I hear my mom's voice grow thick and know it hit her. She tells me how she had an amniocentesis as well as a PUBS test when she was pregnant with me. She doesn't get into any feelings, just the science from thirty years ago.

"I'm sorry you're going through this. I know it must be hard and I'm sorry my genes passed to you which ultimately went to your baby. Did you learn the gender at least?"

She knows I've been anxious wanting to know the gender and I tell her I'm not telling anyone, not even Dean. She actually laughs at me and tells me good luck with that. I like to think I'm okay with keeping secrets. I kept my sister's surprise birthday party a secret for two full weeks.

I'm at a loss of words right now. I'm about to say goodbye when my mom says, "I feel I'm to blame that you're going through this. I wish you weren't going through this but you are. If you need me to be with you today, I will come up."

My mom and I are close. I even called her my best friend in high school. Throughout college I stopped communicating with her as much. Once I met Dean I spent a lot of time with him at his family's house. My mom was a bit hurt by it, especially since I didn't talk with her a lot. Ever since she knew I stayed at Dean's, things have been a bit different since she feels I replaced her. How can you replace your own mother? I could never do that but I can't change how my mom feels. I can only keep telling her I love her.

Unfortunately, whatever I say to connect with her doesn't work. As she gets older, I worry about her being alone. She stays very active by walking with friends and going to museums. However, when I talk to her it seems she forgets bits and pieces of what we talked about previously. I don't know if it's just me but I worry about my mom's health.

I see a number I don't know calling me and I tell her I have to go. It's UMass scheduling a sonogram and amniocentesis. I'm grateful they called so soon as I can schedule both after work.

Chapter 5

It's the day of my sonogram and amniocentesis, and holy halibut, I'm terrified. I'm not good with needles and Dean can't be with me due to COVID regulations. He said he would go to the hospital regardless so I will see him when I get out. I told him that was thoughtful but not necessary.

I wish I had said yes. One, I hate driving in Worcester. Two, new places give me anxiety about not knowing where to go. Three, I have a needle going into my abdomen tonight. I shudder at the thought.

I cannot think about needles right now as I turn into the hospital entrance and up the hill toward the parking garage. I roll down my window to grab a parking ticket. I drive in and don't have to drive very far to find a spot as it seems coming here at five at night is the best time. As I park, I take a deep breath to calm my nerves.

I place a hand on my stomach and say, "We always have to do things out of our comfort zone Sookie. In order to grow, you have to do things you may not want to do. Right now, Mama does not want a needle in me but I have to, to learn more about us."

I've been trying to talk to her more as she is growing and growing more rapidly than I thought. It's crazy how time has flown since I found out I was pregnant.

I shake my head in wonderment of the human body. I'm walking through the hospital and follow the signs. I somehow made it to the right place without having to ask for help. I call that a victory in my book. I'm glad I'm wearing a mask because I've been whispering to Sookie this whole time about my random thoughts.

It's just me in the waiting room plus the receptionist who checked me in. I'm unsure of what to do and know I can't keep talking to Sookie.

I take my phone out to let Dean know I made it. I contemplate whether to bring up social media or not, and decide against it. I'm so on edge that my mind is racing for once. I wonder if this is what it's like in Dean's mind. He has ADD and says he thinks of many things all at once.

Thankfully a tech comes in and calls my name. I'm a bundle of nerves as I walk across the hall to get my tests done. I remember to breathe as I lay down and situate myself.

The tech gets to work and rambles on about something as I'm half paying attention. I'm staring up at the screen mesmerized by how adorable Sookie already is.

"When will I feel her movements?"

"It depends. Everyone is different but I bet you will feel her soon."

There is a pause and the tech continues. "I didn't feel my baby till I was at least twenty-four weeks pregnant. My baby was delayed, so they say, in developing but now my son is four years old and giving me a run for my money!"

I have worried about Sookie ever since I heard she may have Down syndrome but I try to push my worries aside. It's hard to push my worries aside because with Down syndrome there will be many challenges for her and our family; medically and emotionally.

"It looks like your girl already has some hair!"

I look closer and realize she does have some hair on her head. "I didn't realize babies can grow hair this young."

"Babies in utero are so impressive. I still see things that I didn't know could happen. Would you like to see your baby in 3D?"

I don't know how different that can be but once she switches, I can't stop staring at the screen on the wall. Sookie is perfectly content with her hands by her face. It actually seems like she is sucking her thumb. I wish I could touch my stomach to feel her move.

The tech is done taking pictures and says she just needs to have her supervisor look at the pictures. I know I'm not done as I still have the amniocentesis testing, but I think I'm more ready now then I was before my appointment.

It isn't the tech who comes back but someone else. She tells me her name but I completely forget as she says they found some things out. It doesn't sound good and I'm anxious to hear what she has to say.

"I reviewed your ultrasound and there are some things I wanted to bring up. Your daughter has what's called a complete AV canal defect. She has a hole that shouldn't be there and the size is a bit concerning. I'm putting a cardiologist on your team to monitor it.

"I also saw a few other fetal anomalies such as her right kidney. It appears to be dilated and not draining. We won't know for sure how severe that is without further testing. She also has an abnormal amount of amniotic fluid, as well as, her stomach being extremely small for her gestational age.

"Your daughter could have many more health risks throughout your pregnancy and with the known risks she may not make it. Are you thinking of continuing your pregnancy?"

I look at her as if she's a lunatic. Why wouldn't I keep her? I know she told me so many health issues but I'm not going to let that stop me. I'm going to fight for Sookie no matter what. Sookie may have some issues but she is still healthy nonetheless. She isn't in distress, or at least, it doesn't seem like it. As I became a sports nutritionist a couple years ago, I know the importance of food and the effects it has on our bodies. I'm going to change my diet dramatically and show this doctor that us Wests can prove anyone wrong.

"Of course, I am. I too have mosaic Down syndrome and am perfectly healthy." Even though I have had many issues with my ears.

"Do you have a significant other?"

"Yes. Dean wanted to be here especially since it's difficult for me to remember all the details in certain situations; this being one of them."

"As you want to continue your pregnancy, he can come to all ultrasounds. This way when there are more findings you both will know. Since this is all new would you like me to write some of this down so you both can talk?"

"That would be great, thank you. I also was told I would be having an amniocentesis done today."

"Yes, you were supposed to, however those are done before five so whoever booked your appointment screwed that part up."

"When I scheduled the appointment, I told her anything after five works best for me." I can't believe I'm not having it done but I'm also happy that I can have Dean with me at least.

"As your daughter's health is important, I suggest we schedule it for tomorrow morning. This way we can have the results on Monday and you and your husband can meet with a genetic counselor with any questions you may have. Plus, we recommend patients go on bed rest for at least twenty-four hours after the procedure."

My preschool is always in need of help and knowing I'm making them short gives me anxiety. I already called out when I heard about Sookie having Down syndrome.

I know I have to do what's right for Sookie so I say the ten o'clock appointment works for us. The doctor hands me the paper where she wrote down the heart condition and I feel the tears coming on. I always thought that if I was healthy then my daughter would be. I feel like such a failure with her already having so many health issues and she's only twenty weeks old. I wish I could take her issues away.

As I'm walking to my car, I make a pact with myself. I'm going to eat more vegetables and fruit, cut out processed foods, and no more coffee. Ugh. No more coffee? Can I really do that? I'm going to have to if I want Sookie to be healthy. I need to do this for Sookie as I can try to save her. She is in my body and what I do with my body affects both of us.

I nod in my head feeling better but sigh. I also need to call work and Dean. I decide to call Dean first but don't know how to tell him. He is going to think I failed our daughter. How could I have not known our daughter is in distress?

A sob escapes and the tears finally come out that I've been suppressing since the doctor told me about her heart. I truly hope I can help her live as I don't want to lose her.

What if she doesn't make it? What if she doesn't make it despite all my efforts? What if I don't hold her and let her know how much I love her? She won't be able to experience all the joys in life and will only know pain, if she is in pain.

I'm in my car whimpering like a dog and am happy it's dark out. I hate it when people see me cry since my face becomes a blubbering mess. I never knew I would be bawling so much during pregnancy. My emotions have been crazy but my pregnancy has not been normal so far.

I need to get a hold of myself and call Dean. He texted me asking how everything went.

I start driving and call him.

"Hey. How did it go?" Dean sounds chipper and I hate myself more.

How do I tell him I'm already a failure of a mother? I know Dean will tell me I'm not a failure but with more health issues brought to our attention, it makes me feel as if I did something wrong.

He must sense that it didn't go well as he says, "I can come to you right now so you don't have to drive. Where are you?"

I take a deep breath and count to ten. "It's worse than I thought. She has a hole in her heart, her right kidney isn't working, her stomach is too small, and there is too much amniotic fluid."

"Okay. Well, how did the amnio whatever go?"
I kind of chuckle as I know he knows what it's called. He is the smart one in our relationship. "They don't do it after five pm. I have it tomorrow morning which means I have to call out. I don't know how to do that. Like, what do I say?"

"You just tell them the truth. Say how you thought the amniocentesis was today but they don't do it after five pm and they scheduled it for tomorrow. You need to take care of our baby and yourself. They should understand that."

I know he is right so I tell him I'm going to call work. The good thing is that if I cry, they will get it. All of my managers are moms.

"Call me once you talk to work so I can be with you during the rest of your ride."

I get off the phone with Dean and with a shaky breath I call work. Why do I have a feeling I'm going to get emotional every time I talk with work about my appointments?

Chapter 6

It's April and I'm in my second trimester feeling like a beached whale. A lot of people say I don't look pregnant especially from looking at me from behind which makes me feel better, but I feel humongous.

Sookie has been perfectly content inside me even though I haven't felt her move yet. It makes me nervous but I try not to think too much about it.

I cut out coffee completely from my diet, I'm eating more broccoli and leafy greens, berries, and no red meat. I rarely eat pizza or bacon which is super difficult. I'm eating beans and less chocolate. It's been arduous but I want Sookie's hole to get smaller and her health issues to resolve on their own by what I do.

I'm currently getting dressed as Dean and I are getting our second COVID vaccine . After, we plan on going out for lunch to celebrate his birthday since it's in five days.

We haven't done much by going out or seeing friends because of the pandemic so I'm happy we are finally doing something. I'm okay with being inside, curled up with a book but I can only look at my walls for so long.

I've always been an introvert but I do like being around people; just on my terms. If I could, I would say parties begin no later than six pm and end by ten pm. Also, standing the whole time and talking while drinking bores me. I would rather play games even if it's my least favorite: Munchkins.

I'm done doing my hair and know Dean needs nudges to get out the door. He is just like his mom and takes forever and a day to leave.
I peek my head in the office and say "Hey, we should be leaving now. We don't want to be late and I will need to stop to pee."

He rolls his eyes at me but he does start moving...toward the bathroom. I really hope he doesn't sit to take a ten-minute poop.

"I'm ready so I will meet you in the car once I'm done in the bathroom."

It's been ten minutes and Dean still isn't in the car. I get out of the Jeep and go into the house where he is in the kitchen giving Lance food.

"Do you have masks?" Dean asks me as he turns around from the cabinets.

I didn't think we would need them but better to be safe than sorry. "Nope." I grab two from the dining room and we both walk out.

I've been feeling a little extra chunky but I'm happy about that since it means she's growing. I know at least four other people who are pregnant with me other than Ellie.

When my brother married Ellie, we weren't very close but on our trips as a family we got kind of close. With her being a month more into her pregnancy it's been nice having her to talk to and her expertise in cardiothoracic surgery has been even more helpful. I just wish they didn't live thousands of miles away.

"You're quiet, are you okay?"

"Yea, just worried about Sookie. I haven't felt her move."

"We know she does move with the sonograms we have. She will move and then you probably won't like it."
"I don't know. I think I will love it regardless."

As we left a bit late, when I asked him to stop so I could pee, he said no. I didn't want to cause a fight so I didn't say more. Dean has been amazingly sweet through my pregnancy. The small things used to turn into bickering but lately that hasn't been happening.

We pull into the parking lot where we are getting our shots. The last time we got the shot, I bled. The paramedic who did it said I was the first bleeder which I highly doubt.

The medic gives me my dose and I start moving my arms to let the dose move. I somehow start moving my arms in a train motion so I start making train sounds. Dean finds it hysterical but joins in. He may think of me as odd but he always joins in with my craziness.

The movement makes me hungry. "Can we look up restaurants around here? Mama bear is hungry."

We start looking at restaurants in the area but we can't seem to find a place we both want to go. Dean says he is starting to get tired so we go to a fast food restaurant. I wait in the car sulking since I do not want processed food. I also did not want to be eating in the car. I really wanted to do something fun and eating in the car is not fun.

All of a sudden, I feel as if somebody kicked me in the bladder making me almost pee my pants. I look down at my stomach in wonder and feel another kick but more on my left side.

"Sookie, did you just kick Mama?" I ask her in wonder.

I think she actually hears me and lightly kicks me again. She is really making me need to pee but I am overjoyed she is kicking me.

I know Dean is still inside the restaurant, but I desperately need to pee now.

"Girlfriend, you are making Mama need to pee. Can you kick somewhere else?"

I'm eternally grateful that these masks can hide so much. Not just facial expressions but me talking to myself.

I see Dean walking to the car as I'm about to get out. "Where are you going?" he asks as I'm about to step out of the car.

"The bathroom. Our daughter finally decided to start moving by kicking my bladder."

Dean's face brightens and he puts a hand on my stomach. "Good girl. You keep growing big and strong, baby girl."

I love how cute he is toward my protruding stomach. I also love how my girl is finally moving. I was honestly worried about why I haven't felt her; maybe she isn't developing enough or maybe I'm carrying a dead baby. All the possibilities that my doctor said can happen.

I know every pregnancy is different and I should count my lucky stars but I wish I had a pregnancy where my baby is healthy and doesn't have all these complications. I see so many other women pregnant, including Ellie, just having side effects, whereas I not only have side effects but a baby who may not have a normal childhood because of her genetics.

It's why I feel so responsible for all Sookie's distress. I don't know if she really is in distress but I know I am. I stress about whether I'm eating healthy enough, drinking enough water, getting enough exercise, and relaxing. Despite changing my diet drastically for her, I have no clue if it's actually working and I just feel so sad all the time.

I sometimes ignore Dean and hide in my books but internally I cry. I ignore my mom's text messages although I feel I shouldn't as she also feels responsible for Sookie's health. I take longer showers because I don't want Dean to know how I feel so responsible for all of Sookie's health problems.

I walk into the restaurant toward the bathroom and try to relax and get off this emotional rollercoaster. I want to remember this day as the day I felt Sookie moving.

Chapter 7

"We need to talk."

I look up at Dean from my book and am in the middle of a sentence so I ignore him to hopefully finish the page I'm on.

"Jackie." His tone has this warning to it but of what, I have no clue.

I finish the page I'm on and know there aren't many pages left. "Hold on, I only have a couple pages left."

He lays down on the bed next to me as I'm lying on my left side curled up into the pregnancy pillow he bought. Lance was curled up at my feet until Dean came in. I decide to put my book down and look up at him.

"Yes?" I ask him with a bit of snark since I hate being interrupted in the middle of a chapter.

"You've been acting differently since we found out Sookie has Down syndrome as well as her various other complications, and I'm just worried about you. I see you reading a lot more than normal and you don't get out much."

"Well, it's hard to go out and stay safe with COVID going on. I don't want to get sick and risk Sookie's health. I know it's May with nice weather and she is due in three months, but you are busy trying to figure out how to teach a subject you didn't even major in so we can't do much. I would love to go on a hike with you but I feel I can't ask you as I don't want you staying up till midnight catching up."

"Well, I got most of my work done so I thought we could go out and go on a hike. Would you want to?"
I actually would but the last time I told him I wanted to do something with him he had to finish his work in the office. "I would but are you sure you can spare the time?"

He looks at me with his green eyes and says, "I would love to spend time with you and Sookie."

He places his hand on my belly and I love the feel of his hand. His hand makes me feel better about things but he won't ever know how deeply I hate myself. I'm glad he didn't really press the matter and thinks it's because I don't get out much.

We both get dressed in workout clothes and sweaters as it's low sixties out. I start to feel a little giddy about going outside and exploring with Dean.

We used to do a lot together on weekends but ever since he started working in special education in the inner city, his entire time is spent on lesson plans geared toward all the levels of his students plus grading, writing IEPs, and calling parents. It's why I've come to hate the school he works at because he wasn't trained to teach English, he majored in History, and he wasn't trained in special education so he doesn't know how to write IEPs. He has become pretty adept at writing IEPs now, but he has a lot of students. It makes me despise his school as he won't half-ass his work. He is a hard worker and will put more than a hundred percent of his effort into his work.

I'm so lost in thought that I don't realize we are already at the park. We normally hike four-thousand-foot mountains but, with being pregnant, I don't think I have that in me.

"Where would you like to walk?"

I didn't really look into the park so I suggest just walking around. We start meandering aimlessly with no destination in mind which is nice.

"So, I've been thinking a lot as I've been finishing the nursery that we should do one thing together on weekends other than eating together. As much as I would love for it to be sex, I know you've mentioned not feeling pretty, which by the way is bullshit, so I wanted to know what you would like to do."

He's been bringing sex up a lot and he is right. I don't feel pretty. It's not that I'm big but I also don't feel like myself. I also don't know how I could even get myself in the mood.

"I would like that. We could play games as we own a lot of board games, just not Munchkins."

I played that game once with our friend Rita and Dean, and I had no clue what I was doing. They had to tell me the rules so many times that I just got so aggravated and annoyed. They were talking and enjoying it, but I wasn't. Dean doesn't know this but I hate being the Debbie Downer. He would just tell me he would explain the game better, but I just don't want to give it another shot.

"I still don't get why you don't like that game, but I like that idea. I could make us some mocktails too!"

He has been making a few for me which have been yummy. Rita has also been sending me a few recipes for drinks as well, and Ellie sent me a book of mocktails when she learned we were pregnant. I have been flipping through that book a lot as I've been craving certain drinks.

"You know I could really go for a margarita or pina colada, also a nice cold beer, but I know that won't happen as the one non-alcoholic beer you found isn't that great."

He has been nice enough to find things I can drink that are non-alcoholic. Unfortunately, the beer he found is just meh. Thankfully, I only have three months till my due date.

"Can you believe that Sookie is due soon? I need to start planning the baby shower."

"I can't believe it. It feels like yesterday we found out you were pregnant. Doesn't your family plan the shower?"

"I don't know. This is my first time being pregnant so I have no clue who plans it. I was going to ask Rita to help because I want two showers. One for friends so I can have an in-person shower and another for family which can be virtual. What do you think?"

"I just want you to be happy, honey. What would make you happy?"

I want to say a healthy baby but instead I say, "To have everyone together in person but COVID makes that impossible since rules state that no more than ten people can be together. I'm not going to be the irresponsible person to get someone sick."

I'm thinking of how people are still having weddings indoors with quite a lot of people there. I like being with people, don't get me wrong, but with how the virus spreads I feel like it isn't safe to gather, especially for me. I would feel horrible if I got COVID. Sookie doesn't need more problems.

"Well, it seems as if you know what you want. Talk to Rita and see what you guys can do together. We don't need to do it soon so just don't stress about it."

I am stressed. I am always stressing and I never know how to not stress. I don't have a normal pregnancy, like Ellie's, and I'm jealous. I hate how I'm jealous, but I am.
"Jackie." Dean says my name warningly as if he knows what I'm thinking and he probably does. He knows me so well which I sometimes hate since I can't keep a secret from him.

When I did the gender reveal for him, I had told him beforehand. I only lasted a day with that secret. I tried my hardest to not tell him the gender but I was too excited. He acted surprised when I took a video of him so we could send the reveal to our family. We tried video chatting with our family but some members were busy.

"Yes?" I try to act all innocent hoping he won't know what I'm thinking and feeling.

"Stop. Stop overthinking. You are doing the best you can with everything. I know this hasn't been easy for you. We will get through this. Together." He emphasizes together. "You aren't alone. I know you are carrying our baby but I am here. You can always come to me."

I look at him and realize I needed to hear that. It is nice having Dean who has been so caring and supportive. He doesn't know what it's like carrying a baby but no male will ever know. I know what he says is true but it is hard. It's so hard and I don't know how to go through this speed bump with him.

"I know I can come to you and I have. I won't keep secrets from you and have been honest. I just…I really don't know how to express myself sometimes. Right now, I'm happy. I love being outside with you and doing our first hike together as a family makes me so happy. I want to capture this moment and remember it forever."

He grabs his phone and snaps a picture of me. It was a bit sudden but I do like chronicling our lives with pictures. I ask him to take it again despite my hair looking a mess. I will cherish this moment despite how I still feel. I know these feelings won't go away overnight. I do have Dean. I need to remind myself I'm not alone in this chapter of our lives.

"Hey Jackie." I look at him. "Why are writers always cold?" He pauses. "They're surrounded by drafts."

"Oh my lanta," I say with more dramatic flair and slap my forehead from his joke.

Dean cracks up and says, "Oh come on! That was funny!"

I need to start being more myself so Dean doesn't torture me with his jokes. Things will start looking up. I have to have hope. If there is no hope then how can I be happy for Sookie?

Chapter 8

"The heart is looking good overall." The cardiologist talks about the flow of the blood while showing us Sookie's heart on the monitor.

Whenever she talks about my baby girl's heart it rarely makes sense to me. It's why I'm so grateful I have Dean with me as he gets it. He asks the right questions and asks for clarification on things. I know he sometimes gets her to explain things another way so I can try to understand what she is saying but I always ask Dean to explain it to me once we are in the car.

I also just hate sitting on these hospital beds with the slimy goop they put on my stomach to look at Sookie's heart. Actually no, I hate the doppler as it tickles me so freaking much.

The cardiologist is still talking and I realize she must have said something that isn't good as Dean's face looks a bit grim. Sookie's AV Canal Defect isn't getting better like I had hoped with my diet. The doctor is saying how the hole is getting bigger. I normally dread the specialty appointments because it's always bad news. I do like how our cardiologist talks about some of the positives of Sookie's heart. Lately, I feel as if the doctors are just relaying negative information. I know it's their job but it depresses me.

I try to pay attention but just can't help looking at her heart. I personally don't see the hole. What untrained professional can tell my daughter has a complete AV canal defect? All I see are the red and blue colors moving back and forth. To me that seems normal but it isn't. My daughter's heart isn't normal. Nor is her right kidney. Or her stomach. Or her esophagus. Or her brain.

What's next? Her lungs? I'm near tears laying on this bed with my shirt pulled up to my chest trying to stay strong while the cardiologist talks about what will happen when she is born.
I know once I give birth, she will have to go straight to the NICU. To be honest, I don't know what will happen after that. My doctor says that she

is happy my daughter is progressing but doesn't know if she will make it full term which freaks me out.

I am a planner. I like having a set plan in place, so not knowing when Sookie will be born terrifies me. Her due date is August eleventh and my doctor wants her inside me for as long as possible so she can grow and not be underdeveloped. I do too but I want to plan if I can. Today I plan on bringing it up as it's only three months away.

All of a sudden, I'm brought back to the present as Dean is asking me something.

"I'm sorry, what?" I can't believe I just spaced out.

"Do you have any questions?" My cardiologist has such a soft voice it's sometimes hard to hear her due to her mask.

"Not that I can think of at the moment." I never have questions because I never get it. "What about you, honey?" I look to Dean for any insight but he also shakes his head no.

"Then I will see you in a month to check Sookie's progress. Keep up the good work, Jackie."

Our cardiologist is so sweet and I do like her. She has three daughters and always talks about them which makes me happy that she is personable. I feel like some doctors are all about the facts and could care less about the feelings.

After all my appointments, I see the head doctor of my case, who I think is going to be my OB for delivery, but it does depend on when I deliver. I've seen almost all the doctors here so I can be comfortable with each one. I personally love and hate it.

Each doctor is great but I just want Sookie to come out alive and healthy. It seems like that is hard to ask for but I'm hoping everything works out.

Dean has been to most of my appointments which I love. I have no clue how I would get through this without him. Despite being near tears earlier, his presence just calmed me. Despite his loud teacher voice, it's soothing. His voice is very melodic at times which I adore.

I hear a knock at the door and my doctor coming in with one of the student residents from a previous appointment.

"It seems like there are no changes other than Sookie growing, which is great. Do you have any questions?"

I'm always nervous about asking the wrong questions but if I'm going to be Sookie's advocate, I can't hesitate anymore.

"Yes. Since I'm a planner and Sookie is due August eleventh I was wondering if I could schedule my delivery. I was thinking of August fifth as it's a Thursday. If she comes within 24 hours everyone will be here on a Friday."

Also, I have a few more paid time off days I want to use up.

"We can certainly do that but I say we wait for now. That is full term which is what we want so good thinking."

That comment makes me swell with pride. I too want to go full term however, I want Sookie to be healthy enough.

"How is my weight? I remember you mentioning that during a pregnancy it's common to gain between fifteen to twenty-five pounds."

"You are gaining a lot of weight. With how far you are, you've gained more than we recommend."

Therefore, I'm fat. Well, fatter than I should be, she's telling me. I guess I need more rabbit food and less chocolate; at least I'm having dark chocolate as it's healthier.

Since we don't have any more questions, we leave for home. I'm a bit miserable as my appointments didn't go well with cardiology or my regular appointment. No woman likes hearing they are fat.

I get that every pregnancy is different, as everybody is different, but really? I look down at my stomach and mutter, "At least we have meat on our bones."

Dean is oddly quiet which is weird since he needs some sort of sound going at all times. I look at his face and it doesn't seem grim or pissed. It's his eyes that sometimes give him away. His eyes change color with his emotions which I love. When he is happy, they are blue. If he is upset or stressed, near the middle it turns brown but the rest is blue. At night his eyes turn green. I still don't know why they turn green but when they turn green, I love it. I like to think his eyes turn green when he is turned on or wants sex.

I hear him sigh and I'm still watching his face. He really hasn't shown much emotion and I hate how he can keep a poker face on.

We normally talk on the way to the cars but today we don't. I have no clue what to say so once we get to the parking garage and to level five, we finally stop.

"I'll call you once we're on the highway." Dean is being very mysterious and I don't know if I like it.

"Okay," I reply and give him a kiss.

We are in our cars driving and I'm hit with sadness. Do you ever have a wave of guilt and despair just hit you? I feel like a tidal wave of emotions and I'm just drowning. My efforts to get Sookie healthier aren't working and I'm getting too fat.

I hate how I always think this but I feel like I'm already failing as a mother.

A horn blares and I look behind me. I don't see anything but I'm glad I'm looking to my left since I'm getting onto the on ramp, where some dumbass almost clips my car by cutting in front of me. I always wondered if I would get sick of driving in Worcester and I have. I truly despise Worcester. All of my accidents, except one, have happened in Worcester.

Once I'm on the highway, Dean calls me and I pick up without saying "hey" but instead with a, "What did you want to talk about?"

"Don't let the doctor's comment about your weight affect you. You are eating healthy and exercising, which is the best anyone can do."

I'm about to respond when he says, "What the fuck? Pick a fucking lane, dude, and use your directional. Mechanics put blinkers on a car for a reason. Idiots."

I smile to myself as his comments about drivers are always amusing. "Language mister. I don't want Sookie going into school swearing like a sailor because she learned it from you."

I hear him exhale and say, "Anyway Jackie, I know you and I don't want you feeling like you have to lose weight. You are growing a baby inside you who needs all the nutrients you are giving it. Sookie needs all the food you are giving her."

He is right and even though I was upset about it, I've moved past it and tell him so.

"I really don't think it was appropriate for your doctor to say that. Even though you asked the question she shouldn't have said what she said. She either tells us that Sookie won't make it or you can do better with your diet. You would think they teach doctors empathy. I'm thinking we should find another doctor."

I had a feeling Dean was going to say that. "I know my doctor hasn't been very positive but she is also being realistic about Sookie's health. Sadly, Sookie has a lot of complications but she is active. Sookie is currently kicking me right now making it difficult to drive. I have no clue how pregnant ladies can drive safely. We should get a pass that says no driving or working while pregnant."

"Can this person press the gas pedal? It's forty miles per hour, not thirty, dipshit."

I smile despite my eye roll toward his comments on other drivers.

Everything will be alright. I just need to stay positive.

Chapter 9

Sasha and I are playing baby shark for the millionth time today as Ophelia keeps doing the sign language for "more" and looking so cute. I'm screwed once Sookie is born because I give in to my kids at school so easily.

I went from being support staff to a lead teacher with Sasha. I love working with Sasha and now I'm with the toddlers instead of the babies. It's also nice to just be myself while teaching instead of holding back who I truly am.

All of a sudden, I hear crying and see Jamie crying. His blonde curls and blue eyes have all the teachers swooning over him. It doesn't help that he has such a soft voice that makes him cuter. However, he whines so much that it drives me crazy. I do work with toddlers so these kids will whine.

I walk over, even though I think I waddle, and squat at his level.

"What happened Jamie? Why are you crying?"

He rubs his eyes and says, "Ophelia took my toy."

I glance at Ophelia who looks down as I do too. "Ophelia, give Jamie his toy back. We have many toy links for every kid to play with. How about we find some for you to play with?"

Ophelia shakes her head and her red hair shakes out of the loose ponytail. Her hair is always coming undone since she is so wild.

I try to think. She loves tumbling on the mat so I ask if she wants to do that. Her head nods vigorously which makes me laugh internally.

Working with kids is a blast. There is normally not a dull moment.

Once I start taking Ophelia's legs to help propel her to roll, other kids come over for some fun. Most of the kids love tumbling so I try to make sure everyone gets a turn.

"How are you feeling?" Sasha asks me.

She must have just finished sending all the pictures to the families since she was so quiet. Every day we use the iPad to send updates to the families which includes pictures of their kids.

"Tired but good. I'm glad I'm leaving soon."

"Do you think you're coming back after giving birth?"

Everyone except leadership has asked me that and I always say yes. To be honest, I don't want to. I just want to stay home with my baby girl and teach her.

"Probably not but don't tell anyone. The drive is a killer and I don't think I can do that with a baby. I already get up at four thirty in the morning to work out and get here. Imagine adding a baby into the mix?" I shudder just thinking of going to bed late and waking at four.

I love to sleep and with a baby I know I won't get much. I don't know how much sleep I will get but I knew what I was signing up for before getting pregnant. I've talked with many moms who mention getting up every three hours the first few months and then it kind of gets better. If Sookie is anything like me, she will sleep through the night once she's three months old; maybe sooner.

"I have no clue how you drive so far. My drive is a half hour and I hate it," Sasha is fixing her hair as she speaks.
I'm actually envious of her hair as I rarely see any flyaways. Her brown hair is normally neatly done but she must have been in a rush this morning as she put it in a messy bun. When I think of my hair, I wish I didn't have so many flyaways. I'm surprised my natural hair color is back

since I've dyed my hair red so many times. I've always wanted red hair but got stuck with dirty blonde hair.

"I love the people I work with here and enjoy working with these kids. Once my baby is born, I'm going to be out for three months, hopefully more because of her surgery."

I can tell Sasha is pouting despite the mask. One of the reasons why I love her is because she is very empathetic.

"I hope you do come back because I will miss you. I can only talk to you about our fart roulette."

I laugh and still can't believe how much we talk about bodily fluids. Fart roulette came up when we were working together in another classroom with the seven-to-twelve-month-old babies. One day I had no clue if I needed to poop or fart and she mentioned fart roulette as it turned out to be a fart thankfully. Now, fart roulette is our thing.

"I will miss you too but I don't think I can drive this far. Plus, with the pay and how much childcare is here, it isn't worth it. I barely wouldn't bring any money home."

"How much is childcare here?"

"Twenty-eight hundred dollars a month. I don't know how much it would be part time but I don't think that would help much."

"It's insane how much childcare is. Do you have a plan?"
I haven't thought too much about it as I truly want to stay home. Dean and I haven't talked much about daycare, Sookie's health, and COVID. As far as we know, Sookie isn't immunocompromised, but I worry. What if Dean or I get sick and she catches it and is hospitalized?

I push my thoughts aside and say, "I've looked at some daycare options in our area which are more affordable but I don't know if I want to stay in childcare. I've always wanted to work in elementary education, so I'm hoping maybe I can transition."

I have so many dreams. One of them is making an impact in this world. I want to leave behind some of my knowledge whether it's my knowledge on fitness, nutrition, books, or self-acceptance.

Before Dean and I moved in together, I applied to a few state colleges that had athletic training for a master's program. Instead of getting my master's, Dean and I became personal trainers and I also became a sports nutritionist. We were called the dream team at our gym. We trained together and helped others with their fitness goals as well.

I always talked about becoming a well-known trainer but that died quickly since I never had a lot of clients and didn't like split shifts. I had too many days of waking at four and going to bed at eleven.

I realized I went down the rabbit hole and Sasha is getting my attention. "Sorry, I completely spaced. What?"

Her brown eyes look at me with concern as she must have repeated her question. "How is Sookie doing?"

Once I told her my favorite TV show, she almost guessed the name. I don't have a great poker face.

I try not to cry as I know she means well, but it terrifies me that I could potentially lose my baby girl.

"She moves a lot which tells me she is fine but Sookie still has four major health issues. I know it could be worse but my doctor keeps saying she won't make it full term and how her life will be difficult at first."

"It's good that she is moving! She's just like you; strong and always dancing."

I smile at that and love Sasha for her positive outlook on my life.

With the ratio being in range for just one teacher in our classroom, I start packing up my things and make sure Sasha is alright. It's been a struggle lifting heavy things but I hate leaving the trash behind. Duties between us should be split and I can't do the closing chores assigned to me. It makes me feel like crap but ever since I had round ligament pain, my back hasn't been the same.

Technically my back hasn't been the same since I slipped down a flight of stairs at my first apartment. I was leaving for work and there was a bad snow storm throughout the night. My apartment had stairs that had carpet, on the outside (who does that?), which iced over. I slipped on the first stair and mostly went down on my back. I tried calling out of work so I could get it checked, but they wouldn't let me. That was the joy of working in the healthcare industry. I went in and started lifting heavy patients with the Hoyer machine. Using that machine hurt my back so much more.

I shudder and turn out of my classroom. The front entrance is where leadership is and they all tell me to have a good night.

I love it here yet I don't want to come back. But they have been so good to me as they have been understanding about what's going on. I've had many crying sessions in front of the principal and she's always there to talk to. It's a pleasure to work at a company where I'm comfortable being myself. I adjust my seatbelt near my belly and look ahead.

As I'm merging onto a jam-packed Route 3, I start getting frustrated with the people in front of me. Once I have Sookie, I can't imagine myself wanting to do this drive with Sookie in the car. I hate driving on highways. I've been in a few fender benders since taking this job because I'm always on a major highway. The massive trailer trucks give me anxiety when I drive by them due to all their blind spots. I mean, I can't be the only one. Those things weigh a ton and if it hits you, you're a goner.

I have seen a lot of accidents on the highways I drive since I started working in Burlington two years ago. All the injured people I've driven by make me shudder. I hate knowing how people suffer in car crashes yet they happen daily.

My mom even worries about me during my commute which is sweet. I love my mom and have gone to her condo after work a few times since she lives close. I haven't since I've gotten pregnant but I know she would love to see me. My mom has taken Sookie's diagnosis hard and I don't know how to make her feel better. I don't know how to make myself feel better. Once I figure myself out, then I can help her.

That is one thing Dean and I disagree on. Dean is always wanting to help others instead of himself and I'm always telling him that he has to take care of himself first before helping others. Once you are happy then you can make others happy. I live by that saying.

I'm finally merging onto the last highway which is Route 2 when he calls.

"Hey honey. How are my girls doing?"

"We are doing good. Super hungry, but good."

"I was calling to see where you were so I could start dinner for you. Does pork lo mein sound good?"

My mouth waters and I say yes. I've been craving Chinese food and spicy foods. Dean loves that I'm finally eating spicy food since I normally can't stand it.

I see traffic up ahead and I start braking as he's talking about his day. He has been happy since he found out I'm pregnant. I finally come to a stop with the traffic and all of a sudden feel myself moving forward.

I start to panic as my car almost hits the person in front of me but I slam on my brakes and lift the emergency brake. Bile rides up my throat as my panic rises. I end the call and try to focus on what I need to do but keep thinking of Sookie. I'm wearing the seatbelt properly, but I'm worried it could have damaged her.

"Baby girl, are you okay? Show mommy you're okay by moving."

I place my hand on my stomach and don't feel anything and start crying. I can't lose her in a car accident. I just can't. Out of all the things to die from I wouldn't want it to be from someone else's hand.

A rap is on my window and I roll it down. There is a woman out there who has gray hair and blue eyes. She is saying sorry and how I jacked on my brakes suddenly making her go into me.

Normally, I would berate the person but I'm too worried about Sookie. I don't know what to do or how to make myself feel better.
Ever since I changed car insurance, everything is electronic so I try to find a piece of paper telling this woman I want to exchange information.

She hands me her business card and I look back and notice it's a company van. I ask for her insurance information and she jots half of it down. When I ask for more, she says to call her since she doesn't have it.

I finally step out of my car and her eyes go wide seeing my belly. I'm only two months away from my due date so I'm quite big. Getting out of my car is actually interesting to watch since my pants are always tight.

"Oh, how is the little one?"

I look at her and say, "Currently not moving, thanks."

"I was in a horrible car accident with my second and he is just fine. I wouldn't worry too much as babies are so resilient."

"My girl already has a lot of odds against her so thanks for the vote of confidence."

I shouldn't be so snappy but this accident is her fault and I don't want her thinking it's mine. I snap a couple of pictures even though I don't see much damage and go back to my car.

I try to calm down but it's difficult as I don't feel Sookie moving. I can tell where she is, which is on my right side. I picture her head resting on my hip as her legs were kicking my left side before the accident.

I merge into the traffic and take deep breaths. I can't believe that just happened. I've been trying to drive so carefully so this wouldn't happen and it did. I'm an idiot for not looking behind me before stopping to see if I needed to put my hazard lights on. Route 2 traffic can come on suddenly as even I have almost collided into someone as I wasn't aware we were completely stopping.

I need to not think about the accident and drive. I realize I hung up on Dean due to being hit. He must be frantic right now.

He picks up on the first ring asking me if I'm okay.

I take a deep breath since I'm still shaking. "We were in an accident. I can't feel her move and I'm still freaking out Dean."

Tears prick the corners of my eyes but I refuse to acknowledge them. I don't want to be weak now. I need to be strong for Sookie as I can't feel her moving. How do I know if Sookie is in distress?

"You know, I had a feeling this was going to happen and I hate how my gut was right. Do you need me to come get you?"

There he goes again thinking of others.

"No, I didn't see much damage to either car. I was stopped when she hit me. With the nonexistent construction it makes people stop. If the workers knew to put away their materials there wouldn't be construction signs everywhere."

I could have kept talking if it wasn't for Dean. "Jackie. Are you ok?" He stresses the word ok and I know he is worried.

"I'm fine. I'm just worried about Sookie. Like I said I can't feel her movement and I'm freaked out. She was moving before I got hit."

"Maybe she can feel how stressed you are so she isn't moving. Or she could be sleeping. I would call the doctors and see what you should do."

I know he is right but a part of me just doesn't think I should. I'm not sure why I feel this way but I do.

"Shouldn't I call my insurance company? I care about making sure this is documented."

"Honey, you have to do what you think is best. How far away from home are you?"

I look at the signs and realize I am in Leominster so I answer about fifteen minutes depending on how slow people want to drive.

I see brake lights so I start braking but don't want anyone else hitting me, so I put my hazard lights on. No way am I getting hit again.

I finally make it home and see a bunch of family text messages in the family chat and one from Ellie asking me how my day was.

For some reason I text Ellie back and not the family chat.

Me: I was feeling good until I was in a car accident on my way home.

Ellie: Oh my God, are you okay?!

Tears form in my eyes as I text.

Me: I'm freaking as I can't feel my baby move. She was moving before the accident.

Ellie: Relax. Our babies do feed off of our emotions so stay calm. I too would be freaking out so I don't blame you. Are you going to report it?

Me: You bet I am. I recently got home so I'm just taking a breather.

Ellie: I don't blame you. I would need that too. I would take a long bubble bath and have a nice drink.

Me: I might take a shower to relax. I'm not a bath person.

Dean is behind me as I'm sitting on a chair in the dining room adjacent to the kitchen. He is rubbing my shoulders as I'm texting Ellie.

"What does Ellie say?"

"To relax as Sookie can feel my emotions."

I know what he is going to say before he says it. "Then what can I do to help?"

I honestly don't know so I tell him I'm going to shower. I'm heading upstairs as I finally feel a little kick. It's not a big kick like normal but it's movement nonetheless. I breathe a sigh of relief as I go into our room.

For some reason I hate sitting on any of our furniture after I get home from work. I'm not sure if it's due to COVID or working with kids, or both, but it grosses me out. I'm thankful our bed frame has a bench attached to the end so I can sit on it. My pregnant body can't balance well when dressing anymore.

I take a few seconds to sit on the bench before undressing. Why does everything happen so fast? I wish life would slow down. Everyone has to rush because I only see elderly people driving slowly on highways now.

I look up at Dean's dresser and the windows on both sides of it are open. I close the windows and the blinds so I can start undressing.

I go toward the bathroom in my underwear thinking I won't want to do this when Sookie is older. I remember my mom walking around in her underwear and I thought it was weird…unless I'm weird for thinking that.

I get to the bathroom which is just ten steps from the bedroom and turn the water on. I wait a bit before fully undressing. Once undressed I look at my belly and caress my stomach. I find it beautiful how my body can hold such a precious life.

After my shower I end up reporting the accident through my insurance company before I forget. The lady barely gave me any information that I can use but my insurance agent says the amount I have is enough.

It's been such a long day that I end up grabbing a book and falling asleep.

When I wake up the next day, Sookie still isn't kicking me as much but is moving. I realized I never called the doctor but know they don't open till eight so I get ready for work.

Dean and I spend a bit of time in the morning but he normally leaves first a little after six and I leave at six thirty. I'm always jealous of others' commutes, but there is another coworker who lives in my town. We sometimes play leap frog but she tends to always get to work first.

I'm at work, finally, and drop my stuff off in my classroom. I head toward the front to see if I can talk to someone first. I see Olive in there and ask if she's free.

Olive has the cutest little boy who goes here and has been amazing to talk to about my pregnancy.

"What's up?" She asks as she closes the office door so we're alone.

"I was in an accident last night." This is where tears start filling my eyes and I try to push them away. I hate how emotional I get, especially now with my hormones going a thousand miles in a second. "I haven't felt my baby move much so I was hoping I could call my doctor."

"Of course! I can go to your classroom to let Sasha know what you're doing and to code once over ratio. Are you ok?"

I realize I'm sobbing as I'm terrified. I'm terrified the accident somehow hurt Sookie and a limb is broken. I try to calm down as best as I can and not think of the negatives.

"I think so. I'm worried about my baby since she hasn't moved much."

"I'm sure everything is fine. Your stomach shields her from a lot and it seems you did the best you could. Let me know what they say."

I nod and leave the room. I go back to my classroom and see Sasha and a few kids. My favorite blonde girl is in, since all the girls have different colored hair. I ask for a hug from her which she gives and I hug her close. When I feel distressed, I always need hugs. I pull away and feel Sasha's gaze.
I grab my phone and say, "I will be back. I need to call my doctor."

I know she is about to ask a question since I'm an ugly crier so my eyes are most likely red from crying. I duck out before she can even ask me a question as I know I will start weeping in front of her.

I go toward the staff lounge but someone is in there so I head to the resource room. No one there, just the printer printing.

I sit down and take a deep breath. I count to ten and call my doctor.

Someone picks up and I explain what happened last night and a nurse instantly comes on the phone. She explains to me that I should come in right away and to the emergency wing. She tells me it's the labor wing but not to worry as it's just a precaution. This precaution makes me feel like I'm hyperventilating. I don't want Sookie coming this early. She isn't due for another two months.

I don't know what to do so I call Dean forgetting he is at work.

I feel bad for calling him at work and am surprised when he picks up. "I'm sorry. I didn't know what to do."

"What's going on? Are you okay?"

"I called the doctor and they told me to go right in. I just got to work. Should I go right in or work for a couple hours?"

"What do you want me to do?"

"Tell me what to do! I don't know." I'm honestly freaking out and my mind is blank.

"If you think you can work for an hour then do it, but I would talk to your manager first or principal. If you need me to meet you there, just text me."

We end our call and I try to calm down but can't. I head to the bathroom and take my mask off so I can splash water on my face.

I glance at the mirror and stare at my reflection. My blue eyes are glassy and red due to the crying. My hair is sticking up all over the place in my ponytail with the baby hairs wispy by my forehead. I truly hate how frizzy my hair gets year-round but love my color.

I look down at my belly. "We always have to do hard things in life, Sookie. Mommy has to do a hard thing and it's figuring out what's the right thing to do right now. Give mama strength, baby girl."

I know I have to leave the bathroom but am scared. I obviously have to talk to Olive. Since the bathroom is right across the hall from my classroom, I had peeked before going into the bathroom and saw her with Sasha.

I finally open the door with much apprehension but I want to set a good example for Sookie. I don't want to be this weak.

Once Olive sees me, she goes out of the class saying she will be back to talk with me.

Sasha looks at me and asks, "What's going on?

Tears go to my eyes so I cover it up by grabbing my water bottle and taking a sip. "I was in a car accident last night and my baby girl hasn't really been moving a lot. My doctor wants me to go in ASAP."

I hear her gasp. "Oh my god. Are you okay?"
I shake my head and say, "I'm a mess. I should leave now but I also want to stay for a few hours as I don't want to use up too much of my PTO."

"You need to take care of yourself. You told me that jobs are temporary and don't bring you the happiness you truly need. Only you can make yourself happy by doing what you love."

I do say that and know I need to take my own advice. I see another teacher who floats around the school to help out in classrooms for breaks, and Olive.

I say bye to Sasha and head out the door to talk with Olive. We go into the front office and both sit across from each other.

"What did the doctor say?"

I'm calmer now than I thought I would be and explain how the doctor wants me to go in as soon as possible to make sure Sookie is alright. I also tell her I'm okay to work for an hour until our other teacher who does breaks for the toddler wing comes in.

"That would be helpful if you could stay for an hour and then leave for the hospital but it is your call. We want you both to be healthy and safe. The teacher that is currently in there can stay if need be but we did have a few call outs today."

I don't know why it was so hard for me but I'm glad I came to a decision. There are times when I can't think straight and need help coming to a decision. I'm happy with myself for coming to a conclusion.

I go back to my classroom and tell Sasha the plan. She hates that I have to leave but she is also worried about me. We decide to let the kids do some free play before I have to leave, which I'm grateful for.

One thing that I love about working with toddlers is how huggable they are. They are very attuned to how others are feeling…at least at times. They don't always feel that way about each other.

Once the other teacher comes in, I grab my things and text Dean telling him I am leaving. He is going to leave work in thirty minutes since the hospital is about ten minutes away from his school.

I hope everything is okay but I have felt Sookie move so I'm not too worried. As I near the hospital, Dean calls me letting me know he is leaving. We somehow make it at the same time and park next to each other. We walk in, hand in hand, and he goes toward the check in for guests as I walk ahead. He somehow catches up to me and asks if I know where I am going. I tell him how I'm always here and know where to go. He lets me lead the way and once I'm on the fourth floor I realize I actually have no clue where I'm going. Dean ends up leading the way and a maintenance guy has to card us in to get to the right side.

I sign in and we are led to a triage center. The gurney I'm lying on is semi comfortable and they hook up two probes to my belly. I know the nurse told me what they are called but I can't remember. All I know is that they are uncomfortable and she can't find where to put the one for Sookie to hear her heartbeat.

We end up waiting for a resident to do an ultrasound to make sure Sookie is alright as the nurse mentioned inducing me today but it's way too early. It's May and I'm due in August. The plan is for Sookie to go full term. I try not to freak out by holding onto Dean's hand.

Once the resident comes in, she takes the probes off my stomach and she sets up to see Sookie with the ultrasound. She does a few tests to make sure Sookie is doing okay. We are waiting for Sookie to breathe a few times but she only does it twice but not rhythmically like the resident wants. The resident says that everything else looks fine and that my doctor will review the pictures and let us know what the plan is. She thinks that we won't need to induce me today but it's up to the doctor.

I sigh and realize it's going to be a long day. I can tell Dean is getting antsy just sitting there so I tell him to go to my car to get my lunchbox as I have lunch and some snacks. Before he leaves, I ask him to connect my phone to the internet so I can read my book on my Kindle App while he is gone.

Dean is finally back and is on his phone talking to his mom. I love how close they are but also hate how many times they talk in a day. A part of me is a bit jealous that they can talk about anything and his mom just listens. Tracy doesn't tell Dean what to do but she gives him suggestions.

I try not to think too much as I need to be positive and not pessimistic.

"My mom says that she will bring some food for us during her lunch break since she only works twenty minutes away."

"That's kinda far. She doesn't have to do that!"

For some reason I don't like people having to drive out of their way to help me. The only person I'm okay with doing that for me is Dean and maybe my mom.

It's the afternoon and the nurse comes in to check on the monitor as Sookie has been moving making it difficult to track her heartbeat. Dean and I have gone through all my snacks and water so he went down to the cafeteria to grab some water and ice cream for me.

It's been a long day so we ask the nurse if there has been word yet from the doctor. Once she realizes that's why I'm still here she makes it her mission to get me out as Dean and I are both restless. I can only imagine how uncomfortable Dean is since he has been in a chair for about five hours.

About thirty minutes go by and the resident comes in again to tell us that the doctor says Sookie looks good and to just monitor her movements for a while longer. I'm thankful I don't need to get induced as I was freaking out about how her organs aren't fully developed and how if she were to come this early, she could have more complications.

An hour later and we are finally walking out of the hospital after being there for six hours. My back hurts from lying on that uncomfortable gurney so I can only imagine how Dean's back is feeling. My mom said she would order us a pizza so we wouldn't have to worry about making dinner once we get home, which is extremely nice of her. I sincerely hope that I'm back in this hospital for my ultrasound in a couple weeks instead of giving birth.

Chapter 10

It's June and my first baby shower is tomorrow. I wanted it to be early since when I was in the hospital, I started freaking out that Sookie would come early. Despite telling Sookie to let her cousin come first, which is July, I don't know if she will listen to me. My doctor keeps telling me that she is doing well despite her health ailments but a part of me keeps thinking that she will be like me and be early to the show.

Rita has been planning my friend shower which is happening tomorrow at my house and my sister, Beth, is planning the family shower which will be held virtually next weekend. I'm excited for tomorrow since I can't wait to be with my friends. With COVID going on I don't want to risk Sookie's health any more than it already is. I keep thinking that when I'm pregnant again I can have another shower and do it better but when I told Rita that she said you only have a shower for your first pregnancy. I find that lame since COVID is going on and I can use that as my excuse but I digress.

I'm working with Sasha and want it to be the weekend already. It's almost time to leave which I'm thankful for.

"So, would you be upset if I didn't come tomorrow?"

The question is so out of the blue that I'm taken aback. Taken aback, I don't know how to respond and don't know why she is asking me this. Yesterday she asked me if she could bring my present early and I told her not to do that. Now I'm thinking she doesn't want to come to the baby shower. I already had my best friend Jackie instantly say no as she decided to not take time off from work. Jackie is married to her job so I wasn't too surprised. I was certainly hurt that Jackie wouldn't at least consider coming to the party since she keeps talking about being an aunt. Jackie has been off lately by not texting me as much and I have no clue why. I'm not upset about her not coming, just a little hurt, but I tried not to let my emotions get to me when I texted her back. She was the first one out of the sixteen friends I invited to say anything.

I look at Sasha and ask, "Why? Does your husband not want to come?"

She looks down before saying, "Yea and it's a bit of a drive for me."

I know she lives in New Hampshire which is a bit of a hike but I do know that some of my friends I did invite who live far away considered coming which was nice. I don't want to be rude especially since I know where she is coming from. I hate driving and if I have to drive more than forty-five minutes by myself, I would go crazy.

"I don't blame you. It would mean a lot to both of us if you would come. Some of my friends are coming from far away so you aren't the only one with a drive. How about you reconsider? It's going to be outside and there aren't going to be a lot of people as I hate big parties."

I already hate how many people said no to this party. Some of them are my camp friends who live in different states which is why I didn't put an end time to my party so people could leave whenever. My sister drove down yesterday so she could come to it with my brother-in-law.

Three of my friends from college all said no but never actually RSVP'd to Rita and Rita had to reach out to each of them. One of them had asked me a couple weeks ago when it was before the invites were sent out and I told her to just wait for the invite like everyone else. She wasn't thrilled with my answer but I told her that I'm having two and wasn't planning them. Ever since, things have been icier than normal with us. We have had many fights in the past eleven years of being friends and I'm not sure what's going on but don't have any energy to try to fix it.

I'm at that point in my life where if a friend doesn't want to be with me and Sookie, then we can part ways. I've always been family focused and I want to give my attention to Sookie, not stupid catfights. That's all my friend ever wants since when we have a conflict, she always goes to Dean who hates getting sucked in the middle. I hate drama which is why I have not been talking with any of my college friends.

I realize Sasha is looking at me and is waiting for a response to something I did not hear. "Sorry, what?"

"You completely spaced out. Are you okay? I was asking what you were going to wear tomorrow."

"Honestly? I'm tired and my college best friends all said no to the party and I'm still hurt by it. My friend Rita and I aren't surprised they said no but it still hurts. As for what I'm wearing, most likely a dress since it's going to be hot outside."

"Is this the friend who got upset at you for saying how you wish you could redo your bachelorette party?"

I told Sasha everything about the Queen Bee of my group of friends from college. The other two just do their own thing and listen to what she says. I have no clue if they believe everything she tells them nor do I care. It's like *Mean Girls* but they are girls in their twenties. I don't even know where I fit in the group. I've always felt a bit of a loner with them as I could care less about gossiping.

"The one and only."

"If I ever meet her, I would probably give her a piece of my mind."

I love how Sasha sees it my way and wish I had met her sooner. She has been such a good friend and I actually forget the difference in age between us. I love Sasha for who she is and hope she never changes.

I also didn't want much for my bachelorette party as I wanted a party bus and to go on a wine tour. The only thing I got was to go to three wineries, with one of them being a place I had gone to with some friends. I know Rita tried her best to make it what I wanted but she kept telling me that some people were making it difficult. It may not have been what I wanted but it's in the past and I spent it with people who will hopefully stick with me through thick and thin.

"Yea but that's eons ago. As for tomorrow, it's going to be low key with food and games. I will most likely be sitting a lot due to my lovely legs."

My legs started swelling around my second trimester and my varicose veins on my left leg have been throbbing. My feet have swelled tremendously that my compression socks leave outlines when I take them off at night. Dean has been a saint by giving me foot massages daily but I wish my legs didn't have to be swollen to get foot massages.

We are finally down to four kids so I pack up my stuff to leave. Sasha and I switch each week as to who leaves first but I wish I could leave first all the time. It sometimes helps me miss some of the traffic on the way home.

"I'll see you tomorrow!"
I wave back as I leave for home.

———

"Have you heard the joke about the daughter of Sean Connery's brother?"

I look at Dean waiting for the punchline knowing it's going to be horrible. Dean is atrocious with his dad jokes but he does have some good ones once in a while.

"Well, it was a little niche," Dean says, in a horrible Scottish accent.

I roll my eyes at him as I wait for Rita and her boyfriend to get here. I don't get half of his jokes sometimes. I try not to acknowledge his joke.

"Oh, come on, that was perfect!" he groans.

I look at him and see some facial hair on his chin and above his lip. I hate facial hair mostly because it irritates my skin when I kiss him but it also does not look good on him. He hates how he can't grow a beard like his brother Jared. Jared does have a nice beard that he keeps trimmed. I'm thankful Dean can't grow as much facial hair as Jared. I think it wouldn't look good on Dean anyway.

"It was alright."

Sasha had texted me earlier still second guessing about coming. I asked her if she had anything else to do and she said no. I told her to come over for a bit and if she doesn't have a good time then she can leave. Sasha is like me in that aspect. I too would have second guessed going to a party by myself where I wouldn't know anyone.

I finally see my sister pull up with Mike, my brother-in-law. I look at the clock and see that they are thirty minutes early. I wasn't expecting them this early but she did text me earlier saying they would be leaving my mom's soon from New Hampshire. My mom has a nice place in New Hampshire by a lake that is big enough for my sister to bring her two dogs.

I grab some flip flops by the front door and head outside. I see the dogs first and Dean putting a table outside for food. He is already talking with Mike and it seems like he already fired off another joke as Mike is laughing.

"Beth! You're early. How was the drive?"

I walk toward her as she is walking the dogs by our firepit. Dean and I want the firepit closer to the house with a patio because it would increase the curb appeal. However, town regulations have a rule about it being too close to the house so I can't get what I want.

"It was okay."

I see Mike with a pizza box and he is eating a slice.

"How come you guys brought food? We have plenty! Dean even bought hamburgers and hot dogs to grill. It's food I won't eat either."

I have given myself a strict diet so Sookie can be as fit as a fiddle when she is born. I refuse to eat processed meat and to only eat lean meat and red meat once a week.

"When I asked you about food, you didn't respond so I thought you wouldn't have lunch available."

I don't remember Beth texting me about food but she probably did. Lately, I check my phone and don't respond right away. I'm trying to break out of that habit as my mom has gotten on my case about it. I can see myself doing that to Sookie too.

"I don't remember that but what kind of party doesn't have food?"

Once I say it, I realize how snarky my comment is and wish I could take it back. It's a good thing that Beth has always been laid back and isn't defensive. Matt and I are not like that.

Beth tries to get the dogs to stay away from the pizza box as Dean is setting out chairs with Mike.

I finally see Rita park behind my sister's car and get out with her boyfriend. She was starting to worry me since she has all the decorations. I see her grab bags out of her car and come toward us.

"Hey Beth!" Rita yells at my sister. They both like each other and got along well when coordinating during my wedding. Rita would be an excellent party planner.

Rita drops the bags by the back door and I go toward her to see if I can help. Rita and Dean both tell me to relax and sit down but she does show me some of the decorations. As I'm obsessed with Harry Potter, she got light up boxes that say "baby" and a banner that says "Welcome Home, Muggle." She also has balloons to blow up to put around the house so people know where to go even though most of our friends have been here before.

Rita heads inside and I stay outside with Beth and Mike. Mike is allergic to cats so he rarely goes into our house. I deep-cleaned our house in case he went in to use the bathroom. Whenever Mike, Matt, or my dad come, I deep-clean this house and even wash our floors on my hands and knees. It's difficult to do that now but I hate when people get sick due to our cat. Lance is a Blue Russian which means he should shed less.

Beth and Mike are already sitting with the dogs in the shade. I take a chair and sit down with them enjoying being outside. I know I'm going to start getting too hot as I've been having hot flashes during this pregnancy.

"So, how've you been, Jackie?" Mike always asks how I am while fist bumping me. If he doesn't do it, then I know he isn't feeling well.

"I'm okay. I feel like a beached whale and my legs look like ones too."

I see Mike glance at my legs which are a bit hairy as I haven't shaved in a while. It's been difficult bending so I haven't bothered shaving unless I plan to go swimming at my mom's place.

"You don't look like a whale to me."

I'm thankful and amused that he says that. I almost weigh as much as Dean and it's starting to hit me. I know I'm carrying Sookie and she is growing really well but I still don't like how much I weigh. I'm just worried it's going to take me forever to get the shape I had before I got pregnant. I worked hard for the body I had before and don't want to have to start all over again.

It takes just a couple minutes for me to start sweating as the sun is on us. I'm comfortable sitting where I am and don't want to move. I can see Mike eyeing me so I know he will pick up on me fanning myself and say something soon.

"I'm hot. Let's move our chairs into the shade."
I knew Mike was going to say something. We move our chairs away from the firepit and closer to the two big bushes in our backyard that blocks most of the sun. As it is the middle of the day, this shade will go away soon but I move my chair with them.

Rita comes back out with the decorations and hangs the banner on the big tree by the bushes. She sets everything up with the help of Dean and it looks amazing.

I'm thankful people are starting to show up as I sometimes have no clue what to say to Mike and Beth, who have been oddly quiet. She's normally a chatterbox but hasn't been talkative today.

It's like everyone comes at once which is good as Rita put everything up in the nick of time. I was starting to worry but the food was out so that's all that mattered to me.

I keep looking at my phone as Sasha said she would text me once she got here. It's as if her ears are ringing as she texts me letting me know she parked across the street. I go toward the front and see her Subaru and Sasha standing by it. She sees me and waves.

For some reason I'm just not in the mood for a party anymore and just want to be inside curled up with a book. When I was sitting with my sister, I could feel my mood shift. I have had mood swings a lot during pregnancy so I hope my feelings subside as this party could go on for quite a few hours.

"Hey! It was super easy to get here other than the insane traffic."

"Yeah, traffic can be a pain on route three especially. I'm glad you made it!"

I bring her to the back and introduce Dean and my sister. Once introductions are made everyone sits in the circle that Dean made. Rita hands out cards to everyone for all the games we are going to play since I love games. I can't stand aimless chit chat. My attention won't hold and I grow restless fast. My college friends love standing around and talking so that's when I always suggest playing a game.

Everyone is filling out the cards that Rita handed to everyone so it's pretty quiet. I realize Dean isn't out here which is another reason why it's so quiet. He would start talking to make things interesting. He is able to get parties started whereas I just stand by myself and people-watch.

I look at all the cards. There is Over and Under where people have to guess whether they think the numbers in the statement are below or above the correct numbers. I'm not entirely sure if I'm doing this one right but I'm just going with it. One is Mommy or Daddy and I remember giving Rita the answers to this myself. Another one is all about me which I do like. Who doesn't like a game that is all about oneself? I see spells and charms questions to see how well everyone knows Harry Potter. The last one is well wishes for the baby. For some reason I have a hard time with this since I want to be serious so Sookie can look back and know how much I love her.

"So, what are we doing?" Dean is back from wherever he was.

I look up at him and want to ask where he was but decide against it.

We are filling out the card of who knows Mommy best? It's twelve questions about me that I love. I remember giving the answers to Rita for some of these questions.

"Hey, what is your favorite TV show?" Shasha whispers to me.

"I'm not telling," I whisper back to Sasha.

Rita yells out time and asks everyone how old I am. Thankfully everyone knows I'm thirty-one. The second question is tricky as it asks where I was born.

"Worcester?" one of my friends' answers.

Another friend shouts, "Boston!"

Rita looks at Beth and asks, "Do you want to say or shall I?"

Beth answers Rita, "Danbury, Connecticut."

We go through a few more questions until my favorite TV show comes up. Beth and a few others guess *Friends,* Sasha guesses *One Tree Hill,* and another friend says *Supernatural.* All of them are great guesses and it makes me happy I can stump my friends.

"It's *Gilmore Girls.* She watches it every year," Dean answers. "How do you guys not know this? She talks about it all the time."

"Well, your bachelorette was *Friends* themed so that's why I guessed it," Beth says.

We move past that question and move onto the cravings which cracks me up. Sasha sees me eat all the time as we work so she guesses most of it but everyone else's answers crack me up.

One of my friends says, "Caviar and sparkling water."

Another friend says, "Okra, pierogies, and peanut butter." This makes me laugh.
We finally make it to the last question of what my favorite color is. Everyone guesses correctly; purple.

"Nice! The last one we have is wishes for baby. Does anyone want to read there's aloud?" Rita asks.

One of my friends raises their hand and Rita calls on them. "I hope you love your family and friends. I hope you learn to experience life. I hope you experience anything you dream of. I hope you find your true self. I hope you laugh until you cry. I hope you respect your parents. I hope you aren't afraid to explore the world. I hope you become whatever you want. I hope you never forget to love life." It brings tears to my eyes that I wipe away.

The last friend says, "I hope you love your family. I hope you learn math. I hope you experience D.M.T." I have no clue what this is but Dean tells me later, chuckling, that it is a drug. "I hope you find a boatload of money." Everyone laughs at this. "I hope you laugh until you pee. I hope you respect everyone. I hope you aren't afraid to fight for the right to party. I hope you become happy. I hope you never forget nine-eleven, never forget."

The games are done so we open presents which are all very sweet. My sister had hers shipped since she bought one of the expensive, and big gifts, which was much appreciated. The changing table will be used many, many times.

After the presents, we start to eat. We tell everyone that we also have burgers and hot dogs since I won't eat them but no one wants one. Dean made cupcakes and I put two different kinds of frosting on them but I'm not in the mood for it. I've been having weird cravings lately and I sometimes don't want chocolate. Somebody mentioned ice cream cake and now all I want is that.

One of my friend's goes to the store to see if they have any since everyone says today is all about what I want. It's nice how supportive my friends are. I know I can be difficult, especially now, since I don't always communicate timely.

I'm sitting while everyone is walking around and eating. My feet are already swollen so I'm starting to feel miserable. I know Dean is going to tell me I should have worn my compression socks but who wears those with a dress?

Rita comes up to me and says, "Want to do pictures? It seems like people are getting restless."

I'm getting restless but taking pictures does cheer me up. I stand up and go over to the tree where people are congregated anyway.

"Who do you want first?" Rita asks, at the tree she set up for pictures.

"Dean first, then my sister. After that, it doesn't matter much as long as everyone is in a picture with me."

We take lots of pictures and when I look at them, I don't like them. I hate how fat my arms have gotten and the angle of my body. I don't say anything because I know the answer I will get. People will say I'm pregnant and I'm supposed to get some excess fat but that I will lose the weight in no time. I don't get how people can say that. How do they know I will lose weight in no time? Do they know something I don't?

Ever since I entered my second trimester it's been difficult for me to wrap my head around things. I get so overwhelmed with little things now. How do I know if a daycare is the right fit for her? Will I be able to work with her health conditions? Will she even make it? Will we have enough money to cover her medical expenses? Am I even being a good mother when all I feel is alone and defeated?

I try to push away these thoughts as today is all about Sookie but it's difficult. Today is about Sookie and I don't even know if she will meet all these people; not because of COVID but due to her health.

I sigh as people make their way to the cornhole game that Dean took out. I have barely been talking to anyone because I can't get out of my head.

"Ice cream!"

Those two words make me perk up. Ice cream does make me feel better. I go toward my house as our friend brings it in. A few others are following behind me.

"So, there were no ice cream cakes and I went to another store too. I figured Friendly's ice cream was better than nothing!"

I am a little sad about no ice cream cake, but he is right. Ice cream is still good. "These are great, thanks!"

I am truly grateful as this will cheer me up. Now that some people are in the house, Dean and I suggest a tour to the few who haven't been here like Sasha. I leave the ice cream behind as we give the tour. I love pointing out the built-in cupboard in our dining room as it is original. Our house was built in the 1940s and still has some special features which is why I fell in love with it. I'm thinking we might move though since I will want an open concept so I can see Sookie while I clean or bake.

Sasha sees Lance walk by and she says, "Hey, kitty."

Lance looks up at her and makes a small hiss and walks away as if he owns the place. "Lance isn't a people person and hates big crowds."

Sasha looks at me and remarks, "My cat is the same way."

We go upstairs into the nursery. Dean finished putting up the decals I bought from Target and it looks amazing. I wanted Sookie's nursery to be all about nature so her walls are green, except the paneling that was there before, with decals of trees, bears, rabbits, deer, and more. Dean did such an amazing job! He put up the changing table that Beth and Mike gave us plus the crib. This room always makes me happy now that it's semi-finished.

Everyone is complimenting Dean and I smile at him. I know a joke is coming from Dean as he always has a joke up his sleeve.

Someone asks which baby monitor we want and Dean answers her question.

"Well, the experts recommend putting a baby monitor in the nursery with your baby. It turns out they don't mean the lizard."

I look at Dean and shake my head in amusement. "Oh my lanta!"

Everyone looks at him as if he has two heads. Somebody says that he needs a better joke.

"Okay. What is Donald Trump's favorite nursery rhyme?" He waits for a bit and pronounces, "Barack a bye baby."

Everyone laughs at that as that was a good one. Somebody asks Dean if he tells his jokes to his students. He jokes when he knows someone is upset. If he is joking around now, that means he knows I'm upset.

Dean responds, "When the teacher asked a question the students were all up in arms."

"You know I wasn't asking for a pun, but that's a good one," Bob says who was the one who got the ice cream. "What are you currently teaching?"

This question is an issue with Dean as he has been having difficulty teaching English. I have been helping him occasionally by looking at his lesson plans and helping with vocabulary.

"Yea, I'm an English teacher. Good thing too as English teachers never write students off!"

I slap my forehead at that pun even though it's a good one. We all walk downstairs and I'm glad to be in the kitchen.

Everyone grabs some ice cream and heads outside. We all go toward the cornhole game and the boys make teams and the girls sit in the shade. Rita is sitting by me and Sasha is sitting by my sister.

I'm content. I'm sitting in the shade with people who care about me and Sookie. These are the people I know are my true friends.

I look around me and even though I'm not one hundred percent happy, I'm alright.

Chapter 11

It's just been a week and it's the day of the family shower that my sister is hosting. I'm surprised she was able to plan as she moved across the country yet again. My sister moves a lot with Mike and at times I'm jealous. All her moves are normally for work or school, for either her or Mike. The places she has seen are exquisite as she has been to India and Australia. One day I will travel the world with Sookie and Dean and make memories to last forever.

Beth is an amazing sister to have and I know I will utilize her when Sookie arrives as she's an occupational therapist. She had her own business with a partner when she lived in Texas and sold her share to her partner due to moving. She is getting her doctorate which inspires me to go back to school one day. I don't know much about Mike's job other than he works at a college. Normally when they move, it's not too difficult finding a job. Last week, they moved to Washington. I'm curious to see what kind of games she found for my party while traveling cross country.

My mom is supposed to be here any minute to help decorate as my sister wanted the decorations to be a surprise. The invites my sister made are so amazing that I already put them in my memory box. The invites were Harry Potter themed with a separate card for drinks such as butterbeer.

Ever since I told my mom about the Down syndrome diagnosis, things have been weird. I've been pushing aside her comments. At first, my mom was coming over a lot and we would go on hikes and get food together like we used to but then things changed in my second trimester. My mom seems to think everything has been her fault with Sookie's health issues. Hopefully today will be a good day.

I hear the front door open and a, "Hello?"
I'm wearing comfortable clothes this time with a nice shirt. I bought a maternity shirt as I figured I could wear it even after pregnancy as it's super nice. It's a dark green flowy shirt that I can wear with leggings. My hair is down for once but doing it's own thing. My hair has a mind of its own as it's kind of wavy.

I walk into the kitchen and say, "Hi Mom!" I try to make my smile go to my eyes but I'm a bundle of emotions.

She drops her bags in the dining room and comes in for a hug. "You are definitely getting big!"

My mom seems to comment on my size every time she sees me. At first it really got to me as it's been a sore subject for me. Once I told her how my doctor mentioned my weight and how it made me feel, she backed off with the weight comments.

I'm less than two months away from my due date and am getting anxious. I have no clue if I put all the things we will need on the gift list. I asked some parents at the preschool I work what they used for certain things such as strollers and cribs. I hope I put everything down as babies need a lot but also grow out of a lot of things fast. I only put a few books on the list as I don't want duplicates of books. I have been to a few baby showers where everyone buys the same book.

"It is two months away." I rub my belly and mutter under my breath. "At least you are healthy and nimble."

"Where is Dean?"

"I'm not sure. I think he is upstairs moving the computer into the nursery."

My mom makes her way toward the stairs as Dean runs down the stairs. "Sorry, I'm here. Hi Allison!"

"Hi Dean. I want to make the drinks. Do you have a pitcher I can use?"

I have no clue why she didn't ask me even though I have no clue where it is. We have a small pitcher and a party pitcher. Dean ends up getting the party pitcher out as well as some vegetables for us to munch on.

Dean and I go upstairs with the decorations that my mom brought with her. She brought balloons to make an arch to put behind us.

Dean starts pumping air into the balloons and tying them together while talking to my mom.

"Do you want to hear a joke about a balloon?"

I look at Dean and my mom says, "No" as she comes into the room. We both know his jokes. I laugh at my mom as we both know it will be corny.

Dean doesn't let it stop him. "Too late, it just got away from me."

I laugh as it was good but won't admit it to him because then he will just continue. He asks if we want to hear more and my mom and I both exclaim, "No!"

"Whatever you do, don't hand Elsa a balloon. She will only let it go."

I roll my eyes and walk out of the nursery and into our bedroom. I want to do my hair as I feel it looks horrendous. I brush my hair and the static goes straight up. I'm glad Dean isn't here to make a joke about my hair.

My mom walks in and asks, "Everything alright?"

I look at her and tell her I'm thinking of doing my hair or putting it up. She tells me it looks fine so I go downstairs for more snacks. I try not to eat too many snacks throughout the day but if I do I make sure it's something healthy. I'm thankful Dean bought vegetables and cheese and crackers.

Dean and I haven't been out in a couple months and I wish we could get away before Sookie is born. I know a lot of people go on baby moons but I don't want a trip. I just need a day out with Dean that doesn't involve hiking as my feet are so swollen. I love going to my mom's lake house and the water is nice for my feet. I'm just so worried that I could go into labor early and be hours away from the hospital. My doctor mentioned not going out of state close to my due date.

"Jackie!"

I jump as Dean walks in and asks, "Are you alright? Your mom is downstairs and there is ten minutes to spare."

I look at him and walk into his arms. I inhale his scent of evergreens. I'm excited about our shower but my worry for my mom is overriding everything.

"Do you think everything is okay with my mom? She seems off today. Do you think she is lonely? Should we be seeing her more?"

Dean looks at me and says, "It's possible. Try not to worry too much about that right now though. She is in a good mood and I will continue to joke around."
I lightly punch his shoulder and comment, "Stop it with the corny jokes. You're just making dead people roll around in their graves."

"You make absolutely no sense but I love you." Dean and I kiss and walk into the nursery.

He turns the computer on and we see my mom and sister waiting on Zoom. Soon my family from all over the United States is hopping on. I even see my mom's sister come on. I'm excited to see at least twelve of my family on, with some of my mom's friends whom I've known all my life. If I had any nerves beforehand, they are gone now.

My sister starts with the introductions and hops into the games. It lasts for about an hour and ends well. I had a lot of fun with the games despite needing help with guessing the artist with the lyrics. Dean is fantastic with music, so I cheated a little bit by looking at his paper. It was all in fun and I could tell everyone had fun. Dean and I both won "guess the movie with the emojis". That was probably my favorite game.

There wasn't a lot of talking as my sister hosted all the games and we entered our answers through an app on our phones. It was a lot of fun but I wish there was a portion where we talked. I enjoyed it but wish I could have aimless chit chat with my family as I barely talk with any of them.

My mom was in our dining room for the shower so Dean and I go downstairs and see her packing up her stuff.

Dean says, "I bought some steak for us to eat for an early dinner. Do you want to stay to eat, Allison?"

Dean is a very hospitable host. I on the other hand could care less. I say short visits are the best. If your home is comfortable then your guests will want to stay longer. My mom sees how I'm not a great host at times as she always comments about it. I do try to make sure my guests are relaxed and happy.

My mom replies, "I thought I could treat you both to lunch. Would you like to go to the tavern in the center?"

I am standing with my back against the counter in the kitchen with Dean at the sink cleaning the pitcher that had the butterbeer in it. My mom is standing in the middle of the kitchen by our island.

We look at each other and I can tell we are both okay with it. "That sounds great!" I don't sound enthusiastic but I'm also tired.

Lately, I have been sleepwalking. Last night I walked around the bed and woke up before I could get anywhere. I was at the foot of the bed so I climbed into bed forgetting I was pregnant and almost hurt my belly. It's been interesting but it's been making me tired waking up in the middle of the night in certain rooms. I'm just glad I haven't walked out of the house. I used to sleepwalk as a kid and at camp I ended up in another cabin almost climbing into the wrong bunk bed. I was mortified.

"Earth to Jackie!"

Dean is in front of me and I snap out of my trance. I look at him apologetically. "Sorry honey."

"Are you okay?" He looks concerned and he has only experienced me sleepwalking once. According to him I have been punching in my sleep too.

"Yea, I'm just tired." I look down at my feet that are beginning to swell. "And my feet are starting to swell so I don't want to be out too long." His phone rings and I know it's his mom. Tracy was trying to call him earlier before the shower started but he was busy with the balloons. He lets it ring which is not like him. Dean always picks up even if it's a number he doesn't know.

"Your mom is in the bathroom and I just need shoes. Are you ready?"

I'm not ready, so I go upstairs to grab my purse and flip flops. I know Dean will hound me about my feet but when my feet are this puffy, I don't bother trying to get my feet into my sneakers.

My mom is in the kitchen when I enter. "You ready?"

I have no clue why everyone keeps asking me that, but I nod my head.

My mom asks Dean if he can drive so we all climb in and head out. I'm exhausted and could fall asleep but it's just a couple minutes to drive there.

With the due date coming so quickly, it feels surreal. I have been waking up and before I even open my eyes, I forget I'm pregnant and am sad. Once I feel Sookie moving inside me, I smile and open my eyes. My body has been sore and tight and no amount of stretching helps. I've been doing yoga and ballet lately to help but nothing helps my body. The movement helps Sookie go to sleep though.

Dean backs into a parking spot and we all get out. I look at my mom who is putting a mask on so I put mine on as well. I actually don't mind wearing a mask as it hides my facial expressions and talking to myself.

We all walk in and I'm anxious. Lately, my mom has been giving me advice that I don't want. I know she is trying to be helpful but I'm starting to get annoyed with it.

"How are things going with you guys? Baby girl doing well?"

I never know what to say to my mom anymore so I let Dean take the reins. "Everything is going well. Baby girl is doing well and the doctor hasn't given any new updates on anything."

I still don't know if that is good or bad news.

"That's good to hear!"

Our waiter comes over to get our drink order. I decide to stick with water even though they make really good mocktails. We all talk about getting an appetizer to split and surprisingly I'm not craving anything specific, except sleep.

Dean's phone rings and I know it's his mom. She has been calling all day so I know he is going to take it because maybe someone is hurt. Dean excuses himself which leaves me with my mother.

"How are things between you two? You seemed tense earlier before the shower. Did Tracy say something to you?"

I never know how to answer my mom's questions. What do normal people talk about with their mothers? I used to be so good at this as we were so close when I was in high school.

"Tracy was having problems getting onto Zoom for the shower for Dean's grandma. I tried to help but you know me. I'm not great with technology."

"Oh. I just worry," my mom says with concern.
"I think it's sweet how close Dean and his mom are. Dean just worries a lot about her since his brother recently moved out."

I have no clue if that's true or not but I do know his brother is just like me and doesn't call a lot. Family doesn't need to know everything. As long as you let your family know through text that you're alive then everything is good.

"Be careful," my mom says, which confuses me.

I take a sip of water. I know she has her concerns like any mother would but her comments throw me off.

Thank God Dean walks in because I have nothing else to say.

"Everything okay?" I look at Dean to make sure everyone is okay as his grandma has been having health problems.

"Yea," Dean rolls his eyes and continues. "My mom didn't know the difference between some game consoles for my dad's birthday. I briefly told her because I didn't want to keep you two waiting for me."

"That is very thoughtful of you honey," I lean over to kiss his cheek as I know he is trying to make everyone happy. He always makes sure everyone is happy before himself.

"Actually, there is some water damage in my condo that I wanted to run by you, Dean, to get your opinion."

I actually roll my eyes and am thankful no one is looking at me. I tune my mother out as she told me what happened and I really don't need to hear this again. She spoke to both of us about this, this past week. This is why I'm worried because she has been repeating herself a lot.
Our food arrives and I dive into my French fries and a burger. Dean got steak which surprised me as we always order the same food without telling the other. At least now I can have a bite of his dish.

Chapter 12

I'm in the bathroom peeing for the billionth time and am bored. Thankfully Dean left his phone in here so I'm scrolling on his Instagram feed. A message pops up and it's his ex-best friend. They had a falling out due to me as his friend thought I wanted to use him when we first started dating. Obviously not the case. I want to click on the message but decide against it. If Dean wants to tell me, he can. We don't hide anything from each other which I like.

My dad is in town for a funeral for my uncle. My dad's family is big and very spread out. He should be on his way as he is staying with us. When he asked if he could stay here a couple of weeks ago, I was a bit hesitant due to potentially going into labor early. It's currently July and Ellie went into labor yesterday. She and Matt texted the family but we haven't gotten many updates from them and everyone is anxious.

Ellie and I have become so close. We tell each other everything and she has become an unexpected best friend. I am glad she was one of my bridesmaids as she has turned into a friend I have needed that I didn't know I needed. I always wanted to be pregnant with a friend and I am so glad it was with Ellie.

I took this Friday off from work so I could spend time with my dad as I rarely see him. Dean and I visited a couple of years ago but as he lives in Florida it is difficult to get there. Teachers don't make a lot of money and, as I work at a private preschool, I don't either. We aren't living paycheck to paycheck as I have saved quite a bit of money, but I digress.

There is a knock at the door and I try to move quickly to get it. As it is a little less than a month away from my due date, I am anxious and I hate being swollen. I actually like my belly but my legs and feet are the size of Alaska. My compression socks don't even help anymore which makes working with kids miserable. The heat, ugh. Don't get me started with the heat. It has been in the nineties but it feels more like a hundred degrees to me. I am constantly hot when I'm working and enjoy being home where it's cool.

"Dad!"

I am actually shocked as he looks younger. He started going gray a couple years ago but his beer belly is gone and he looks slim. He has a bit of stubble on his chin but facial hair has always looked good on him. His eyes even look bluer than normal. He must be happier in the warmer weather in Florida.

"Jacqueline. Despite being pregnant, you look good! You make pregnancy look doable."

I laugh as I know he is being genuine. My dad and I have a weird relationship as we don't talk often but we normally don't hold back which I like.

"Funny. I'm a beached whale and would like to be on a beach. Preferably in the water to stay cool."

"The heat is getting to you?"

"You have no idea. It makes me miserable but there is nothing I can do about that unfortunately."

"It is summer. Next time make sure you are due in the winter."

I chuckle as I don't plan on being pregnant again. "Not going to happen."

"Just one and done?"

"Most likely. I love baby girl and being pregnant really isn't that bad, but with all her health complications, I wouldn't want to chance it with another one."

"That's understandable. So, where is Dean?"

As it's Thursday and it's July, he isn't working. Dean ran out to the store so he can continue working on the downstairs bathroom that somehow took a hiatus while he was working.

"He ran out to the store to grab some things for the downstairs bathroom. He should be back any second."

"How are you feeling?"

I have told my dad mostly everything about Sookie's health concerns and he and my stepmom went through almost the same thing with the twins. My stepmom has two girls, Sophie and Sabine, and Sophie had a few health concerns. Sophie is now sixteen years old and very healthy. She is very skinny in my opinion but I know she eats.

I swear Dean knows when I talk about him as he just walks inside.

My dad and I walk to the kitchen to say hi and I tell Dean that I was going to show my dad the bathroom. Dean takes over showing my dad what he has done with the house. I gave him a honey-do list to get done before the baby arrives.

Having my dad ask how I am meant a lot. No one except Dean has asked how I truly feel. Dean knows how I feel but I don't know if he knows the full extent of my feelings. I don't know how ready I feel to care for Sookie with all her medical complications. I don't know how I would feel if I lost her. I have loved her since I found out I was pregnant and I would do anything for her. My heart literally aches thinking of how I set her up to fail in this world if she comes out and none of her health issues have gotten better. As her mother, I am bound to protect her. I am bound to nurture and love her to grow big and strong. I feel I am already failing as a mother to help her grow the way she should.

"What do you think, Jackie?"

I look up and see my dad looking at me. They must be talking about food as it is a little after six in the evening and I am starving. I needed food an hour ago.

"I like that idea!"

I literally have no idea what we are talking about but I swear I heard food and anything with food is a good idea.

"I was thinking we could go to that restaurant that overlooks the river? It's a few towns away I believe. I think it's called Glen River Lodge?"

Dean knows what he is talking about instantly which is good because I have no clue what my dad is talking about.

"Yea, we went there for Easter with your mother Jackie. You liked the food!"

I normally like food anywhere unless it gives me food poisoning which I haven't had yet in this life, and hopefully never.

"Great! Let me get ready and call the house just to check in. I will be out shortly."

My dad goes to the guest bedroom and Dean and I are left to our own devices. We are literally glued to our devices. There are times we will message each other when we are just a few steps away from each other.

"I'm going to get changed." Dean was at my mom's painting to earn a little extra cash. He is still covered in a bit of paint on his arm.

He normally landscapes but he decided not to this year due to the baby. He wanted to but I told him it would give me anxiety if he was working and I was at home by myself or at work and couldn't get to the hospital. I am a bundle of nerves about when my water breaks. Where will I be? Dean and I have talked about it, but you can't really plan these things out fully. Everyone works and people take vacations.

My Dad finally comes out of the guest bedroom and we all make our way to the restaurant. I always sit in the front due to motion sickness but now it's every second sickness. My motion sickness came on a few years ago and my family likes to joke about it. I let it be as it's mostly my head that gets heavy and very faint.

We all get into the rental car as my dad drives and Dean talks about the car. I have picked up on a few things about cars due to Dean's knowledge on everything. My husband's knowledge is absurd. I don't even know how he remembers everything but he always says a mind with ADD can be useful at times.

Once we park, I remember coming to this restaurant a few years ago. My memory is not the greatest, especially now that I'm pregnant.

We walk in and are instantly seated. My dad instantly orders a few appetizers for us to share which is good because I'm so hungry I could have been indecisive. I don't know how I get more indecisive about food when I'm hungry. My mind doesn't think well with so little food inside me, apparently. Sookie must be soaking more than just the food in me.

We are all looking at menus but then my dad asks, "Do you think Matt and Ellie's baby has arrived yet?"

"I hope so! I hate waiting!" I really do hate waiting. It's the youngest sibling trait. I may have half siblings but I don't share anything with them so I act like the youngest.

"I hope everything is going well with them. I think the baby has arrived and they are just in the moment." Of course, Dean is more rational and realistic about this than me.

My dad grabs his phone and answers a text. He has been on his phone a lot tonight. I can tell he is preoccupied as he seems more distracted. I hope everything is going well with him.

Looking at him makes me grab my phone for any updates and it's just an update from the family text of my mom, siblings, in-laws, and Dean. This chain blows up so much I have to mute it or it gives me major anxiety. I love texting and prefer it over talking but group messages put more pressure to respond. When it's a lot of people in the chain and everyone is saying the same thing, it makes me wonder why bother responding when someone else said the same thing? Who needs five congratulations or happy birthdays? Some people may like it but I find it annoying in a text message. If it is a message from each person separately, I appreciate it better. I feel like other people also feel obligated to respond so their response isn't as genuine.

"What would you like to order?"

I haven't even looked at the menu. I have, but I'm debating between two entrees.

Thankfully my dad responds, "Can we have a few more minutes? We have been preoccupied. My son is waiting for his first baby to arrive any moment."

"That is so exciting! I will leave you to it."

I go back to looking at the menu but then my dad starts talking again. "What do you think they named their boy? Matt has always liked strong names."

"I like the name Logan but that's just me." I am also obsessed with Gilmore Girls and would name all my children after that show if I could. Dean and I want three kids so I could get my Lane and Logan. If I want more kids. That's still up for debate.

"I could see them using William as that is a strong name but it's Matt and Ellie deciding." There goes Dean again with his logic. I sometimes find it annoying but tonight I'm too tired to care.

"They sent a picture! Roland Luther. Huh. Not the kind of name I thought they would use." My dad looks shocked. "That is one clean baby after delivery. It must have been a cesarean but they don't mention details."

I look at the text and he is right. It is a very clean baby and quite cute. That baby looks exactly like Ellie with my brother's nose. Sookie has quite a bit of hair and I'm shocked Roland doesn't. Roland also is a name you don't hear often but it is unique. I love unique names but I also love nicknames. How can you get a nickname out of Roland? Ro? Land?

My dad is right about the baby being clean. I know Ellie wanted to have a natural birth so I'm curious if they waited a few hours to take a picture or if she did have a cesarean. I hope I can push Sookie out but I'm not opposed to a cesarean. I just want to try my hardest to push her out as much as I can.

We finally ordered our food after being here for probably fifteen minutes just talking. I feel bad but the dining room isn't too full. There is a decent amount of people here but it isn't crowded on a Thursday night.

My Dad and Dean start talking about the trees outside which bores me. I always wonder how Dean learns all the miniscule facts about everything. He is a walking encyclopedia and if I need an answer I know he can give it to me. If he doesn't know something, he looks it up and retains it for life. I'm quite jealous of his memory but it's one thing I love about him.

Our food arrives swiftly. I've never received my food so quickly and I'm still a bit full from the appetizers. It's a good thing it took us a while to order our food. We are all quiet as we eat and I somehow manage to finish my food. My Dad asks if I want dessert but I don't think I can stomach any more food.

Knowing Ellie and Matt had their baby makes me nervous for Sookie's arrival. Despite my doctor being open about everything, I have no clue what to expect. Will I be able to hold her? Will her heart be okay? What if her organs are worse than the doctor's predicted? I can't help thinking about all the what ifs but I don't want to be so optimistic thinking I will be able to walk out of the hospital with Sookie in a day's time. I need to snap out of thinking this way because it makes me sad.

I don't want my dad or Dean to know what I'm thinking so I try to figure out if I can slide into the conversation without them knowing how depressed my thoughts are. They are talking about cars now which I know nothing about.

Dean mentions something about muscle cars and I try to interject into the conversation. "I saw your favorite car the other day Dean. It's the Firebird, correct?"

"That's one of them, yea." He continues talking with my dad and I'm glad I at least said something.

"Are you ready to leave Jackie?"

I nod at my dad, thankful that we can go home. I'm having fun but when people talk about things I know nothing about, my eyes glaze over.

As we are leaving, a group asks us if we can take their picture. It is extremely pretty here but I just want to get home and leave. Dean, being the gentleman he is, says yes. Now I have to wait, which I hate doing, especially since I'm not wearing the proper footwear to be standing for too long. I grabbed flip flops on the way out because I didn't want to put my compression socks on. I don't care that I run the risk of my varicose veins popping.

Dean gives them their phone back and they say thank you. I glare at them as selfie sticks were made for a reason. I realize I'm being a hypocrite as I do ask people to take pictures of Dean and me when we hike but when you see a thirty-seven week pregnant lady, don't make her stand and wait for her husband.

I'm happy Sookie hasn't arrived yet. I have told her that her cousin has to come first if she really wants to be early. Thank God, Ellie's son came two weeks late as I would have been a basket case if Sookie had come at thirty-seven weeks.

With all her health complications I still don't know how we both will survive. The past month, if I don't think about her list of health issues, I'm fine. If I do think about it, I cry.

What if she can't swallow food? I know the doctor mentioned surgery but she already needs open heart surgery. What if more complications arise when she's born?

I wish she could stay inside me for more months but she is gaining weight. At least I'm doing one thing right in my life, eating healthy. My OB and the cardiologist are impressed with Sookie gaining weight already. It gives me hope that our life isn't completely doomed.

Chapter 13

It's a week later and I'm sitting on our couch while Dean works in the bathroom. I'm lucky I married such a handyman as pulling the tile off the floor and wall would have been expensive. On the other hand, I bet my bathroom would have been done by now. Although, saying Dean did all the work is worth it.

I'm getting bored of sitting on the couch while Dean does renovations. My mind wanders and my body aches. Normally Sookie wakes me with more kicks but she wasn't very active this morning. This has happened to me a couple of times but once I start eating food with more sugar, she starts moving. It's a good thing Dean always buys me ice cream.

Despite doing all my tricks to get her to move more, I have only felt her a handful of times in the past three hours. I haven't said anything to Dean but I'm freaking out thinking she's stuck on her umbilical cord not breathing. Thinking that, I start crying believing Sookie is stuck and could be in serious danger.

I pick up the house phone and call my doctor's office. I speak with the nurse who tells me to lie on the bed and try to count any movement in the next hour while waiting for the on-call doctor.

I already did that which is why I walked downstairs to grab some water. When I'm anxious I pace and I'm now pacing in the kitchen. I hear Dean in the basement and can tell he is about to come upstairs so I hurry as fast as I can upstairs so he can't tell how nervous I am. He knows me well and I don't want to worry him if this is all in my head. Sometimes as I am an emotional thinker, I make things grander than they are.

I lay on our bed and try to even my breathing by counting. I last ten seconds before asking myself how others can do this.
I pace our bedroom staring at the phone that I left on the bed waiting for it to ring.

"Please tell me you're okay, baby girl. You're scaring mama."

I don't feel her move and I try not to cry but I broke the dam earlier so they flow freely. Reading normally distracts me so I grab my book but reading about World War II will depress me further. Historical fiction is great but I need to be in the mood.

The phone rings and I instantly pick it up.

"May I speak with Jacqueline West please?"

"This is she." I try to make sure he can't tell I was crying by leveling my voice. I have no clue if it worked.

"Tell me what's going on. You mentioned you haven't felt your baby move in the past couple hours?"

I nod as if he can see me. I clear my throat and say, "Yes. I tried laying on my left side counting how many movements I felt and only felt one." I know my voice sounds shaky which I hate.

"I think it's best if you come in so we can monitor the baby and go from there. I would bring your labor bag just in case."

That's reassuring.

I hang up the phone and my mind is blank and tears are streaming down my face. This is not how I envisioned my labor. I thought my water would break and I would be a mix of happy and anxious. Now I'm terrified and don't know what to expect which frightens me more.

I walk toward the kitchen and almost walk into Dean.

"What's wrong?"

I don't know where to start so I say, "We need to go to the hospital now."

"Okay, let's go." He doesn't even ask questions. My worried face must have him on autopilot.

My bag has been in my car for the past month so I grab a pillow and my Kindle. I hope I have everything so how can you be fully prepared to give birth?

I look at Dean who is dressed in jeans that are torn and a ripped tank. He doesn't even think of changing. I don't even know if he has had lunch as it's well past noon. He always works for hours on end without breaking for food. That's something I could never do.

I'm in the car and he comes out with the baby car seat. It's a smart idea as I didn't even think of that.

"So, are you in labor?"

That's a loaded question as I have no clue but I could be or Sookie may be in trouble. "I don't know. I called the doctor's office when she was not moving and they told me to come in."

Dean is quiet as he drives. I look at the speedometer and see the speed going to eighty miles per hour when it's posted at sixty-five. He is either anxious, nervous, or both.

As it is a Sunday, we get to the hospital in record time and head to the labor triage. I don't go the wrong way this time but Dean is also leading. I haven't learned how slow I go in flip flops.
They bring me to bed number one which makes me feel special. I look at the time and it's close to three in the afternoon. I have no clue what to expect as I am scheduled to be induced in just two weeks. Sookie does not get how I like to plan things but despite these thoughts I rub my stomach anticipating meeting her…just in the near future. Like two weeks in the future.

One of the technicians walks in so we can look at what Sookie is doing. She is currently sunny side up on my right hip looking peaceful. It looks as if she's sucking her thumb. I have a picture of her doing that in an album. Soon the technician leaves to go talk with the doctor and I know that will take a while. I remember being in here last time after my car accident lying in this bed bored out of my mind.

For the next hour I read while Dean plays games on his phone. When someone comes in, I jump in anticipation.

"Looking at the sonograms and the state of Sookie we plan on inducing tonight. We are currently waiting on a delivery room to be available for you as today seems to be popular to give birth. Do you have any questions?"

I don't have any, just nerves. I didn't expect them to do it this soon. I really don't think I'm ready. Can I really push a seven-pound, seven-ounce baby out of me? I remember my friend gave birth to her nine-pound daughter but that was her second and I've heard your second baby comes faster than the first. I just don't know what to think. What kind of mind space do you need to be in for this?
I know Ellie pushed for a while and then had a cesarean. I never asked her many questions about it and now I'm regretting it. I could text her now but a part of me is debating whether that's a good idea or not.

"How are you feeling?"

I look at Dean and don't know what my face looks like. "I'm nervous. I don't know what to expect or how long it's going to be. What will happen once I push Sookie out? Will she be healthy enough for me to hold her?"

"We will see. We won't know that, but I do know you did everything you could to make her as healthy as possible. I wouldn't worry too much, Jackie. You are strong and so is Sookie."

I know Dean is right and hope everything goes smoothly.

It's almost midnight and I've been stuck in this bed for hours. Dean is in the next room sleeping while we wait for a room to be available. One of the nurses brought me a sandwich and snacks since I've been ravenous. This waiting is killing me and I hate how I eat when I get bored.

A different nurse I haven't met comes in and asks, "Are you ready?"

I have no clue what she's asking me but I somehow say yes despite not being ready for any of this. I'm terrified out of my mind.

"Are you alone or is your spouse around? We're moving you to your room!"

Now it makes sense. I wasn't expecting a room as I thought it would take another day at the rate everything was going.

"Dean, my husband, is sleeping in triage two."

"Perfect, I will go get him. You stay here."

Dean walks in a minute later looking all ruffled. I have no clue how he can sleep when we are about to become parents in a day or two.

"I just got woken up by a very chipper nurse. What's going on? Did they finally find a room?"

"Yes. Where did she go? Did she tell you her name? If she said it to me, I completely forget."

"I don't think so."

She finally comes back in with a wheelchair. I'm happy to get out of this bed. The triage beds are not very comfortable after a few hours.

The nurse talks on the way to the room. As it is early in the morning, I do not know how she has so much energy. I do like her as she cracks jokes at Dean who is being a good sport about it. I know he doesn't like people joking about him but I think he is as nervous as I am.

She helps us get settled in the room and goes about her business. I'm now in a more comfortable bed but not as comfortable as I would like. I ask Dean for a pillow to prop myself up a bit. The nurse told me to relax before they induce me and I have no clue how that happens. That would have been a great question to ask.

She comes back with some sort of contraption that makes me hesitate about what's to come. I'm beginning to think I should have just waited to come to the hospital since Sookie was fine…despite failing her breathing test.

"Are you ready?"

I look at her unsure how to answer that question. "I guess. I kinda have to be."

"So this is a Foley balloon and I'm going to insert it into your cervix to induce your labor. I want you to lie back and get comfortable as this can be uncomfortable."

I don't know how she expects me to get comfortable knowing something is going to get shoved up my vagina. She tells me what she's doing but I would rather she get it over with. I feel it inside me and it's not that bad, just uncomfortable.

"Is it normal for me to need to pee after this has been inside me for a while?"

"You can use the bathroom. It will help us to see if it worked!"

I waddle to the bathroom and go pee, however the balloon falls. I ask if that's normal and it isn't.

Once I'm back in bed she inserts another one. This one feels different and I feel something on my leg.

"It worked! You are officially in labor, my dear."

Oh boy.

Chapter 14

It's been three days that I have been in this bed with minimal sleep and with contractions ten minutes apart. It feels like I've been in this hospital forever. I just want Sookie to come out. I've been trying to bounce on a yoga ball and even squat her out but she's perfectly content in there.

I hear her heartbeat all the time which is very comforting but I'm getting extremely antsy. I've learned that the nurses mostly work twelve hour shifts which I find horrifying. These poor nurses are probably exhausted.

Dean has been supportive and helps the nurses when he can. Even though I'm in labor, he is still telling his horrible jokes. I've told him I'm unable to walk away from his jokes and he should spare me but these nurses are too nice and laugh at his jokes.

A new nurse comes and introduces herself as Gail. Most of the nurses tend to introduce themselves and look at everything. Sometimes they give me more Pitocin to speed along the labor. Gail does that as I set my book down. I try to read but I can't focus. My mind is either racing with thoughts or a black abyss.

"What is your book about?"

I tell her it's historical fiction based on World War II and how these two sisters are fighting in their own way. I just read how one sister climbed a mountain with fallen soldiers to get to a safe place before going home. She tells me about a book that she recently read when a sharp pain just goes through me. I squeeze Dean's hand tightly as it passes.

"Did you feel that?"

"Oh, I felt that. She has had a few contractions but she has never squeezed my hand that tightly."

I glare at Dean but it happens again and I squeeze him again eliciting an "ow". A part of me is glad I was able to hurt his hand that badly.

"I'm going to get your doctor. Your daughter's heart rate is elevating which could be due to the Pitocin. Try to relax so she can relax."
Gail comes back with a resident doctor who takes a peek at my cervix. She says I'm four and a half centimeters dilated and to drop the Pitocin a bit due to the stress it's having on Sookie.

I still feel the pain of my contractions but after a while they go down which relieves some of my stress. My muscles relax a bit but my body aches from being in the bed so much. I'm used to moving and working out, not lying down all day.

The contractions aren't as strong and I lie on my left side. One of the nurses had me laying in certain positions to speed up my labor but I'm still here. The position she had me in was weird as my top leg was hanging off the bed but my lower leg stayed on the bed. It was very uncomfortable.

"Let's decline your feet to see if that will help a bit."

I let Gail do her thing as she does this for a living. I haven't been questioning anything and I'm not sure if I should.

I feel another contraction but I have been feeling them sporadically. Ever since Gail came in, I have felt more contractions which excites and terrifies me. I'm ready for Sookie to arrive and finally meet her. I just hope I will be a good mother to her.

"Your contractions seem to be getting closer together. Are you feeling them?"

"Oh yea." It's hard not to but it doesn't last too long.

Gail excuses herself and comes back with the same resident doctor. She exclaims I'm seven and a quarter centimeters dilated. The resident asks if I want to do a practice push so I decide to with my next contraction which is now every two minutes.

We don't wait long and I push for ten seconds by holding onto Dean's hands. Gail gets a bar to attach to my bed for me to hold onto during a contraction. Holding the bar feels better as I push.

Gail tells me to relax and to save my energy for pushing later on.

"Do you do yoga?"

I look at Gail quizzically and answer hesitantly, "Yes…"
She tells me to stay on the bed but to flip around holding onto the raised bed. I start doing the cat and cow poses hoping that Sookie will flip.

The reason why my labor is taking so long is because she is sunny side up on my right hip and seems perfectly content. She doesn't understand that she's already giving Mama a hard time.

I seem to be doing the poses for a good ten minutes when I ask Dean to help me flip.

"You did that for a long time. You also had a few contractions. How about you rest and I get you more grape popsicles?"

"Thanks." It's been weird not eating anything but I've not been hungry. I haven't had a real meal since Sunday night and it's almost Wednesday night. Let's go Sookie. Mama wants real food as she misses it. I hope she hears my thoughts as we are technically one right now.

My contractions are starting to feel stronger so I'm hoping Sookie is ready. I really don't know how much more I can take. I'm used to running marathons but this is completely different. This seems like an Ironman but longer.

Gail comes back with the popsicles and looks at my catheter. When she checks my catheter, it makes me think back to when I was a nurses assistant. Gail is funny as she always comments on how well I pee. I should tell her I'm used to drinking a gallon of water a day.

"Dean?"

"Mmm?"

"I can't finish this. It's making me feel queasy with the contractions."

I hear Gail's chair and see her coming over from the computer in the corner. She told me it shows her my contractions, Sookie's heartbeat, and my blood pressure.

"Your contractions are getting closer together. I'm thinking we can try speeding up your labor by upping the Pitocin while I monitor Sookie's heartbeat so it doesn't skyrocket again. Sounds good to you guys?"

I nod my head as I'm ready. I didn't feel ready on Sunday but I feel ready now. I just want this to be over.

The contractions are starting to get closer and closer together making it more painful. They finally drug me as the time has come. The doctors asked if I'm ready to push despite not being ten centimeters. I don't know if I'm being impatient but I feel like I can do this. I did a few practice pushes which felt good but weird. I'm glad I did many squats and held each for ten seconds. I found a great workout program as I feel ready to push. I'm hoping I can put the workout program to the test.

I have no clue how long I've been pushing but the whole team is here and they all keep telling me how close Sookie is. They keep telling me how red her hair is which motivates me but I feel so spent. I feel like an elephant is sitting on my chest making it hard to breathe. I want to be strong and be a good example but everything hurts, especially my lungs.

Dean is holding my hand while I pant. I feel a contraction but I just can't push. I physically and emotionally just can't. If someone could tell me Sookie will be out of me in five minutes with a few more pushes, I could probably keep going despite how my body feels.

"Your daughter is right there, Jacqueline, but your heartbeat is high. There are some devices we can use to help you deliver Sookie safely."

She tells me my options and I'm leaning toward the vacuum but don't know if it will help or not. How do I know if it's the right choice? What if I pick it and end up damaging our daughter even more?

I look at Dean for answers. "What do you think?"

"It wouldn't hurt. Your grip has become loose so maybe this will help. We could try the vacuum and if you don't think it's worth it, then we stop."

I nod my head and wish I could have more painkillers. It wore off at least an hour ago and I've been feeling it. I whisper to Dean, "Do you think you can ask for more painkillers?"

"Do you guys think you can give her more painkillers? It could probably help her."

One of the doctors answers no, but I don't hear the reason.

"Are you ready, Jackie?"

I nod my head and wait for a contraction. Sookie is ready and I push. I hear people encouraging me and Dean counting to ten. I release my breath at ten seconds and go again. I feel Sookie's energy and think I feel her about to come out.

"Her head is almost here! Keep pushing, you got this!"

I push but it's as if a fly swatter zapped all my energy as I feel dead. I try to push but release it in just two seconds. Dean stopped counting and I feel woozy. Everything starts to feel fuzzy and I see specks of light around the whole room. Everyone seems to be far away.

"Jackie?"

I hear Dean and something snaps me slightly out of my daze. I look up at him and whisper with tears in my eyes, "I can't."

I feel so defeated. I have no energy. I'm near tears but can't even cry. Silently I'm crying as this is not how I pictured my labor going. I gave up which I hate myself for. I have always gone through life trying everything and not being a quitter. I already wish I could turn back time to redo my labor and wait till I was ten centimeters.

Chapter 15

Sookie is being held against my left shoulder so I can see her. Someone unwrapped my arms from the side so I could touch her. I don't even know how I feel as Dean told me I pushed for eight hours and Sookie Olivia West was delivered at seven oh one in the morning. She weighs exactly seven pounds and is the cutest thing I've ever seen.

Right now, I don't feel anything and hope they keep giving me painkillers. I stare at her face and she opens her eyes slightly. Blue eyes just like mine but prettier. Of course, my girl has to outdo me, that would be a me thing. Her red hair is striking and I hope it stays forever.

They take her away and I hear Dean at the door with one of the nurses. I'm glad he is following Sookie but also a bit sad.

"Let's close her up. Do you want to take the lead?"

I'm still open? Thank God I can't see anything or I would probably tell them to hurry it up. It's a good thing they made this dome around my head so I can't see them work on me. I'm shaking and want to be close to a furnace. I've been shaking ever since they wheeled me to the operating room. I don't know if it's due to shock, cold, or lack of energy. I feel all three so maybe it's a combination.

I realize they are taking the dome away and are about to transfer me to a bed. I try to move my legs to help but I physically can't feel my legs. I can only feel my arms. They transfer me with ease but it sent a sharp pain through my abdomen. The feeling is coming back but I still feel…clumsy.

I'm brought to a room with a few other beds and a nurse gives me crackers and ginger ale.
"Eat up, sweetheart, as you need your strength."

I take the crackers and nibble on one not feeling remotely hungry at all. I take the ginger ale and almost drink the whole thing.

I feel so alone despite the nurse being in here and wish Dean were here. I can feel the tears about to come as I gave up. I gave up on Sookie by not continuing to push. If I had just kept going, I wouldn't have needed a cesarean.

Dean comes in and walks over to me. "How are you feeling?"

I look at him as if he's stupid. How does he think I feel? I gave up on our precious daughter and am recovering in a weird room. I can't really eat and am drugged.

"Sorry. I wanted to follow Sookie to make sure she was okay. She's up in the NICU so I can bring us there when you're cleared."

I'm not even capable of seeing my daughter. How am I going to be able to see her?

Dean seems to realize he keeps saying the wrong things as he says, "Sorry, honey."

He strokes my hair making me realize I must look a mess. I haven't showered since Saturday and it's Thursday. Ellie told me it took her almost three days till she showered which makes me feel almost better.

I can't believe I'm worrying about my appearance when I know nothing about Sookie. "How is she?"

"She's good. Sookie woke up and looked around and went back to sleep. They mentioned doing all the tests for her kidney, esophagus, and head. We won't be able to see her as they are doing those tests now. She's beautiful, Jackie. You were amazing."

I look at Dean and can tell Sookie stole his heart. She's not even a day old and already has Dad's unwavering love and loyalty.

I can't wait to see her and hold her in my arms. I look at the crackers and eat a few so I can see her soon.

"Okay. Someone should be collecting you shortly to bring you to your room. Congratulations." The nurse from the corner comes over to relay the news and promptly leaves.

I smile and say, "Thank you" before she exits the room.

It's a couple hours later and the pain is intense. I thought I would be able to see Sookie but no one tells you how your body will feel after pushing followed by a cesarean. Although, I'm not sure how I would describe it either. It's excruciating and I can't imagine moving. I'm glad I have a catheter. They can leave that inside me till I'm able to walk.

"What's your pain level right now?"

I don't want to say ten and be a wuss so I say eight as I love even numbers. Odd numbers seem to be unlucky for me.

She tells me I'm on quite a few painkillers that are overlapping for pain management and the nurses will ask my pain level every shift. She also told me the catheter is coming out so I don't get an infection and I want to cry. I'm terrified to walk anywhere after being cut up.

The nurse leaves and Dean is by my side. I feel unsteady as if I'm ready to collapse even though I'm laying down. I try to scoot up in the bed but the movement makes me gasp. Tears well in my eyes due to the pain, but I think of Sookie who is a fighter and needs her mom. I blink the tears away hoping Dean won't notice.

I realize I need to use the bathroom and grab my phone. The nurse gave me a cell number to text whenever I needed anything. I'm curious if it's faster than a call light.

"You need help in the bathroom?"

I feel stupid for asking but I have no idea how to get out of this bed. I nod my head.

"My suggestion is to grab onto the bed rail and swing your legs to the side. The first time getting up, you will feel unsteady. I also have pads and liners for the bleeding."

If I didn't do any birthing classes, I would have no clue why you bleed so much after labor. When I did the class, it explained how your body gets rid of extra blood and tissue that helped grow your baby. The bleeding can last up to a week but if it's longer, and still heavy, it's not normal. Another thing the doctors ask is if I've pooped since I just had major surgery. I'm just hoping I poop in a day or two, or they could keep me longer. Thinking of the bathroom makes me need to go even more.

I brace myself and stand up. I feel extremely unsteady, lightheaded, dizzy, and in tons of pain. I don't even take baby steps. I shuffle toward the bathroom due to the pain. Once I'm on the toilet, it's awkward. Leaning back hurts like a son of a bitch as well as leaning forward. I'm leaning sideways onto the toilet paper dispenser. I feel humiliated with how I'm handling the pain.

The nurse hands me a pad and liner for the weird underwear I'm wearing. It's insane how much blood is coming out of me. She gives me some sort of bottle to squirt at my vagina. The wonders of life after labor.

I feel a little better and don't shuffle my feet this time. Getting into bed is a bit easier than getting out of it. I need to remember to really train my body if I do this again. I've never felt so weak in my life. I've also never experienced so much pain in my life.

Dean would most likely understand the pain level as he tore both his ACL's.

It's currently past dinnertime and a wheelchair was brought in so I could visit Sookie. I walk a few steps to the chair.

"Did you want to visit your daughter?"

I nod and she says she will call the NICU to let them know we are on our way up. She puts a sheet on the chair which makes sense as I could stick to it. It's surprisingly comfortable.

All three of us go up to the NICU. Dean has his phone so we can take pictures. I'm finally going to see my daughter. I'm both excited and nervous. I'm in so much pain that I don't want to drop her.

I'm being wheeled into Sookie's room and I stop breathing. She's so tiny and sleeping in a tiny incubator with so many wires attached to her. I try to stay strong by not crying but she looks so fragile yet peaceful.

"Sookie recently went down and she's been doing great with her bottles. She certainly loves to eat as she just guzzles it down. I'm Denise and will be taking care of her tonight."

"Thank you," I whisper. I don't want to wake her. I'm scared to touch her due to all the wires and with how small the bed makes her look.

Denise looks at the monitor and asks, "Do you want to hold her?"

That's a loaded question. I do but I don't want to hurt her if she's somehow too much weight for me. I hate thinking that as I used to powerlift. I've never felt so incapacitated in my life. I look at Dean hoping he says yes so I can touch her.

"Yes, we do."

I'm grateful he answers and holds her first. Although I guess he held her earlier when she was born. I try not to be jealous but I can't help it.

Denise expertly picks her up and places her in Dean's arms. She quietly leaves the room for us. I look at Sookie and she looks so tiny against Dean's bicep which isn't that hard as his biceps are as good as Vin Diesel's.

She looks so peaceful in his arms. Dean gets out his phone and tells me to get close. He snaps a picture of all of us. It's the cutest picture and her sleeping face makes it so adorable.

"She has my face. She even looked at me earlier and she even has my eyes!"

"She's your mini me. Although, her nose is cuter and she has my forehead."

Her nose is cuter and, sadly, she does have his big forehead. I want to hold her but I'm terrified. I don't want to drop her or somehow hurt her. My pain isn't too bad sitting but I do feel pressure by my incision area. I currently have a pillow there applying pressure which feels nice.

"Hold her. I will be here in case you need help."

I look at Dean and hold my arms out for her. Dean places her in my arms and untangles the wires that bunched up. I look down at her and just stare.

I can't believe how she was inside me for eight and a half months. I can't get over how beautiful she is. She's all mine. My daughter. My precious baby girl. I want to hold her forever and not let go but my pain is starting to come back.

"I want to keep holding her but my pain is starting to increase. I don't want to hurt her." Dean comes over and takes her from me. "Wait!"

Since we have to wear masks, I pull it down and give her a butterfly kiss with my nose. She moves a little bit but doesn't wake. I don't want to leave but I must as I'm due for medicine since the pain is really intensifying.

Dean leans down to give her a kiss goodbye and wheels me off. We get back to my room and flowers and a massive Godiva chocolate box is waiting. It's from Ellie and Matt which makes me feel bad I didn't do anything nice for them once Roland was born. I feel like a horrible sister but the chocolate is calling my name. It's hard for me to feel bad or even depressed if I have chocolate.

We turn on the Olympics which has been on all week. It was very motivating when I had my contractions. I kept thinking how training for these sports is just like giving birth. The intense training these Olympians endure to get to where they are is wondrous. Most of the athletes train eight hours a day, seven days a week. I fall asleep thinking of labor as an Olympic sport and I win!

I'm woken up by a nurse telling me it's time to take some medication which I gladly take. She asks if I need anything so I ask for more apple juice. I look at my phone and am surprised there are no messages from the family. I know Dean was keeping them up to date throughout the whole delivery.

The nurse comes back and I ask her for help to the bathroom. It's still painful to walk by myself. I hate having to hold onto someone while walking. I'm getting into a rhythm of taking care of myself in the bathroom which sounds humiliating but I'm proud of it.

I'm awake and it's six in the morning. Nurses kept waking me every four hours for some kind of medicine. I'm glad they are staying on top of my pain management but sleep is awesome too. Dean is somehow still sleeping but I'm starving.

I look at my bedside table and see a tissue box. I throw it at him which misses his head. I'm terrible at throwing as I always miss my target. I look for something else and see a cup. I throw the cup which hits him but not in the face. He doesn't even stir. I pick up my phone and hope his phone is on. It vibrates but doesn't wake him.

I finally whisper, "Dean!"

"What?"

"I'm hungry and I want to see Sookie. The nurse told me there's some sort of menu and phone in here. Since I'm currently an invalid, I need your help."

I hear him sigh but he searches and finds a menu. I can't order till seven. I have us jot down what we want but the options aren't a lot.

"I can always run to Dunkin Donuts to grab coffee and breakfast sandwiches. Want me to do that?"

I don't want to be alone in case I need to pee but I'm extremely hungry. I haven't had an actual meal in almost a week. Popsicles can only take you so far. I weigh the pros and cons as I don't know how long it would take the kitchen here to get everything ready and brought up when it is seven.

"That would be great. Just hurry, okay?" I really don't want to be alone and I also want to see Sookie.

I would have stayed with Sookie last night but needing medication every four hours makes it difficult. I need help walking to the bathroom which I hate. I hate asking for help. I don't know why asking for help is a form of growth. Maybe I can't grow as a person but I like trying things myself. If I fail by myself, I will look at the situation and consider different ways to get it done. Some people say I'm stubborn but I say I'm ingenious.

"It's across the street so I will try to be quick." He gives me a kiss on the lips and takes off.

I finished the book I was reading so I grabbed my Kindle while I wait for Dean.

My phone vibrates waking me and it's finally seven. I pick up the phone and order some food. I will never say no to free food. I still order the coffee here to see if it's good or not. I'm starting to need to use the bathroom and am worried something happened to Dean. He has been gone for a good half hour and it's early in the morning. I wonder what I should do about going to the bathroom. I could try to go myself as I'm on medicine so it doesn't hurt as much.

I decide to go for it. I have to be a strong mom and make tough decisions so I'm going to go to the bathroom myself. I certainly sound like an invalid. I scooch myself to the edge of the bed and prop myself to sit on the edge. So far, so good. I stand up and tentatively step forward. It does hurt but not as much as yesterday. The urge to pee is real and I try to squeeze but I waited too long. A little comes out and I'm glad no one is around to see it. My friend was right when she said your bladder is never the same after a baby. I've never wetted myself before. Thankfully, it was just a tinkle but I'm still embarrassed about it.

I make it to the bathroom and plop onto the toilet. I'm curious what my scar looks like down there and where exactly it is.

"Jackie?"

"I'm in here!"

He opens the door and asks, "Did you get to the bathroom yourself?"

I proudly say yes and don't even mention how I slightly peed myself. He has already seen enough with the soaked pads and more importantly, the doctors cutting me open. I'm quite envious he got to see it.

"I'm proud of you. I know how much pain you've been in and I know how painful surgeries can be."

His praise makes me feel good. I haven't felt strong due to all the medication I've been given and not walking well by myself. I hope this feeling goes away because I want to be a strong mom for Sookie.

"Coffee and breakfast sandwiches. Sorry about the coffee as they poured so much in the cups that some of it spilled out. That's why it took me so long."

I wash my hands and look at my reflection. I flinch as my hair looks greasy and matted in places by not being washed in a week. Hopefully I can shower soon because I look horrendous and probably smell.

I walk toward my bed and Dean comes by my side. "I can do it. I'm just really slow." I swat his hand away from my waist to emphasize my point.

"Okay. I will just stay close just in case."

I roll my eyes but internally am grateful I'm lucky to have such a nurturing husband. Hopefully, I don't lose him with my mood swings. I sit in my wheelchair instead of my bed for our breakfast. As we eat, I start to get uncomfortable and think it's due to not having any medicine in quite a while. I decide to text my nurse since I want to see Sookie after eating and don't want to be in pain while holding her.

"Hello! I'm Reya and will be your nurse till three. I have your pain medicine as well as your vitamin C and iron pills. Your blood work came back saying you're anemic. Were you aware of that?"

I wasn't but as I had surgery, I can see that happening. "No but I bet I lost quite a bit of blood. Being anemic after surgery is normal, correct?"

"Every person is different but it isn't always a cause of concern. We will do another blood test before you leave on Monday just to be safe."

Now I'm a bit worried. Dean never had any issues after his surgeries so I don't know what to think. I try not to think of it now as I want to see Sookie.

"Can I see Sookie after this?"

"Of course! I know lactation wanted to see you. Someone should be by shortly as it's probably to see what kind of pump you want."

I completely forgot about that. Sookie must be having formula which is good to know she likes it. The nurse last night said she was guzzling it down. Already showing the doctors who is boss. My little boss baby. I smile thinking of her upstairs in the NICU eating and sleeping. I know she's in great care but hate how I can't be with her.

Soon Reya is gone and the lactation consultant is in. Thankfully I didn't have to wait long but I haven't really had my breakfast yet. I also have to use the bathroom again because coffee goes straight through me.

I realize I missed her name and she's still talking. "...so I suggest pumping every two to three hours for ten to fifteen minutes, just to make sure you feel empty. I'm going to leave the pump here for you and the brochures about the pumps for you to look at. I can come by tomorrow to see if you picked a pump to bring home!"

I never thought of pumping. I always thought Sookie and I would breastfeed but I guess I can pump since I'm not always with her. I also don't want to nurse her in the middle of the night if Dean is awake. He normally doesn't go to bed till eleven so he could easily feed her.

I look at the pump and at Dean. "Am I supposed to hold them both in place while I pump? How do people normally do it? "

Reya walks in and sees me eyeing the pump. She must have heard my question as she answers me instead of Dean. "There are pumping bras you can wear but we can take one of these bandeaus and cut some holes in it. My friend took an old sports bra and cut holes in it."

I take it from her and put it on. It's definitely interesting but once I put the pumping materials through it, it works like a charm. I thank Reya for the suggestion. Despite getting the news about being anemic, it's been a decent day so far.

Once everyone leaves, I take the pumping materials off. My boobs started leaking during my third trimester so when I look down and see that I made three, almost four-ounce bottles, I'm happy with myself. Dean can't stop telling me how I should sell my milk. Before leaving to see Sookie, I use the bathroom and, holy halibut, it hurts just to poop. I'm happy it didn't take me too long though. Exactly twenty-four hours after my surgery and I poop. Now everyone can stop asking me if I've pooped.

Dean and I go into Sookie's room and she is awake. She looks beautiful. My baby girl with her red hair and sparkling blue eyes! Looking closer at her eyes I see a silver tinge to them toward the middle. I'm cradling her close to my chest and am not afraid anymore to hold her. I was foolish thinking that because even if I somehow lost my grip I wouldn't drop her. Dean takes her from me and holds her himself to get some love from her. She is so tiny and precious.

A nurse comes in and introduces herself. At this point I've stopped learning all their names because it's someone new every day.

"Sookie had a great night. She kept eating every three hours. She has gained some weight! Her stats are looking good however we do want to see her SO2, oxygen saturation, number higher. It's currently in the eighties and it should be between ninety-six to one hundred. She has 'coded' a few times over the night but I say that loosely as she moves a lot and her sock comes off making her numbers not normal. Do you guys have any questions?"

Dean and I look at each other and say no. I never know what kind of questions to ask in situations like these. Despite being in the healthcare industry for a while, I don't know what kind of questions to ask in the heat of the moment. My questions come to me afterwards when no one is around and I have to ask Google.

"Hello, I'm Dr. Jag, one of the genetic counselors here," a tall woman walks in. Something about her makes me tense up which makes me grip my pillow in my lap in pain.

"Have you spoken to a genetic counselor before?"

"Yes, we have. It wasn't very informative. It was like I was back in high school learning genetics even though I already knew it." Holy crap. I just sounded like a bitch but it's true. Our session was not informative. It was boring and gave us no answers about anything.

"You need basic understanding to learn why children are born with Down syndrome. Looking at your daughter I can easily distinguish many characteristics of Down syndrome. For instance, she has low muscle tone in her neck. Her eyes are close together. Her hands and feet are extremely small. The way her lips part as well as how her tongue sticks out of her mouth."

I really want her to stop talking because babies with their tongue out of their mouth is common. I have many students who stick their tongue out and they don't have Down syndrome. Playing with your tongue as a baby is normal.

She starts touching Sookie without warning and starts doing things while talking. "Her muscle tone is extremely low and she could have possible hip dysplasia already. Since she has heart, kidney, and esophageal issues those are also common for Down syndrome babies as well. We do have a clinic for Down syndrome kids and families for support. I have a lot of pamphlets here for you both to review with my card in case you have any questions."

I look at this doctor and really hope she feels my hatred. "Actually, we want to do more testing to see which type of Down syndrome she has. I do not see her eyes being close together like a Down syndrome baby and as a pre-k teacher I have many students who stick their tongue out so that characteristic should be reviewed. Furthermore, I have Down syndrome which is why she has it but I have Mosaicism. I also know there is a condition called translocation. Also, each person is different intellectually and developmentally regardless of whether they have a disability."

I can't believe I just said that and I'm proud of myself. This doctor has not helped us by talking about the main characteristics of Down syndrome and saying my daughter has it. I don't care if my daughter has it or not. I love her and she won't be treated any differently than any other baby in this world.

I look at Dean who looks completely stunned. I normally don't talk back to others but I can't stand down. This lady can't be going around being so cold toward parents who went through labor to deliver a baby who instantly gets whisked away to the NICU.

Everyone sits in silence and I have nothing left to say...unless she has more snide comments about my daughter who is perfect to me. Her heart may have a hole in it but she is all mine.

Dr. Jag says goodbye and leaves. I stick my tongue out toward her and say, "I can't believe I just did that. Did I sound bitchy?"

"A little bit but it was well deserved. Who does she think she is coming in here and saying all that shit about Sookie? Low muscle tone? Small hands and feet? Don't all babies have small hands and feet?"

I know he is pissed off just like me and I'm happy I'm not alone. We don't have time to talk as a few people come into Sookie's room. One of them I remember from yesterday which makes me feel good that the team almost stays the same.

"We have some good news and some bad news," the woman doctor announces after introducing herself. I really won't remember her name in just a few minutes, especially after what she has to tell us. "What would you like to hear first?"

I answer the bad news as I don't want to hear it at the end. "The bad news is that the foramen ovale never closed. That is the normal opening between the two chambers that should close after birth. Sometimes it does take a couple days so we are monitoring that. The good news is that her feeding test came back negative which means no surgery on her trachea! The other test on her kidney also came back negative which means her right kidney is fully functioning. However, she will need more testing for her kidney but that can be done as an outpatient. We are monitoring her heart for the foramen ovale to close as well as her weight gain. She seems to be doing well with the latter. I know I just sprung a lot of information at you. Do you guys have any questions?"

Dean asks them a question about the heart and refers to cars which makes me tune him out. I know why he asks questions regarding subjects he likes so he can retain it but it makes me stop paying attention…sometimes.

The doctors seem impressed with his knowledge as I hear one of them ask, "Are you a doctor?"

I'm proud that my husband is smart but he makes me feel stupid sometimes. I hope I look like I'm paying attention as I'm lost to what is being said.

"Well, in that case if you guys have any other questions let us know. I tend to be up front by the doors."

Everyone leaves, leaving Dean and me alone with Sookie. I stare at Sookie and tears well in my eyes. I'm glad her kidney and stomach are working but I hate knowing that her heart isn't functioning well. I don't get a lot of what is going on but I do know she has to work ten times harder than any other baby.

I touch her hand and wish we were home. I wish we were on our couch with Sookie in my arms. I wish she didn't have this heart condition and that I could take any pain away from her. I hate feeling like a failure but I do, which makes me hate myself more. I have to keep telling myself to be strong so I can be a good role model for my daughter. I feel Dean's eyes on me and look away.

"It's okay to cry Jackie. I hate it too. The good thing is that Sookie is getting excellent care here so you can get better."

I'm still in a lot of pain which makes myself hate how weak I am. It's a vicious cycle of emotions inside me and I don't know how to control them.

All I know is that when I'm in here with Sookie I feel like a horrible mother who can't take care of her daughter. When I'm in my room, I feel weak and distraught and can barely walk around my room. My nurse tells me to walk around as it will help with my recovery but it hurts. My incision stings and burns. It feels like it's being ripped apart with every step I take. I know they sewed me well but I worry that I could be damaging the work they did by walking too much. I just don't know anything anymore.

Chapter 16

"Do you have any questions about any of the information I gave you?"

I look at my nurse and am overwhelmed. I'm going home today and I don't want to leave. I got into a good routine and was able to see Sookie whenever I wanted. If I leave, I will be away from her. I was hoping to leave this hospital with her, not empty handed. I know it could have been worse, as there are women who give birth to stillborn babies. I, at least, am lucky I gave birth to a beautiful daughter…whom I can't bring home with me.

Dean has been at the house all weekend finishing the downstairs bathroom as stairs will be hard for me the first day. The doctor says to take it easy but to walk. I personally don't like the pain and would rather be sitting but I'm also getting antsy. I miss doing things but the searing pain is still there when I walk even a hundred steps.

I realize she is waiting for an answer so I try to think of a question. I asked about stairs but can't think of anything else. "I think I'm all set."

"Good, if you think of anything else let me know."

Reya has been my day nurse quite a few times and I like her. The nurses on this wing have eight hour shifts. The nurses on the labor and delivery side work for twelve to twenty hours which boggles my mind.

I'm worried I'm going to forget to take my medicine while at home and be in a lot of pain. They are bringing me home with oxycodone but I'm still worried. I wonder if this worry will ever go away. I'm starting to worry about even eating on time.
Dean is currently getting the car out of the parking garage and bringing it to the valet. Now I'm starting to worry about being in the car. I hope it doesn't hurt as much since standing up is still hurting. I realized too late that I should have asked about managing my pain in the car. The seatbelt would be on top of my incision that flares up in pain without warning. I know my pain is due to it being stiff as it's new and needs to be gently

stretched, therefore everyone tells me to walk. Not bend, or squat, or lift, but walk.

The agony this incision gives is unreal. I'm worried about sleeping in our downstairs bed. It's too soft for my liking and makes you sink toward the middle. I still use the bed railing here so how can I get out of bed at home? I know I'm thinking too much now but I can't help it.
"You ready?"

I jump as I wasn't expecting Dean so quickly and am still packing. I've been slow due to the pain, but mostly because I don't want to leave. I don't want to leave Sookie behind. My jump makes my incision burn, making me put my hand there to add pressure to lessen the pain.

I add the rest of the pads the hospital provided me and zip my bag shut.
"All set."

Dean picks up my bag and looks at me. "You okay?"

I don't understand why people ask me that. No, I'm not okay. I'm in lots of pain still and worried about being home. I'm scared that I will do damage to my incision by either doing too much or too little. I definitely don't want to leave my daughter behind but have to. I'm a mix of emotions that when I go this crazy my mind becomes blank. I space out of everything completely.

"Jackie?" Dean comes up to me and touches my arm.
"Not really but I'm moving." He looks confused at my answer but I don't know what else to say. I don't lie to Dean and I know he also is upset that Sookie isn't coming home with us.

"Do you think you can walk or do you want to use the wheelchair?"

"The wheelchair. I'm not that strong."

"You are strong, Jackie. You just gave birth to a beautiful baby girl. Yes, it sucks she can't come with us. Fuck, I'm a mess too Jackie. I wanted to leave this hospital as a family. I had no idea she would have to stay in the NICU for longer than a couple days but she's alive and thriving.

"It's not what we expected but I'm grateful to be a dad and have two strong, fierce ladies. Stay strong Jackie. We can get through this together."

I look at Dean with tears in my eyes and don't bother trying to swipe them away. This is why I love Dean. His loyalty never wavers.

I sit in the wheelchair and tell him I'm ready to leave. We both know I'm not but if I don't leave now I never will.

He wheels me down and outside to the valet. We have never done valet so he stands with his ticket waiting for someone to be free. The guys are just standing by their booth just talking to each other.

"I think you just need to go up to them honey. They aren't mind readers." I try to nudge him so we can get going.

He gets his keys and he wheels me to the passenger side. I grab onto the handle and hoist myself up into his truck. Neither of our cars is low to the ground but mine is closer. It's difficult maneuvering myself into the seat as my incision burns. I take the seat belt and realize how this is going to hurt. I make the seatbelt extremely loose by holding it out and Dean notices. He grabs the pillow that I've been sitting on in the wheelchair to put underneath the strap. It cushions it enough that the belt doesn't hurt. I sigh in relief.

Dean drives away from the hospital and I look out the window with tears in my eyes. I hate leaving my daughter behind. I did not envision leaving the hospital without her and it is tearing me apart. Dean takes my hand that is resting on top of the pillow and squeezes. I know he knows I'm crying despite me looking outside. He knows me too well.

"I would try to make you laugh but I know you told me laughing hurts. What can I do to take the pain away?"

"I don't know." I hate how hoarse my voice sounds when I cry.

"I hate seeing you this way. It hurts me too but she is in the best care possible. Her nurses are taking good care of her. That's what we have to think about."

I know he is right but it hurts. He drives over a bump which makes me gasp in pain. The pain shoots up to my lungs and burns. He takes a turn at the light and my abdomen squeezes making the pain even more intense. I have never experienced pain like this before and I would not imagine it on anyone. I grip onto the handle above the door to keep myself straight. Whenever he nears a bump or a turn, I try to loosen my body as when my body goes rigid it hurts like a son of a bitch.

I know Dean asked if I was alright but I am now definitely not alright. "Can you stay on the highway next time instead of going on the windy backroads that have a gazillion potholes?"
"Sorry. I didn't realize it would hurt you."

I didn't either but the highway has less turns. Thankfully, we are almost home and I can relax. I think of home and the nursery. I don't want to go home. I don't want to see the nursery. I don't want to see all the cute baby toys we have been receiving. I wish the tears would dry up and disappear but I know they won't. All of her medical problems are my fault. I wonder if we had conceived her last year, would she have all these issues? If only I ate healthier from the get go and didn't have almost an entire bottle of wine the week after she was conceived. I hate myself for giving her a crappy start of life. I wish I could take her pain away. I wish we could trade lives so she doesn't have to endure open heart surgery and to be able to come home like a regular baby.

I remember seeing the other babies in the NICU and a lot of them are tiny. One baby looks to be the size of my hand. One baby sounds like a pig. Another has so many wires attached to him that I worry about him as well. I don't see many parents besides the other babies and wish I was next to Sookie right this second.

Our house is in front of me and I know I have to get out of the car eventually. I already have to pee and have no clue how I'm going to get around our house. I'm thankful Dean has the summer off because I would not be able to be by myself. When I'm sick, I need all the help as I'm a wuss with pain and taking care of myself.

Dean opens the door and says, "My lady."

I roll my eyes but am thankful he is here to assist me. I grab his hand and slide down the seat and into the driveaway. I grab ahold of his arms as I walk up the three stairs to our front porch and wish we didn't have these stairs.

We walk inside and it smells stale. I have been in the hospital for over a week. It feels weird to be home. Dean told me that Lance had a few accidents while we were away and his mom tried to take care of him. Lance runs to the door and I try to bend down to pick him up but it hurts squatting down.

"I got him." Dean picks Lance up and I can hear him purr. We do our family hug with Lance in between us while we scratch his face.

"Oh, bubba. How I missed you." I really did miss him. It was weird being away from him for as long as we were gone. We had only been gone from Lance for at most two days when we got married.

I normally like to unpack right away but I'm curious where I will be most comfortable here. Our couch is a bit deep to sit on but so is our chair. Dean said he finished the downstairs bathroom for me so I wouldn't have to go upstairs until I was ready. It was really sweet of him but I hated being by myself in the hospital. I was lucky one of my friends came by with doughnuts and stayed for a while. The crazy thing is that my friend also delivered her girl at the same hospital with the same doctor as she was high risk due to her diabetes. It was interesting when she came to see me as my doctor was in there checking up on me.

"Jackie? You kinda spaced out right there. Are you hungry? It's only about four o'clock but we can have an early dinner, maybe watch a movie?"

I honestly want to be by myself but not. It's a weird feeling. I don't want to say no and hurt Dean's feelings but being here without Sookie is making me feel weird. I also know I should pump so Sookie can have more milk but the doctor's told me to rest and not worry too much about that.

"I want to pump first so I can bring a lot of milk in for Sookie. Can we find the pump first?"

The lactation specialist told me to pump every three to four hours for fifteen to twenty minutes and I plan on doing that. I know I need to take care of myself but with Dean here I can ask for his help and take care of Sookie first.

When I pumped for the first time it was extremely weird. I'm very sensitive and every part of my body is ticklish and so are my boobs. Apparently, whenever I had a letdown, which is milk coming out fast, it tickled. I'm one odd duck but I certainly don't want to be normal.

"Here you go honey." Dean hands me the pump and I look around trying to figure out where to sit. "How about you try the couch? Maybe put a pillow behind you?"

I sit on the couch but without a pillow behind me it hurts. The doctor said any activity that engages the core will hurt but won't do any damage. I hate pain so I won't do any activity that will engage my core if I can help it. I just didn't realize that engaging the core happens all the time.

Dean puts a pillow behind me and it feels much better. "This is good. Thanks honey." We don't always say unique pet names but when we used to write letters to each other we were honey bunches and oats. We never spoke it out loud much.

As I'm putting my pump together Dean is looking at the pump I asked for. Once it starts running, he starts talking about how cool the settings are and starts pressing buttons as I'm pumping.

I swat his hand away as I say, "Knock it off. It felt good before you started pressing buttons. Go do something."
"I have nothing to do. I don't even know where I will be this school year. If I prep for history, it could be a waste of my time if I don't teach it."

Due to COVID, he taught from home while I did house projects, ran, and worked out. I helped him with work such as vocabulary and grading. It was a lot of fun. I have always thought of being a teacher but when I see how much Dean has to do at home that thought runs away. Teachers bring so much work home. I give Dean a lot of credit for what he does as I really couldn't do it.

I look at him and at my pump to see how much time I have left. I don't feel very hungry but when I'm sad I don't eat much unless it's ice cream. I will always have room for ice cream.

"Can you bring the bags upstairs and get me some pajamas then? I wouldn't mind taking a shower so I will need my shower things."

My first time taking a shower was scary. It hurt like hell and my body was shaking even though I wasn't cold. I was in a lot of shock due to the pain and my whole body was trembling. Dean kept trying to help so much that I almost bit his head off. I only washed my hair and he got my backside and that was it. I couldn't stand much and sitting hurt too much. I'm hoping this shower will be okay and am thankful our downstairs shower is a stall. Upstairs is a tub so I would have to climb in. I know I'm not ready for that yet.

"I can do that. Do you want anything in particular?"

I look down and know a lot of my clothes still won't fit me. "Maybe my pregnancy clothes? Pants though because I'm a bit chilly."

I hope I can start working out at the six-week mark but I know every body is different. So many people have told me that I will get my body back within the first year but I'm doubtful. I know having a baby will change everything. I know my time will be dedicated to her and her needs, especially with her health condition. I also know every baby sleeps differently and hope Sookie is a good sleeper just like me.

Dean leaves to go upstairs and my pump says I've been going for almost twenty minutes. I hit the end button and start taking everything apart. I didn't think breastfeeding includes pumping but I enjoy it. Since I can't be with Sookie, I'm glad I can still do this. I did try breastfeeding but she just nuzzled up to me and I almost lost it. Looking at her and how warm she was. I just fell more in love with her. I didn't even care that she didn't want to drink from my boob. Once the specialist came in, she suggested a nipple shield to help Sookie. It did help some but Sookie didn't stay latched on. I was always on the fence with breastfeeding just due to the demands and with how people judge. I plan on trying a bit more but I'm not going to force it since Sookie will be in the hospital so much. I don't want others looking at my boobs while she nurses. Even if I have some cover-up, I would feel so weird.

I take the bottles to the kitchen and fill up three four-ounce bottles and feel satisfied. I've been told not many mothers start making milk right away or make this much. The specialists told me I'm an over-producer and to make sure I pump on a schedule to stay safe. She didn't explain what she meant so I hope it isn't anything bad. Everyone has told me to take care of myself but mentally I need to know I'm taking care of my daughter first.

"Are these okay?" Dean comes downstairs with workout shorts that will be too tight and a workout shirt.

"The shorts are workout shorts. My pjs are in the top left drawer of my dresser. You can put those back where you got them as I won't be able to workout in a while."
"Oh, okay. You didn't tell me where to look so I opened a few drawers."

I realize that now. "Sorry. Can you also bring down a bra? Maybe a sports bra?" I feel like my boobs have grown so I'm not sure what will fit. "Maybe grab some big ones?"

"Got it. Those are where?"

"On the left side but in the middle? It's right below my pjs."

My dresser has staggered drawers so I have no clue why I'm confused describing it to Dean. If I've always wanted to be a writer, I don't understand why it can be so difficult describing details to him. If it's someone's features, it's because I rarely remember the minor details. He also knows me so well that if I describe someone that we both know he will know who I'm talking about in under thirty seconds. Even when we play charades, he sometimes knows what I am. Unless I get a zebra, that's when I kick my leg back and do a little sashay. Dean just looks at me and has no clue what I'm doing, but now he does.

Dean disappears to go back upstairs and I wait for him on the couch. I'm nervous about taking a shower at home but I have to get over myself. To be a good mother, I have to set good examples. I don't want Sookie not trying something due to low self-esteem.

"Okay, how about these?" Dean holds up long pregnancy pants and a shirt.

"Much better."

We both walk to the bathroom and Lance walks behind us. Once he hears the water from the shower he scurries away. The chair is in the shower and I wonder if I really want it. Sitting up straight makes me use my core more which ends up with me shaking. If I stand, I can have my body be limper but still wash myself.

"Can you take the chair out honey?"

"Are you sure?"

"Yea, it's easier for me to just stand."

Getting undressed is still tricky for me as, when I bend for the pants, my incision tightens and the pain intensifies. It makes me fear that my stitches are going to fall out and I will need surgery again. Dean says doing things helps the tightness go away and the pain lessens in time but my impatience is going to make things worse. My fear, on the other hand, is going to make things worse.

I step into the shower and I jack up the heat. I normally love cool showers but I don't want to scare Dean if my body is trembling like it did before. When that happened, I realized it was because my body was in shock. My body wasn't used to standing for that long or even sitting for a prolonged amount of time.

I don't stay in the shower for too long. I quickly wash my hair and my upper body. As I'm turning off the water Dean pokes his head into the bathroom and then fully emerges.

"Do you need help? I can get your back for you."

That does sound nice. I end up turning the water back on and he washes my back for me. He also tries to rub some of the tape off my stomach and arms from the needles I had in me for days. I'm definitely not having another child as the whole ordeal was not fun. Sookie will be fine being an only child and playing with her cousin.

I must have sighed as Dean was saying something. "Honey? You spaced out there. Are you okay?"

"Yea, sorry. It's just weird. I'm having all these thoughts. The pain, Sookie, pumping…my emotions are just all over the place."

"You just gave birth. Of course, your emotions are haywire. I would make a pun but I will refrain myself as I know laughing hurts."

"Much appreciated. I know you joke about things when you are stressed and you can talk about it. We are in this together."

"I know but I'm fine. I like being strong for you and Sookie. It makes me feel good."

"Well, if you need to talk, I'm here."

He helps me with my pants as I put my hand on the doorframe to steady myself. We go out to the kitchen and he has already started dinner so I flip through Netflix seeing what's on. I don't want a funny movie as that will hurt but I don't want to be scared as I don't want to jump. Action movies are normally our go-to but I don't see anything that piques my interest. I used to love flipping through Netflix and watching the trailers of each one but now I'm just getting aggravated.

"Did you find anything to watch?"

There was one that looked interesting. It was an animation with singing that looked adorable. I tell him about it and he tells me to play it. We spend the night eating and watching TV. I forget about how I'm going to get out of bed. Dean and I practiced earlier but the bed is so soft that it hurts. The height of the bed also makes it difficult for me to try the couch. Sitting up is so difficult especially since my doctor told me not to overwork my core muscles which is freaking difficult. The core is the powerhouse of the whole body. It centers us and makes us not fall over. How am I supposed to not overwork it when we use it all the time?

I end up sleeping on the chair I watched TV in with two pillows behind me.

I wake up at five and have a mini breakfast and pump. I want to wake Dean but he looks adorable sleeping with Lance on the guest bed. I know he didn't sleep much when I was in the hospital so I decide to wake him at six. It's currently six and I'm standing over him as he is snoring lightly. I actually don't miss sleeping next to him because his breathing sometimes tickles me. I hate how ticklish I am.

"Dean." I poke him. "Dean, wake up." This time I throw something at him which doesn't help. "Dean!"

He opens one eye. "What?"

"It's six and I want to go see Sookie. Plus, I need your help getting dressed."

Dean takes forever getting out of bed. He lays there and does a little stretch but stays there. Once I hear him fart, I know he will get up. For some odd reason, once he farts, he then gets out of bed. I don't know if it's a guy thing but it's weird.

Watching him isn't interesting as he moves slowly in the morning. He says he is a morning person but he is more a night person. He is sluggish in the morning and takes a while to wake up. He can wake up early but getting him out at a certain time is difficult. I'm normally the first one out the door for our day trips.

"Thanks for making coffee."

"Of course. You can also put it in a travel mug and bring it with us. Speaking of, what do we have to pack my milk? I want Sookie to have enough milk to drink."

I haven't been pumping every three to four hours as I slept through the night but once Sookie is home, I will keep to a schedule of pumping religiously. I actually enjoy pumping as I tend to read while I pump to occupy the time. I think of when I saw Sookie for the first time and it makes me happy.

"Give me a minute. Let me have some breakfast first and then I will pack that up, okay? Relax first."

I don't want to relax as I want to get out of this house and see my daughter who is all by herself. I know babies sleep a lot but I want her to know that Mama and Dada will always be right there whenever she needs us. I hate the thought of her crying and no one going to console her. I try not to go down that rabbit hole or I will cry. I need to stay strong for my baby girl.

Chapter 17

It's been so difficult coming to the hospital and it's only been two days that I'm feeling so helpless. I feel like all I do is hold her and she can't come home. She is gaining weight well and even though her flap still isn't closed, I don't understand why she's still in the NICU. The doctor's keep saying the same thing. We need to monitor her levels to be on the safe side. I've been in the healthcare industry for ten years. I want to tell them I know the signs to look out for if we need to go to the ER. I wouldn't let my baby suffer.

Dean and I have been going every day and stay almost all day but we don't do much other than hold her and have her do tummy time on dad's chest. I love taking pictures of her but I hate how she has all the wires on.

When I look at friend's pictures of their babies, they are home and smiling. Sookie doesn't smile but she does look at us with those silver-blue eyes. Her red hair is getting longer so I'm starting to play with it. I try to think of those two things when I look at other babies but I long for Sookie to be home and in my arms. Every time I hold her, I can't contain myself and kiss her repeatedly. I want her to know how much we love her and hope my love heals her quickly.

Sookie and I try breastfeeding but I get so frustrated that she doesn't latch. She nuzzles into me or just looks up at me. I don't stay frustrated as looking at her makes my heart melt. She turns my heart into messy chocolates that were out too long in the summer weather. Dean has always said I'm a prude and I can't see myself sticking my boob out in public for Sookie to nurse so I haven't pushed nursing a lot while she has been in the NICU. I can try it again at home as that's where we will be most of the time anyway. I can cocoon her to keep her safe from any harm that has been happening in this world.

I shift as I slept on the couch last night instead of the chair in the living room and I slept so much better. I know I need to get up since I really need to pee. The last time I held my pee in too long I actually peed myself and I would have been humiliated if anyone else was there besides Dean. Thankfully, he helped me and even cleaned up the pee that got on the floor. My blood also got on the floor and the toilet. I felt bad that he cleaned up after me so much after my surgery. It must be retribution from all his surgeries.

Dean was smart and tied my gait belt onto the couch and tucked it behind the pillows. It helped me when I had to get up during the night to use the bathroom. People really don't kid when they say your bladder isn't the same after giving birth. I grab onto the belt and hoist myself into the sitting position and instantly everything blurs together and I see stars. I try to blink hoping it makes everything go away but I feel extremely faint and very unsteady, despite me sitting down.

"Dean?!"

I know he won't get up if I scream even though he is still sleeping downstairs. I'm terrified. I have no clue what's going on with me and it's not getting better.

I slowly get up from the couch and my head feels so heavy. I can barely feel my body as I walk through the dining room and into the guest bedroom on the left. I don't stop since I still have to pee but now if I yell Dean will hopefully wake up.

"Dean!" How much louder do I have to be to get him up?

I barely have any energy to yell but I'm scared that I will topple over onto the floor from the toilet I just sat on. That would be a sight to see. A lady half naked, passed out on the floor. That would be wholly embarrassing.

"What?" Dean says groggily from the bed.

"I don't feel good. I feel extremely faint."

He comes toward the bathroom and looks at me. "You look pale. Have you had anything to eat or drink since you got up?"

"No, I just got up. I tried getting your attention before I walked in here but you were dead to the world."

"Sorry. You know I'm a heavy sleeper."

"Yea, I know. It's why I threw stuff at you in the hospital." It was fun throwing things at him to get his attention. I was irritated that he wasn't waking up but I was able to get out a lot of aggression.

"I'm not sure what you want from me."

"I don't know. Advice? It's only six in the morning so I can't call a doctor."

"How about you sit there and I get you some water. If you still feel this way in two hours when offices open you call your doctor. I know you like being at rounds to hear about Sookie but we don't need to be there all day. It isn't healthy and we don't spend enough time at home getting things done."

"What things?" I have been reading a hardcover book and my Kindle to go through my list of books to read that are never-ending.

"Things that you shouldn't be doing. I have to do the yard since it hasn't been done since you returned from the hospital. I think I will get that done while you relax and drink some water."

I do like it when he takes care of me. He always makes me feel like a princess. Dean comes back with the glass of water and I sit there sipping it. I feel weird just sitting on the toilet so I get up and still see stars but my head doesn't feel heavy. I feel light-headed now. Dean helps me walk back to the couch. I sit down on the couch with the hassock by the edge of the couch for me to relax. Thankfully, I don't have to pick my legs up anymore to help swing them into or out of furniture.

"How are you feeling? Your color is returning."

"I feel a little better. My head is now light-headed and I still see stars but better."

"Stay here and only move if you need to. I'm going to make you breakfast. What would you like?"

"I don't know, food?" I know he hates that answer but I have no clue what we have for breakfast.

He sighs and says, "Really? So a slab of beef is fine?"

I look at him and give him a face that says really? " Eggs then, asshole." I stick my tongue out at him.

"You are a pain in my ass." He flips me the bird.

I look up at him and smile. "Thanks, I know I'm number one."

He looks at me as if he has something to say. I'm curious what he is thinking about. He walks toward the dining room and turns around. "Want to hear a joke?"

I never know why he waits for me to say something because after being with him for over ten years I stopped saying yes.

"I told my wife that a husband is like fine wine: we just get better with age. The next day she locked me in the cellar."

I chuckle and my incision burns. He really needs to stop telling me his horrible jokes even though that was a good one. I always have to look on the internet to learn some good ones.

"Oh my lanta. Your jokes keep getting worse and worse." I shake my head with a smile on my face.

I have been texting Ellie nonstop about pain, bleeding, and even Sookie's health. Ellie has been a lifesaver that I will be eternally grateful to her till the end of time. She says the pain goes away but I have no clue why I'm still taking oxy when she didn't have to. I know I shouldn't compare myself, especially since I don't deal well with pain, but it's hard not to compare.

"You're supposed to stay happy, not go solemn."

"Sorry, laughing just hurts and Ellie mentioned how her pain went away. She even mentioned how she started stretching to get rid of the tightness but I can't even bend, let alone get on the floor."

"Everyone heals differently Jackie and your labor was one intense show. You remember what Tolstoy wrote in War and Peace?"

I read that book eons ago so I hope he isn't looking for an answer but it seems he is. "No."
"'The two most powerful warriors are patience and time.' Just give it time and patience and you will heal."

I hate how he is always right. I also don't remember quotes well from books since I read for pleasure not for study. My memory also can't remember quotes well but my patience is always thin. Right now, I want to eat and leave.

"Right now, I just want to get ready and go see Sookie. I know you have things to do but I don't, so I want to be out of here no later than ten. Deal?"

"Deal."

We left at ten o'clock and found Sookie opening and closing her eyes. We got a good report from her nurse so I'm happy she's thriving. I want my baby girl to be healthy and happy. I brought more milk in and they told me I have brought in so much that they should be good till she leaves which gives me hope.

I need more hope in my life as it's been three days of being apart from Sookie. Every day she gains weight but it's her heart that is keeping her here. If only I could have eaten better and worked out more. Working out always improves health; it's why doctors always recommend it.

She makes a sound that warms my heart. Looking at Sookie brightens my mood, especially when I am holding her. I can tell she has gained weight as she is starting to get heavier in my arms. I love holding her but I know rest is good for her. I reluctantly put her down and stand over her. Every time we leave, even for food, I give her a butterfly kiss.

There really isn't much for us to do here but I hate being away from Sookie. Her vibrant red hair, her silver eyes, and her precious face. I can't get enough of her. I stare at her while she sleeps so peacefully. The doctors and nurses normally just let us visit and only come in if it's urgent. All I'm having to do is suck it up and deal with it. The way I'm dealing with it is by reading so I can be in a world where I don't have to feel like a horrible mother.

"Hey."

I look up at Dean who has been playing a game on his phone and playing in my wheelchair. I am still in a lot of pain but I have been walking more and have used the stairs. I used the stairs yesterday since Dean does not know how to find clothes for me.

"What's up?" I have a feeling he wants to leave because I know how much this is killing him too. The waiting. The constant beeping from the monitors. It grinds our gears relentlessly.

"I know you love being here and could sit here and read for days but we should get home. It's not healthy just sitting here. How about we pack up and get going?"

I sigh. I know he is right because I do get a little bored from being in this room every single day but leaving her is hard. I try to think if she will be eating soon but she ate about thirty minutes ago and will be sleeping for a while.

"I guess."

"Hey." Dean gets up and walks over to me. He grabs my hands and puts them on his shoulder. "I know this is difficult but she is getting better day by day. Sitting here for hours will drive us crazy. We need to see the sun instead of being in this dark room." He hugs me and looks into my eyes. "Okay?"
His eyes are green today and I love and hate them. Looking into his eyes makes me see things his way. I don't always like it. I like being right.

"Fine." I refuse to give him the satisfaction that he's right.

We pack up our things and head out. We say our goodbyes to the nurses so they know we will be gone for the day.

I hate this hospital. It makes me depressed. It makes me feel like I can't be a real mom. Ellie is home with her baby and spends all day with him whereas I have to visit my girl if I want to see her. I don't understand why life can be so cruel. Have I not been a good person? What did I do to deserve this?

I can tell Dean is looking at me even though his eyes should be on the road. It has been getting easier being in the car as I just let my body loose on bumps or turns.

We pass a car that has two couples in it that are elderly.

"They must be on their way to bingo."

For some reason that makes me laugh, giving me a shooting pain in my lower abdomen. My incision burns and I clamp a hand over it.

"Stop making me laugh. You know it hurts."

"Sorry. Think of dead squirrels falling from trees then?"

For some reason the image of squirrels falling is hysterical. I feel like it could come from a Stephen King novel. I try not to laugh but can't help it. Dean looks at me as if I'm crazy.
"Dean!"
"What? How is that even funny? You are one weird woman." I can hear the amusement in his voice.

I am weird and proud of it. I have always said there is no such thing as being normal.

We get home and Dean starts doing things around the house as I sit on the couch and read. This has become our normal. Waking up, eating breakfast, being at the hospital for at least two hours, coming home, repeat.

Chapter 18

It's been a week and the nurse told us yesterday that Sookie should be able to go home today. It's Thursday so I'm hopeful I can finally have my moment of bringing my baby girl home to meet her brother Lance.

Sookie's nurses have been showing Dean and me how to do baby care like giving her a bed bath. I would like to say I'm a professional but Dean has me beat with swaddling. He is a natural at it and Sookie looks up at him with her big eyes. The adoration pores out of Dean and Sookie returns it tenfold. They are a sight I want to see for a lifetime.

I don't see what that genetic counselor was talking about. I don't see how close her eyes are at all. All I see is my beautiful baby girl who looks just like me when I was a baby. My mom sent Dean and me a picture of me as a baby and it's crazy how similar Sookie and I look. I have my mini me I have always wanted; it makes me happy thinking about it.

Her heart isn't perfect as the patent foramen ovale never closed but Dean and I already knew she would need surgery for her complete AV canal defect. I'm already impressed with my daughter as her right kidney is fully functioning when it wasn't functioning while inside me. There was a laundry list of what was wrong or not functioning while she was inside me and everything works fine now. Unfortunately, she has a lot of appointments to double check all these "issues" after she is released from the hospital.

"Okay, West family. I would suggest getting an appointment set up with Sookie's pediatrician as soon as possible. This will help speed up the process of releasing her."

She is finally coming home! My heart surges with hope and I meet Dean's eyes. His eyes are also sparkling with hope as well.

"I will get right on that." Dean has been going to a family practice down the street from us that said they are accepting patients.

Dean leaves the room and I am left with Sookie. I don't want to get my hopes up as just a couple days ago they had mentioned her leaving but it never came to be. It might have been a miscommunication since the nurses say Sookie is doing amazing and doesn't need to be here but the doctors want to keep her due to her heart.

I'm just happy that Sookie is thriving and showing these doctors who is boss. I did it as a kid. As I have mosaicism for Down syndrome, I was tested for my cognitive abilities and the doctor said I would never go to college. I proved that doctor wrong by going to college and graduating. I know doctors don't know everything and can be wrong. Nothing is set in stone. We have choices in life. I could have either accepted what the doctor said and not tried, or accepted what the doctor said and said challenge accepted! I just chose to flip him the bird and do things my way. I decided not to let others tell me what I can and cannot do. I hope to teach Sookie that too so she can forge her own path.

I look down at Sookie sleeping in the bassinet. I love how her lips pucker out as she sleeps so peacefully. I could watch her for days and be content. The love I feel for Sookie is stronger than the love I have for Dean and I hope that doesn't hurt his feelings. This love is different though. A mother's love and a relationship love are two different feelings.

Sookie starts moving and I look up at her monitor. The monitor has gone off before but she never seems in distress. Fortunately, I know the signs to look for if she is having difficulty breathing but I have no idea what I would do if I was faced with that challenge.

Her eyes open and I say, "Hey honey bunches. Mama is here. I love you." I press my nose against her and give her a butterfly kiss.

She looks up at me and doesn't smile but I don't expect a smile until she's a bit older. I can see she loves me just by how she looks at me.

"Well, that was a bust. The practice I go to doesn't accept infants so I called the hospital down the street as they have a pediatric office there accepting patients. Sookie has an appointment on Monday at eleven."

"Sounds good to me. You are coming though, right?" I don't need a wheelchair anymore but I am slow as molasses.

I start feeling a bit nervous having to bring Sookie to appointments by myself with the pain I'm still in. I feel useless and defeated as this pain is literally kicking my ass. You would think that being a fitness buff would help you recover from surgery but apparently, I am not as strong as I thought. Once I can start working out, I will have to train myself harder in case I have to go through this again.

"Yes, I am coming. I wouldn't leave you by yourself."

"Okay, good."

Being married to a teacher has its benefits as I would be screwed if I had to do this all by myself. I pat myself on the back for meeting Dean about twelve years ago.

The resident doctor comes in and he stands at the door. "I was told you guys have an appointment made for Sookie. Can you tell me the doctor so I can write it in Sookie's chart and confirm it with the place?"

I look at Dean and he looks sheepish. Of course, he doesn't remember because when something is sprung at him, he doesn't always think of doing everything.

"It's at the local hospital in our town. I can't remember who but I believe it's with the nurse practitioner since it's short notice." Dean is scrolling on his phone looking up the name.

"No worries. I can look that up myself," the doctor says. "Thank you. I will come back if I hear when she will be released."

I instantly text Ellie. Ellie has been an amazing friend and even told her friend who works here about us. It's nice knowing a cardiovascular physician assistant. Her friend was even nice enough to bring me lactation cookies and fuzzy socks. I have a thing for fuzzy socks and instantly texted Ellie's friend thank you since I didn't actually meet her.

Me: Sookie is being released! I have been waiting for this day but I'm so nervous. Were you this nervous too?

I wait hoping for a response as Ellie normally responds to me right away, especially recently since my family has been wanting updates on Sookie. Everyone is surprised and in love with her red hair. I don't blame them. I'm in love with her too.

Ellie: Yes, I was extremely nervous bringing Roland home. We got into a routine though and so will you.

Me: I thrive off of a routine so I plan on doing that anyway.
A knock is at the door and the resident comes in. "I checked with the pediatric office and that checks out. We are waiting on confirmation that Sookie is okay to leave. I personally think she's ready but it's not my call. Do you guys have any questions?"

I just want to know when I can bring my baby home. Lately, Dean has been asking all the questions. I look at Sookie who is currently sleeping while we're talking. At least now I know she can sleep through anything.

"Not at the moment. Thanks Doc," Dean says for us. I look at him with a smile.

My nerves are going crazy. I want Sookie home as that's where she belongs but what if she stops breathing? Or doesn't gain weight? What if more issues arise with her health? With COVID happening she could get deathly sick and then I could lose her. I just got my baby and barely spent any time with her. I wouldn't want to lose her.

Dean slips his arms around me. "Breathe Jackie. Sookie will be alright. She's coming home with us soon. I'm as excited and nervous as you are."

I don't know how he does that. How does Dean know what I'm thinking most of the time? I swear he is psychic.

I feel his arms around my waist and wrap my arms around his waist. I snuggle my head against his chest and try not to cry. It's been difficult not to cry as it's so hard seeing Sookie here. She has less wires now and right now the monitor only has the heartbeat showing.

I take one deep breath into his chest and push back. I leave my arms around him and feel his back arch. I look at Dean and see the crinkles in his eyes. I don't dare try to think what he is thinking as a person with ADD thinks of a million things in a minute. Our conversations are always about a lot with me trying to make sense of it all.

"You make me stronger. I don't know how you stay stoic but I envy you. With all the news we have gotten I try to hold everything in."

He looks at me and says, "I stay strong for you and Sookie. You both are my lights in this dark world. I would do anything to keep you both happy."

I tighten my hold around Dean and squeeze him tighter. I realize I haven't hugged him a lot. With the pain management and pumping schedule, it's been tiring. I feel like my body has become a milk machine instead of my own. I love pumping and watching Sookie grow. Watching her eat makes me happy as she loves it. I would do anything to make sure she is happy and healthy.

My head is on Dean's chest and I feel his muscles tighten. All he has been doing is working out and I can tell. His chest is harder. Dean hasn't always been this built. When I met him, he was scrawny but now when you look at him, he looks like a powerful man. Most people think he has, or is, serving the country with how jacked he looks. His torso is burly and toned with strong shoulders making him look bigger. His legs are powerful as he can run for miles. With Sookie, I can't see us working out together unless Sookie is in a playpen which we do not have.

"What are you thinking?" His voice is low and soft which is extremely rare. Dean definitely has a teacher's loud and slightly commanding voice.

"How different our life is going to be. I knew having Sookie would change things but it's going to drastically change it this coming year."

"That's why we have each other. To lean on each other."

"I know that but I mean we won't get a full solid eight hours of sleep anymore. No more going out for the next six months; maybe more due to her upcoming open-heart surgery. I already feel differently about myself."

Dean lets go of me and stretches his back by twisting back and forth. I hear a pop and sigh of relief.

"Jackie, it may not be the same but our lives will be fuller now. Don't focus on the future. Focus on now. Time is precious, and even though Sookie has a lot going on, I know Sookie will pull through and we should make every moment count."

I know he is right and I nod my head. I look at my Garmin and realize it's been an hour. We didn't plan on staying here for this long so we have no lunch packed. My stomach is rumbling and I will need to pump soon. If Sookie is coming home, we shouldn't leave her room but my stomach is doing a dance.

My face must be looking guilty because Dean asks if I'm as hungry as he is.

"I just don't want to leave and have them think…something. I don't know. If she's coming home, wouldn't we have known by now? My departure was rather fast. They told me in advance and I was out in less than thirty minutes."

"How about I go out and ask what's going on before we do anything?" I nod my head in approval. Dean has been going out there to ask questions a lot while I stay and watch Sookie. Sometimes I lay a hand on her chest to feel her heartbeat. Sometimes I can't believe she is here and is all mine. I truly hope she isn't in pain or suffering. Her cardiologist has said she will have to work harder than other babies until her surgery and could fall behind physically. With her diagnosis of Down syndrome, she is already labeled by doctors no matter what she does. To me, she is my life. She could have webbed feet and I wouldn't care. I will love her no matter what and hope others will too.

I hear the door slide open and Dean comes in as he slides the door closed.

I look at him expectantly. "Well?"

I have no clue why he doesn't just start talking about what he learned. I also don't want to know what he thinks half the time.

"The nurses haven't heard any news so I say we grab a quick snack from the cafeteria and come back up."

I like the plan so we say our 'see you later' to Sookie and head out the door. I always wonder if I will see anyone I know here as I went to college in Worcester. Despite it being a big city, it's a small world.

We make our trip very quickly as we want to go home as a family. I try to move as fast as I can despite the discomfort I have. My incision area is extremely sore, still making my legs weak and my core extremely unstable. There are times the pain shoots up my right torso making me cringe and lay still. When I first go to bed my whole body spasms.

I had a follow up appointment with my doctor earlier today and I asked her about my pain. She said it's normal and my body is taking a slow time recovering. All I got for an answer was to walk and start stretching to help my spasms lessen. I tried stretching earlier and I'm definitely tight since I barely do anything. It didn't seem to help much as my body trembled with the basic stretching poses I was doing that she gave me. Even Ellie had mentioned a few different stretches to do.

I beeline it to Sookie's room saying a quick hi to the nurses as I walk past them. I try to be courteous since they work hard but I just care about spending as much time as possible with my daughter.
I open the sliding door and leave it open for Dean. I see her eyes open and I say, "Hey baby girl, Mama is here." I place my hand on her chest. "Mama and Dada are waiting to hear from the doctors about bringing you home. It would be nice to sleep in your own bed, huh, baby girl?"

Those piercing silver eyes. They melt my heart. So big. So precious. I just want to eat her up and never let go.

Dean finally walks in and asks, "Any word from anyone?"

"Not yet. Normally, patients are discharged in the morning but the NICU could be different as I don't always see parents here. Maybe babies can be discharged at any time."

Dean shrugs and walks over to us. "Hey love bug. You are getting so big." He strokes her face making her look tiny compared to his hand. "Daddy loves you baby girl."

We got used to saying baby girl while I was pregnant so we wouldn't give her name away and it stuck. I find it so funny that we name our children and then have so many nicknames for them. She will forever be my princess Sookie.
The door slides open and the resident doctor walks in for the third time today. "I spoke with the head of Sookie's team and we are going to keep her here for tonight. I have high hopes she will be able to go home tomorrow and you will be able to spend the weekend as a family. It helps that you have the appointment on Monday so keep it scheduled. I'm sorry it's not today. Sookie really is doing well."

I knew not to keep my hopes up but I did. I really hope he can't see the tears in my eyes even though I have cried numerous times in this room. I know these doctors see parents crying but I refuse to dissolve into a crying buffoon. I need to stay strong in front of Sookie. I know crying isn't a sign of weakness and is good for the soul, but personally I hate crying in public. I guess I have to wait another day but I won't be holding my breath this time.

Chapter 19

It's Tuesday and Sookie is still in the hospital. Dean and I are going in but I don't know how much longer I can take the false hope. Each time we are there we get good reports but can't bring her home. It's eating me alive with the nurses and doctors saying different things.

"What's your favorite animal?"

I have no clue why Dean is asking me this as my answer doesn't change. "A dolphin. You should know this as I have a collection of dolphins."

"Well..." now I know what's coming and I'm already cringing. "Dolphins have no sense of porpoise."

I roll my eyes internally but do a soft chuckle. Dean always jokes when he is down or someone else is. He has been cracking jokes all the time making my incision burn.

"Honey, you've been cracking jokes all week. Don't you think it's time to give it a rest?"

"Seven days without a pun makes one weak. At least my jokes about German sausage are the wurst."

"Ah!" I exclaim and slap my forehead.

At least he cares but internally I'm dying. Dean helps as much as possible but jokes are not what I need. I don't even know what I need if Sookie is in the hospital longer. I read an article in the bathroom about a baby being born extremely prematurely who weighed just a pound, maybe two. That baby was there for one hundred days and the parents visited every day. I would visit Sookie every day but for one hundred days? I would be crying every single day.

"Hey, it's going to be okay. Sookie is growing and is thriving. There are so many babies here that do need to be here. Sookie is strong just like you. I have a feeling she will come home today."

I brighten up but not much as I don't want to get crushed.

"You really think so?"

"I have this feeling and I'm ninety-five percent certain."

"Well that means there is a five percent chance of her not coming home."

"You used to be a half full kind of woman but now you're a half empty glass. Jackie, none of this is your fault. Her heart, not your fault. Her Down syndrome, not your fault. Her other problems aren't even problems anymore despite needing more testing done with the kidney. None of it is your fault and you need to believe that."

Whenever Dean tells me this I always start tearing up. Deep down I know all this but at the surface I do blame myself. Sookie's health is my fault. With caring for her for the eight and a half months I had time to rectify her health complications. Obviously, I failed as she has been in the NICU for a week and a half.

"Jackie. I know nothing I say will make you believe me as you need to believe it yourself but at least be happy knowing how beautiful our daughter is. She is the spitting image of you."

I smile as he is right. I have always wanted a twin and Sookie is basically my twin, just thirty-one years younger than me.
"She does look like me and I hope you know I plan on twinning with her."

"I don't doubt it."

We finally are at her door and it's a bit chaotic in the NICU. Nursery beds are moving yet most of the babies are sleeping except for one who is crying. The poor baby who is crying sounds like a pig squealing. It makes me feel like he is here due to low oxygen levels.

I walk into her room and see she's awake. I scoop her up in my arms and give her a butterfly kiss. She just stares up at me but I know she is smiling. When she stares at me, I can tell she loves me.

"Hi baby girl. Mama and Dada are here. I missed you so much but our home is ready for you whenever the doctors say so. Even Lance, your kitty brother, is ready to meet you."

She stares at me and I instantly just know I will never be able to say no to this adorable face. Those big blue eyes and chubby cheeks. I just want to squish her face and kiss her all the time.

Dean walks in and the resident doctor follows in shortly after.

"I'm glad you're here." This does not sound good. "Do you have your car seat?"

We have left it in here for the safety check and it stayed hoping that she would come home soon. It's been eleven days but who says I'm counting?

He must have eyed it as he continues. "Good! Sookie is all set to go home whenever you're ready. Do you have any questions or concerns?"

I'm not sure if I'm openly staring at him with my mouth open as I'm shocked. I love and hate how Dean was right. That son of a monkey! I know he is celebrating both victories, being right and Sookie coming home.

"Is her kidney appointment already scheduled as an outpatient?"

"Yes, next Thursday. It's on the portal in her name. Any other questions?"

I shake my head 'no' to signify I had no more questions and look at Dean.

"I think we're all set. Thank you so much." Dean shakes hands with him.

I feel like this is all a joke being played on me as it doesn't feel real. I feel like I'm being punked. I've been waiting for this day and now that it's here, I feel stuck. My feelings are in between shock and…nothing. Since I feel like this is a joke it doesn't seem as if it is really happening.

I realize I am standing there doing nothing once the doctor leaves and Dean is packing up all the papers that have accumulated for Sookie that we left on the bed. I go over to Sookie and try to imagine her in our house. I see her in the swing that a family friend bought for her. I see her crawling around the living room trying to chase Lance. I see her in her crib looking up at me trying to reach for me. I see her in our house but it doesn't seem palpable.

"Here is all your milk in a bag. It's insulated so it should stay cold until you're home. There isn't a lot left but enough for Sookie for today. Do you guys have any questions or concerns?"

I try to think and realize we don't have any diapers. Since she never came home with us, we didn't buy diapers.

"What size diaper is she? We need to buy some on the way home."

"She is a size one but just barely. You can take as much as you need from us to tide you over for the next few days. She is great at making dirty diapers! Also, take some wipes too. Don't forget the clothes you brought." She is opening the drawers that are connected to the bassinet. "You can also take the leftover formula she has been using as well. That way you know what kind to get to fortify your breastmilk."

I'm so thankful for this nurse. I feel bad for not remembering any of these nurses names but they have been a lifesaver to us for taking care of Sookie. I try not to cry as it's so surreal packing up Sookie's belongings to finally go home as a family. It's starting to hit me and I'm so happy.

My phone goes off and it's Rita. Her grandmother was admitted to this hospital a couple of days ago and she is here. Rita has formula that she got from a donation bin at work for Sookie to use. I'm not sure if it's the same formula Sookie uses but it's still free formula.

Me: We are packing up Sookie's things and heading down in a couple minutes.

Rita: Okay, I can meet you in the lobby by the elevators.

Me: Sounds good! Sookie can't wait to meet everyone.

I put my phone away as Dean is telling me to get off the phone and start walking. I didn't realize everything was packed and he was waiting on me.

"Sorry, I was texting Rita as she is in the lobby waiting for us. I think she wants to give us formula or she may just want to be the first person to meet Sookie. I don't blame her. Sookie is quite amazing."

I look at Sookie who is looking around in her car seat. She looks tiny in the car seat and a little scared as she has been used to being in the hospital for so long. I don't blame her for being scared as I hate stepping out of my comfort zone.

"Jackie, pay attention."

I realize the elevator doors are opening on a floor we do not want as I almost stepped off. A couple comes in and congratulates us on our baby. Now when people congratulate us, I am happy to show off our baby girl. Before, I was a mess as I saw other couples bringing their baby home when I couldn't.

We make it to the lobby and I instantly see Rita who sees us. Her face suddenly lightens up as she sees Sookie.

"Oh hello, you precious angel. Auntie Rita has been praying for you. Why aren't you the cutest?" She looks at us and asks, "How are you guys doing? Excited to bring her home?"

"Excited and nervous. I'm hoping we can get on a schedule," I chime before Dean interjects first.

"It's easy to do a schedule for the first couple months but then it's whatever they want. One of my clients' sisters doesn't nap some days and naps all the time on other days."

I hope Sookie will nap as I would be worried if she doesn't. I know how much extra her body is working due to her heart condition.

"Well, we should get going," Dean says as Sookie starts fussing.

"Text me if you guys need anything."

Rita has been amazing throughout all of this. When I was on bedrest for a weekend, she bought our groceries so Dean could focus on the house work. She has been an amazing best friend during this whole ordeal. I'm hopeful we won't need any help and we get into a rhythm of a schedule.

"Bye Rita!" I say and wave behind myself as we walk toward the parking garage. I almost trip over myself doing this.

I keep looking at Sookie who is looking everywhere. I finally feel like a mother being released from the hospital after giving birth and having my walk of fame. People look at our beautiful daughter and I can tell they see how adorable she is. Her red hair is a little crazy and her blue eyes are wide taking in her surroundings.

I'm surprised at how quiet she is during our walk and as Dean gets her into the car. I'm finally doing a bit better getting into and out of cars but my incision is extremely tight and spikes of pain shoot up my right side of the body everywhere. I still feel like I'm somehow damaging the incision but I try not to think about it.

Dean and I are in the front and Sookie is in the backseat looking around. Once we are out of the parking garage and driving she starts crying. It's not a high shriek but it's loud.

I try to shush Sookie which doesn't work. I try to turn around and look at her but it hurts my incision. I start to sing 'Twinkle Twinkle Little Star' but it doesn't work.

"Dean, how about you pull over here so I can just sit with her."

"I can't pull into there. It's a one-way street."

"Then pull over somewhere so I can console her."

"Give me a minute then."

"I don't think Sookie wants to wait a minute, Dean."

"Jackie, just give me a damn minute. You know I can't focus with her crying."

"I don't know because this is the first time she has cried outside of the hospital, Dean." I say his name with emphasis so he knows how pissed off I'm getting at him.

This is the first time we are all out together and I'm already about to cry. I hate when Dean and I fight, which is rare, and when I'm upset I cry. I try to settle my breathing and think of Sookie. Despite her crying, I'm able to focus on my emotions and calm down. My tears go away as I blink them away and I try to sing again.

"Dean, we're getting close to the highway. Can you please stop somewhere so I can sit with her?"

Despite my attempts to soothe her from the front of the car she is still crying and it keeps getting higher. I'm worried she is straining her heart too much and I want to get back there even though I know it will hurt my incision. At this point, I don't care about the pain and want Sookie to be happy. I would take away her pain or frustration so she can be happy and content.

Dean sighs dramatically and pulls over. "Happy?"

"Almost." I unbuckle and get out of the car to go into the backseat. I sit next to Sookie with a pillow giving me cushion from the seatbelt. "It's okay sweetie, Mommy is here."

Sookie looks up at me as I take her small hand in mine. She stops crying and looks at me with those gorgeous eyes. Dean starts driving again and Sookie just stares at me. I can't do much as the incision still hurts which is annoying. I feel like a broken record constantly thinking about it.

Sookie sleeps all the way holding onto my finger. Seeing her tiny hand makes me melt. I never fully grasped how many emotions motherhood would give me till now. And this is just the beginning.

We pull into the driveway and I climb out albeit ungracefully due to being in the backseat and being a weakling. Dean is taking the car seat out and one of the bags to bring inside.

"Wait!" I try to yell but quietly so as to not disturb Sookie. "I have been waiting for this moment for almost two weeks. I want us all to walk in together." He looks at me as if I have two heads. "You know what I mean. I know we can't all fit into the doorway, dummy."

"I know, Jackie. I'm just messing with you."

"Okay, sorry." I sometimes can't tell with Dean if he is being sarcastic or not. A trait I hate as I can be oblivious.

Dean walks up to the front door and I'm saving this moment in my memory. Our white house on this sunny day with Dean carrying Sookie into the house and me hobbling behind them. I wouldn't change anything, even the pain. This is where we were meant to be.

I walk into the house and Dean walks through the rooms to place her in the living room. Lance rubs up against me and looks at the car seat. He tentatively walks toward Sookie and sticks his nose out. He sniffs the seat and Sookie, and stays there. I instantly grab a picture to send to the family. Sookie shifts and Lance gets scared and runs away. I roll my eyes at him as he is such a scaredy cat. That cat gets scared of his own reflection.

Dean comes back into the house and I didn't realize he had left the house. He must have gotten the other bags from the car as he walks into the room. Dean looks good wearing his orange shirt and khaki shorts. I helped him buzz his hair just a day ago and it looks good on him. His long hair isn't bad but he looks more handsome with a short cut and clean shaven. I hate his facial hair as it scratches the living daylights out of me. I look at him and love everything about him, even the things I hate.

He helps me stand up and asks, "Is this what you pictured?"

"Everything plus more."

He wraps his arms around my waist and I do the same. We stare at Sookie who is still sleeping peacefully in her car seat. I feel content and hope it stays with me.

Chapter 20

It's been a week since Sookie came home and it went too fast. I felt like I couldn't spend any time with her since she had so many appointments. I'm thankful Dean was with me as it would have stressed me out big time. Due to her diagnosis of Down syndrome, her pediatrician wanted a weight check on her two days after her appointment which I thought was insane. I want Sookie to be healthy but she eats well and looks healthy. While she was in the NICU she constantly grew so I didn't think her weight would be an issue.

One of her tests was for her kidney and she had a catheter for at least two hours since the machine broke down before her test even started. Sookie just lay there while Dean and the doctor were talking. After the voiding of her kidney and bladder, we got some images of her abdomen too. This girl went through so many tests for her kidneys, stomach, heart, brain, and ears in just one week that it made me feel dizzy, but she barely cried during any of it. I kept calling her 'super baby' since she took it like a champ. I, on the other hand, would have cried since I hate pain. My daughter is definitely like her father when it comes to pain and I'm thankful for that.

I haven't even looked at any of her results online as I fear that something could be abnormal. No doctor has called so I assume that if something was wrong, we would have had a call by now.

I check the baby monitor on my phone as Sookie doesn't cry when she wakes so it's difficult knowing when she's up. I have to pay close attention to really hear her as she just moves a lot when awake. She kicks her legs a lot but I already knew that from when she kicked me so many times inside me. She is still asleep so I go back to cleaning the house. I'm surprised she isn't awake as I've been vacuuming the house for a while now. Rita kept telling me to do loud things around the house while she slept to get her used to it but I think being in the NICU made her into a good sleeper.

With Dean working it hasn't been bad, just Sookie and I. I was extremely stressed with handling my schedule of pumping and taking care of Sookie but so far it's been okay. I keep feeling like a failure when I look at social media and see babies near Sookie's age who are cuddling up against their moms or smiling or reaching. Sookie sleeps a lot due to her heart defect which worries me. I check on her constantly just to make sure she is still breathing. I already feel terrible that she has to work harder than most babies to breathe and wish I could do everything for her.

I plop onto the couch and just stare at the blank TV. I didn't think parenting would be so challenging emotionally but movies and social media only highlight the good things. I know I could have it worse than what it already is. Some moms are pregnant and may have to abort due to medical conditions that could damage their babies or their bodies. Other moms know their baby died and still have to give birth knowing they will never see their babies smile. I try to think of the positives like having Sookie in my life and I am grateful. I'm so grateful that she is beautiful and alive. I just have no clue if she is in pain. What kind of mom am I if I don't know my baby is in pain or not?

I've been finding it difficult to be happy emotionally when Sookie is sleeping. My thoughts just go dark as it terrifies me that she won't wake. I've been talking with Ellie about this and she mentioned how she is anxious as well. Dean says my emotions are valid with Sookie's health issues but I feel like I should be doing more. I've been googling everything as the parenting books my sister gave me aren't helpful in my case. Are my emotions valid? Do I need medication?

I sigh in frustration and walk around. My pain has lessened and I'm barely taking any medication which makes me feel better. It cramps up when I do too much but I'm back to pacing around the house getting steps in. Sookie loves being outside in her stroller so I go on walks when I feel up to it. The sun does help my mood but only for the time we are outside.

I'm also just going crazy being home all the time and walking in our neighborhood. I need different scenery and feel cramped in our house. If

COVID wasn't around, I would ask Dean if we could go to the store with Sookie or to a park. I feel confined and trapped within our four walls.

Our house is eerily quiet and Lance is hiding somewhere. Lance has been extremely cautious around Sookie and will sniff at her head at times. He doesn't know what to think of the little human but she isn't loud like some babies can be. Sookie does cry at times but not a lot which I'm thankful for. It's nearing two hours that she has been asleep so I get ready to go into the nursery to wake her for a bottle.

We bought a bottle warmer so I take some of my milk out of the fridge and plop it into the warmer. I go upstairs to the nursery and peek my head in. Sookie is turning her head and her eyes look at mine.

I smile and say, "Hi baby girl. I started your bottle." I unswaddle her and pick her up. I nuzzle my face into hers. "Let's change your diaper and go have your bubba."

I really hope I'm not the only mom who talks about everything to their baby. Sookie is my only interaction with the human species. If Lance was walking around, I would pick him up and talk to him too.

I change her and go downstairs. I put her in the swing so I can put some formula in her bottle. I can't remember how much formula to put in so I add half of a scoop which seems to be fine for her. Dean hasn't said anything to me when he sees me make her bottles, so I assume I'm doing it correctly.

I walk into the living room with the bottle and grab the boppy. I put everything on the couch so it's right there. I pick Sookie up and prop her against my left side. I stare at her angular face with her hair sticking up everywhere. Her eyes bore into mine and I smile.

"Hi, sweet girl. Are you ready to eat?"

She just stares at me as I feed her. I encourage her to bring her hands up to her bottle but I know it's too soon for her to hold it. I don't want her to be behind any milestones and want to be her biggest cheerleader.

Whenever she eats, I constantly kiss her head. I can't get enough of her. I really could eat her up as she is so cute.

Once she's done eating, I put her onto the carpet and lay out the quilt my mom made for her. I grab the smaller boppy for Sookie to play on. I'm used to babies screaming or not wanting to do tummy time for long yet Sookie doesn't seem to mind it. I lay her down with her face facing me. I smile and stick my tongue out at her. I hope for a smile but just get a cute little smirk. At least her lips move into something even though it's not exactly what I want.

She waves her arms around and I put Alexa on with some nineties music. I don't always know what to do with Sookie but I try to keep it entertaining. If I get bored, I assume she gets bored as well.

Chapter 21

Sookie has been home for two weeks and it's been wonderful being home as a family. I didn't think about how to manage my pumping schedule with her feeding schedule and I don't know what to do. I want to spend time with Sookie but also make enough milk for her to eat. I've been trying breastfeeding with the nipple shield but she falls asleep on me. I'm glad she is comfortable with me but it makes me feel as if I'm doing something wrong.

Ellie breastfeeds Roland and she had no issues whatsoever. I'm over here feeling stressed out and sad that Sookie won't do it. It has been difficult as I can't always try it every feeding with all of her appointments. I didn't realize how many appointments Sookie would have last week. She had one every single day! It was insane and I was so overwhelmed despite Dean with us. I'm not the kind of person to whip out my boob in public, even with a cover-up. I would feel awkward and self-conscious. My boobs have become their own people. They are heavy and I'm constantly touching them. One morning I woke up and they felt so solid because I slept through the night without pumping. That was the last time I slept through the night, especially with Dean working.

I sigh and look at Dean who is getting ready for work. I'm currently sitting in the living room pumping while reading a book. I'm wearing the makeshift bra the nurse made for me so I can pump simultaneously which has been a godsend. I would be so stressed if I had to pump each boob separately.

I look up as Dean enters the living room. "Hey beautiful."

I grimace. I don't feel beautiful. While wearing the makeshift bra and shorts, I look down and see a fat stomach. My thighs are massive as I can't work out. My arms are back to having bat wings. I know my back muscles are completely gone due to not working out in the past three, maybe four months. I don't feel beautiful and when I look at myself, I don't see it. If I told Dean this, he would tell me how I'm wrong and mention how strong I was when I gave birth to Sookie. That is not a good reason to be beautiful. That tells me I am strong mentally because it was such an ordeal.

"Jackie?"

I look up at him from my book and force a smile. "Yeah?"

"Are you okay? You seem stressed."

"I am stressed, Dean. You're back at work and I have to juggle pumping every three hours, making sure she's fed, she sleeps, and she is happy. I don't want to mess up our only child. I want Sookie to be happy."

"Hey. Listen to me. Sookie is happy. I see how her eyes light up when you hold her and feed her. I see her look up at you when she is on your chest doing tummy time. You are an amazing mom. We made a plan for your pumping and you will make it work. If Sookie's feedings interfere with it just adjust it by ten minutes. Ten minutes won't kill you."

"It doesn't take Sookie ten minutes to eat, Dean. It takes twenty minutes for her to finish her bottle. I get what you're saying, so I guess I will have to do that. Hopefully, she continues to wake at six-thirty in the morning and goes down every two hours."

"Relax and breathe. You got this. Life doesn't always have to have a schedule. I have to go get dressed for work but if she wakes, I will get her so you can finish pumping."

I nod my head and say, "Okay."

"Good. Stop stressing yourself out and relax."

I nod my acknowledgement as he walks away. I never knew exclusively pumping would be so challenging. Despite trying to breastfeed at every feeding, I got myself into a routine of pumping and have a good stash going. I feed her mostly fresh milk but I freeze some too. Ellie sent me a

Facebook group dedicated to moms who just pump. It has been a lifesaver with tips but also I don't feel so alone.

Ellie has also been a lifesaver. I'm still spotting from giving birth and it's annoying. There were quite a few things I did not know about post-op that I wish I had known beforehand. At least now I know if I decide to do this again. At this point, I probably won't do it again or I will just do it differently.

I still look back and think what if I had waited to push and then wouldn't have had a cesarean. I also think I was somehow overreacting when Sookie was not moving and had to be induced. What if I didn't call the hospital? Would Sookie have come when I scheduled my appointed time to be induced? Would her heart have closed naturally? Would she be healthier?

I feel tears running down my face and I brush them away before Dean comes down and sees me crying. I have been thinking this way a lot recently and know I shouldn't. It won't change anything as it's in the past but I can't stop myself. I truly hate myself for messing everything up. Dean would say I didn't mess up and everything turned out the way it was supposed to. He would mention how Sookie is beautiful and healthy. She is beautiful and healthy but she could be healthier. I could have eaten healthier and worked out more. It was just one more week we both had to wait for my scheduled induction.

I sigh and stop the pump. My life right now is perfect. I get to stay home with my daughter, play with her, snuggle her, and read while she sleeps. I have been using Instagram to post pictures of all the books I read and I have talked with some amazing people about Sookie. Everyone has commented on how stunning and strong she is. I have shared about her heart defect because it's been difficult for me to cope and I feel like I have no one to talk to. Ellie and Dean are amazing but they would just tell me to stop feeling this way. These people on Instagram tell me it's normal to feel this way and it takes time to adjust and adapt to everything. I have found a place where I feel accepted for my feelings.

I hear noises coming from our bedroom and try to hear if Sookie is up. Sookie has been sleeping in her bassinet right next to Dean in our room in case anything happens. It also helps me sleep better at night knowing she is still breathing.

Dean just sleeps right through her cute noises, whereas I wake up whenever there is a sound. Sookie barely cries so I'm happy I can get the sleep in between feeds.

I hear Dean cooing and know she is up. Sookie is just like me. Every day she wakes up at six-thirty on the dot and kicks her legs as if she's a mermaid. She really is my adorable mermaid. Sookie also has some strong legs as I remember her kicking my bladder.

Hearing Dean with Sookie is so heart-warming. The way he interacts with her makes me gush to whomever I'm talking to on my phone which is usually Ellie. My book friends are right there with Ellie though.

"Who's the cutest little baby ever? You are!"

Sookie hasn't smiled or started babbling but I know, with how much I talk to her, she will. Whenever I feed her, I talk about whatever is on my mind. Lately, I've been talking about all the vacations I want to go on with her but how I would have to work insane hours or win a million dollars in order to do what I'm talking about.

Dean doesn't have to leave till about sevenish so it's nice having him around in the morning but it means I don't get to see him until after four in the afternoon. I'm waiting until he is back at the high school instead of the middle school as it will be helpful for me and he can have more time to spend with his daughter.

Dean walks down the stairs with Sookie in his arms. I have her bottle ready for her on the side table.

I smile at them both and say, "Aren't you two the perfect picture?"

Sookie looks tiny in Dean's muscular arms. He has been working out a lot lately and it's showing. I jokingly say he is taking steroids as he is getting as big as The Rock. I know Dean idolizes him and I don't blame him.

Dean hands Sookie to me and says, "I changed her diaper but obviously not her outfit. She looked too cute in her pajamas."

"I don't blame you. She is adorable in anything she wears." I stare down at her in my arms and snuggle my face against hers.

Her warmth melts all my worries away and I'm filled with happiness. Sookie always puts me into a good mood. If I'm stressed, I look at her and instantly become happy. She is my light in my dark tunnel.

"I'm off. I will have my cell on so if you need me just text me."

I nod at Dean and say, "Okay. Hopefully I won't need anything."
He leans in for a kiss and we kiss briefly. He kisses Sookie and says, "Bye baby girl. Be good for Mama."

Sookie looks up at Dean with those gorgeous silver eyes. Looking at her makes me smile but a part of me feels empty. She brings me joy but staying home by myself stresses me out and fills me with anxiety.

As I'm feeding her, I look down and see her looking up at me. Whatever I was just feeling, vanished. We are staring at each other and my feelings wash away. I don't even know what was making me stressed as looking at her makes me happy.

Once she's done with eating, we play. I try to have a little schedule of what we do at each awake time but with her being home for just a while I try not to sweat it. I just want to make sure she is learning and can tell all the doctors to suck it who have told her that Down syndrome will make things harder or nearly impossible for her to do.

I remember a specialist telling me that I would never go to college and if I did then I wouldn't graduate. I may have started at a community college but I transferred to a state college and graduated with a major in health education and minored in English. Am I currently using my major? No, but who does? Other than Dean, of course. Most teachers do use their degrees.

Sookie looks up at me and I say, "You can be whatever you want to be. An engineer, an astronaut, or a ballerina. Although, a ballerina goes through rigorous training so maybe something not so intense. Not that you can't do intense since you need open heart surgery sometime this year but still. Listen to your mama ramble." I roll my eyes at myself. This is common: me rambling to my daughter.

She just stares at me no matter what I do. I know she hears me but sometimes I wonder what goes on in that adorable head of hers.

I look at the time and see that I have to pump. I set her in the swing so she can rock and enjoy the vibration. I place everything next to me and start pumping. A couple minutes into it, Sookie starts crying. I start singing "Twinkle, Twinkle Little Star" to no avail. I sing "Old McDonald" and still nothing. I start singing randomly and placing her name into songs I know which somewhat helps but she's still crying.

I have no clue what to do. Should I continue pumping or stop? I could take my pump and sit next to her until the end since it isn't plugged in. I grab the pump and make sure everything is secured as the makeshift bra isn't very tight. As I'm walking, the suction goes away on the left but I sit down with Sookie and readjust. I place my hands on the swing and stop the swing. She stares at me with her red eyes and her button nose scrunches up. My heart literally melts. I cannot stand how cute my daughter is. No matter what she says I will most likely say yes.

Her lips start to tremble and I shush her. "It's okay, sweet Sookie. Everything will be okay. Mama is here. I'm making more milk for you to have in a couple hours."

Sookie looks at me and her eyes soften the slightest. I think we are okay now but my pump is not. The suction seems to be off still despite me fixing it earlier. I don't want to mess with it too much and stay where I am. I only have a few minutes left and Sookie seems to be calm now. This crisis has been averted despite my heart rate being elevated.

I suspire. "Try not to stress Mama out, okay? I'm trying my hardest and I'm new at this. There isn't a handbook for this even though I wish there were."

I have read quite a few parenting books but they can only tell you so much. Every child is different and every circumstance is different. Sookie is special with her holy heart and wide eyes. Some of the tips and tricks may not even work on her.

Sookie starts to fuss so I take the pumping parts off of me. Once I clean everything in the sink and let it air dry, I go back to Sookie. She is moving her arms up and down making her swing bounce even more.

"Okay, okay. I see you and hear you, baby girl."

I wonder if I'm the only mom who talks to her baby like this. I really hope I'm not or else I would definitely feel weird.

I put her on the quilt and have her try to roll but it's difficult because I can't even lie on my stomach. My incision makes everything uncomfortable and my boobs still feel ginormous despite just pumping. My body doesn't feel like mine anymore. It feels alien. I really hope I can lie on my stomach again as that used to be my favorite way to sleep at night.

Sookie stares at me and I stare back. "Well baby girl, it's you and me against the world. What do you want to do despite stressing me out while pumping?"

We end up playing with some stuffed animals and her singing unicorn. She loves music so we end up singing and dancing all day. Hopefully, she will understand Mama needs to pump so she can continue eating my milk.

Chapter 22

I'm pushing Sookie in her stroller and the sky is luminescent despite it becoming dark. Sookie looks frail in her shirt and shorts that I put on her this morning. I look around yet my surroundings aren't very clear despite it being light out. I feel as if someone is watching us so I speed up my pace. I forget what street we are on and it doesn't look very familiar to me. I look around and only see houses here and there.

In our neighborhood, the houses are close together. Here, they are sparse and far between. I look around for some sort of landmark that I may know but I don't see anything. My breathing hitches and I try not to have a panic attack. I am okay. Sookie is okay. I just need to figure out where I am and get us home.

Sookie smacks her lips as if she is hungry and I know she is hungry as it's been three hours since her last feeding. "Hold on, lovebug. Mama will get us home. Just hold on."

I have no freaking clue where we are and I'm petrified. I hear footsteps behind us and I quicken my pace. I also can't remember leaving the house without my phone or keys as I feel nothing in my pants pockets. Surprisingly, the pants I'm wearing have pockets.

I stop and look around so I can figure out if the figure behind us is a friend or foe.

What. The. Hell?

"Susan?"

Susan is Jared's fiancé, so my almost sister-in-law. Her blonde hair and long legs always give her away. They are exactly like Barbie and Ken except Jared always has a mustache which he keeps trimmed.

"Jackie! I thought that was you but wasn't sure as this isn't your neck of the woods."

You aren't kidding me. I somehow ended up in my in-laws neighborhood without any recollection. I feel my head for any bumps or bruises but don't feel anything.

"Come with me! Can we have a snack? Are you nursing? Would you like some wine?"

I have been craving a margarita for months but I won't do that to Sookie. I know I could have a drink and still pump, but with her heart I don't want to risk anything. I don't even want to pump and dump.

I hesitate about what to say but I am hungry and so is Sookie. "Sure, I would love a snack. Thank you, Susan."

I follow her to her house and love the interior. It's a big Victorian house and they have a room for everything. It's a dark gray with green trim and it dates back to the nineteen hundreds. The inside is dark as the light from outside is almost gone.

We walk from the foyer, into the hallway, to the kitchen. I bet some history went down in this house based on how old it is. The lighting in the kitchen is dark too. Something doesn't feel right as I push the stroller into the house.

"Susan?"

"Yea?"

"Where should I put the stroller? I normally don't bring it into the house."

"Oh, that's fine. It's probably easier to stroll her around, isn't it?"

I look at her as if she has two heads. It is, but the stroller is tracking in dirt from outside. I wouldn't want that in my house. I wonder if Dean is here as he would put my mind at ease.

Sookie is starting to fuss so I pick her up but she almost slips out of my hands. I gasp as I thought I almost dropped her. She is fine and I am fine. It was a close call but I'm a bit shaken. Something still doesn't feel right. Sookie is so tiny. She seems tinier than before. Almost paper thin. She somehow lost a considerable amount of weight which terrifies me. Her heart condition could be worsening and I'm not even doing anything about it.

"Are you okay?" Susan is behind me as I gasp out loud not expecting her to touch my shoulder. "Sorry. I didn't mean to scare you."

"It's okay. Sookie looks tinier than normal."

"She looked this way earlier before I left for work."

Apparently, I saw Susan this morning and I don't remember it. What the hell is going on? Sookie is skinnier than normal and I'm in Dean's hometown despite not knowing where he is. I'm starting to get frustrated and annoyed.

I'm holding Sookie as I follow Susan toward the dining room which has sliding doors. I don't remember the sliding doors so I'm curious if they are new. Sookie stills and I look down and see that she is asleep. My bouncing must have put her to sleep.

I sit in a dining room chair as Susan places food in front of me. This is not a snack. This is a meal. Susan placed a chicken dish in front of me with mashed potatoes. My mouth waters as I love mashed potatoes.

Sookie is taken from me and I'm about to protest when Susan interrupts me. "Oh, hello little princess. Your Auntie is holding you now."

She was asleep just a minute ago but I shrug it off and dig in. Whatever this is, it's amazing. I didn't realize how hungry I was before I started eating. I look up and see that Sookie is gone and Susan is sitting across from me and her mom joined us at some point.

I panic looking around the room but don't see Sookie. "Where is Sookie?"

"Oh, I put her down as she was tired." Susan tells me and I relax.

I'm still feeling tense as something just doesn't seem right. Everything seems too staged. Susan also has an answer for everything which isn't always the case. Susan is smart but she normally takes a while to answer and tonight she has rapid fire answers to my questions. I try not to be too suspicious but it's hard not to be when Sookie has disappeared.

"I'm feeling tired myself. I should take her and go home."

"Why? You guys just got here. Besides, Sookie just went down for the night. Stay the night."

I really hope my eyes aren't too narrow. "I've never stayed here. Do you guys have baby things here?"

I highly doubt they do as Susan is twenty-seven so her mom wouldn't have much. I know my mom kept a lot of my baby things but that was mostly books and some clothes that were holiday-themed. My mom also made some of those clothes as well that I plan on putting on Sookie.

"Oh yes! Sookie is already in the nursery. Up the stairs and a couple doors down on the left. Your bedroom is adjacent to the nursery! It's super cool."

I didn't even know rooms like that existed anymore. I thought adjoining rooms were more of a hotel style. I go out and toward the elegant staircase in the foyer by the front door. It takes up most of the foyer but its architecture is exquisite. I run my hands along the animals carved into the banister as I walk up the stairs. I never noticed this before. I also have never been upstairs before and didn't realize how many rooms are up here. There has to be at least eight doors. I walk along and open the second door on the left like Susan said.

The door opens to a dark room with light music playing in the background for Sookie to sleep too. I see a mobile hanging by the changing table as I walk toward the crib. Sookie hasn't slept in a crib before as she is only a month old. With how small she is, she fits well into the bassinet we received as a gift.

Sookie is sleeping peacefully so I guess I should push my doubts away and go into the next room to sleep. This has been a weird day as I still have no clue how I ended up here. I also don't know why or how Sookie lost so much weight as she looks deathly skinny to me. It worries me as I gently touch her face. She is breathing lightly as I caress her face.

"Goodnight baby girl."

I open the door to my room and see a tall, frail man sitting on the bed. I try to close the door and go back into the nursery without him seeing me but he turns. His face is paper white and his breathing is ragged. Terrified, I shut the door with a gasp. Susan's grandparents live in the south and never come up here so I have no clue who that is.

I turn toward Sookie but she isn't in the crib anymore. I spin around trying to see if she's in the room even though she doesn't know how to roll yet.

I try to calm my breathing down but this whole night has been bizarre. I run down the stairs to get Sookie and go home. Dean obviously isn't here and I can just go to his parent's house.

I round the corner and see Dean holding Sookie in the dining room. I relax my shoulders and let out a deep breath I was holding.

"Dean! I was wondering where you were." I'm so happy to see him and kiss him on the cheek.

He turns around and his eyes are brown. That's a new color but his eyes do change color so I disregard it and look down at Sookie who is eating from a bottle. She looks even more frail in his arms. I stroke her face from her forehead to her chin worried that she's losing too much weight.

"I was helping out at the barn, remember?"

I obviously didn't but it makes sense as he will help anyone, even a stranger on the street.

"I forgot. I'm glad you're back. There is some old man in the room adjacent to the nursery. It kind of freaked me out." I'm downplaying it as it felt like I had a heart attack.
"An old man?" Susan looks perplexed which worries me.

"Yea. Thinning gray hair and he looked sick too as he was extremely pale."

"I have no idea who you are talking about. My grandparents only visit during holidays."

Now I'm worried she has some old pervert in the house or I'm seeing ghosts. I could be seeing ghosts as I have seen one before but that's another story entirely.

"Maybe my sleep-deprived mind is playing tricks on me then."

I hear Sookie burp and Dean whisper, "Good burp."

"You should get some rest. Don't worry about Sookie as we got her."

I hear Susan gasp and her eyes go wide. Dean shifts in his chair to look at what Susan is looking at which is right behind me. His face goes pale suddenly and he looks panicked. He looks around frantically and I look at them and am worried about them.

"I think you guys need some rest."

I turn around and I see the old man who was sitting in the room adjacent to the nursery. Now I feel like I'm not going crazy as they see him too. I don't know what to think. Should I run or stay? I look at the man and he is holding a knife. He swings but I feel nothing.

Chapter 23

I wake up in a cold sweat as my dream felt so real. I've always had vivid dreams and this is my first dream with Sookie in it. I've been stressed about her health as the doctors have been worried about her weight progression since she was born early and has health issues.

Lately, I've been having an issue of my own. My bleeding increased a ton when it was barely spotting just a week ago. My six-week appointment was supposed to be this Friday but it's today, Tuesday. This bleeding is heavier than my periods so now I'm even more worried that something ruptured. I have no clue what kind of complications can happen but this bleeding is excessive.

One of my friends, Meg, is watching Sookie as I couldn't find someone at the last minute. My mom was going to help on Friday but unfortunately, she was busy today when I switched my appointment. I love how much my mom wants to help as I know I need help. I just wish she would cook meals that aren't so healthy and bring them over instead of pinto bean salad. Give me chicken marsala or dumplings. I don't mind being healthy but I like splurging. I love food and so does Dean. My mom also makes enough for just one meal for Dean and I as Dean eats for two, maybe three, people. At least she thinks to make something and bring it over. I am thankful for that!

My alarm is about to go off so I swipe on my watch to turn it off. I have never been a huge fan of clock alarms as they are loud. They startle me awake and then I'm in a mood after being awakened so suddenly. My watch is just a vibration that wakes me slowly. Dean thinks I'm weird, that I hate clock alarms, but I can't deal with them.

I roll out of the bed and make my way downstairs to pump. Every day since Sookie came home, I've been pumping at four A.M. and then every three hours. I've been pumping even when I feed her throughout the night. Dean wakes up so I can pump at one in the morning and feed Sookie. I don't ask him for more help since I can't imagine having to work with little sleep. I go to bed at nine, sometimes even before, so I can get some sleep. I've been getting into a routine but I stress so much about pumping while Sookie is awake. I haven't found how to calm her down while pumping if she cries. I don't want her attached to me twenty-four seven as I want her to fend for herself.

My mind is in such a jumbled mess that I shake my head. I start making the coffee and go and pump. I grab my Kindle and read for the next twenty minutes. This has been the life which I like. I like the peace and solitude before everyone wakes. I also never thought I would enjoy pumping too, but I don't mind it since I read.

I go through the morning routine of pumping, reading, and drinking coffee. Dean gets up and we do our dance in the kitchen of making eggs and eating together. We don't talk much as Dean takes a while to wake up. Sookie gets up around six which is coming up soon and I love it when Dean gets her.

Dean and Sookie are the best things in my life. Sookie still hasn't smiled or laughed yet but she has been moving her body and I feel like she will be rolling soon. I may be an infant teacher but I don't know milestones. I'm trying to be patient, but I also can't wait to see her smile and hear her laugh. It's hard taking my own advice. I tell Sookie that patience is a virtue and I need to remind myself of that.

I hear thumping upstairs and know Sookie is awake. Dean is currently making eggs so I make my way into our room and go around our bed. Sookie is kicking her legs up and down and looking adorable as always.

"Hello Sweetheart. Did you sleep well?"

She looks up at me as I wheel her bassinet into the nursery. We do our normal routine of changing her diaper and keeping her pajamas on until after her first nap of the day. I find it easier and it's stuck.

Sookie looks up at me with her blue eyes and my dream comes back at me. I have been worried about her health but I try not to dwell on it and live in the now. I know I can't do anything except make sure she is loved and fed. I bring her to her appointments and there are a lot as we see her cardiologist weekly as well as her pediatrician. I'm happy the laundry list of other ailments has been discarded . Now it's her heart and hoping the foramen ovale closes on its own. Her other hole, the heart defect, will need surgery. Her cardiologist is thinking the surgery will be at six months of age but her heart is being monitored for any changes. It terrifies me that anything can happen. I don't lose sleep over it but when I'm awake it's all I think about.

Sookie smacks her lips and I smile. She has been starting to play around with her lips which I love. She has started making some cooing sounds as well. I try not to worry as I know every baby develops at their own speed. I don't know when I hit certain milestones but I know I was delayed due to many ear infections. I gave my mom a run for her money.

I realize I'm staring at Sookie and not doing anything other than us having a staring contest. "Sorry, baby girl. Ready to go downstairs for a bottle?"

Sookie blinks as I cradle her in my arms. She grabs my finger and holds on as I go downstairs. Sookie found my finger a couple days ago and held on tightly. For a month old, she has a strong grip.

"My baby girl is already up?!" Dean looks at Sookie adoringly. "I started your bottle so it doesn't have long to heat up." He kisses her forehead and then mine.

I smile at Dean. "Thanks, honey."

I know things have been chaotic with all the appointments but my love for Dean has grown. Dean has been patient and level-headed through all my crying about Sookie's health. I don't know how he stays so strong but I'm glad he is as I feel weak with my constant crying. I try to hold it together with him and Sookie but when I'm by myself and not reading I can't help but wonder about all the what ifs.

The bottle heater beeps and Dean grabs the bottle to add formula. Since Sookie's one month appointment, we were told we didn't have to add the formula as the NICU only did it for her to gain weight. We are adding it so she can have more weight on her, for her upcoming surgery, whenever it will be.

I bring Sookie to the couch and nuzzle my head against her head. Her warmth spreads to my chest as I sigh. Holding Sookie is my favorite thing in the world. Kissing her head is another favorite. Love is the best medicine so I pepper her head with kisses all the time. A thought flies through my head about not knowing how much time I could have left with her as well. I could lose her before, during, or after her surgery and I want to treasure every moment I have.

I try not to cry by blinking my eyes. Dean comes in with her bottle and coos at her.
"Are you okay honey?"

I look at Dean. "Yea, why?" I hope I sound convincing as I don't want to worry him.

"You look like you were crying."

"No, I'm just loving Sookie. How could I cry when I'm holding her?"

Dean cocks his head to the right and doesn't look convinced. "Okay. You have your appointment today, right?"

I give Sookie her bottle so she doesn't have to wait too much longer. "Yea. Meg is coming over to watch Sookie."

I have a good support team that I'm grateful for. Meg texts me at least once a week to check in on me. She has her own daughter whom I hope will become friends with Sookie.

"Good. It will be nice for you guys to hang out."

"Well, I have my appointment and she does have work, Dean. I'm lucky she has time to watch Sookie."

"If you need anything, let me know. I'm gonna go get ready." He kisses my forehead and Sookie's.

I had a telehealth appointment a couple weeks ago and was cleared to drive right in time for Sookie's one month appointment. The pain has subsided but I still feel a tightness in my incision, especially when I do too much. That has been difficult to cope with since I love being active. Carrying Sookie to and from the house feels like a marathon.

I had a friend from work come out to help me with Sookie's one month appointment to carry Sookie for me. It was great having her there because she was asking questions that I forgot to ask. She asked about next steps for diagnosis as Dean and I want more testing on which type of Down syndrome Sookie has. It's something Dean and I will talk about it as the doctor said the testing can be done at any time.

I know I have Mosaicism for Down syndrome and my mom had multiple tests done to figure that out. My mom doesn't have the paperwork but I believe her since I don't show any signs of having it. It affects my learning and that's what I hope Sookie has too. She could also have translocation which is why I want testing done. With the three kinds of Down syndrome, I would like to know which one but a part of me is okay not knowing either. I just hate how some of the doctors have been labeling Sookie.

You can't tell Sookie has Down syndrome. Sookie looks just like me when I was a baby except for her forehead and nose. She doesn't have my nose or Dean's. Her nose is the cutest and I'm a bit jealous of it as mine is a bit big for my head. Sookie whacks me in the face making me look down. She has been moving her arms so much while eating that one of these days she is going to give me a concussion. This girl has a good arm. Yesterday she threw a toy across the room by accident, but it was impressive.

Sookie finishes her bottle and I position her on my shoulder to burp her when she belts one out. "Good job!" She is good at burping herself.

Dean is coming down the stairs and I know Meg will be here in a couple hours.

"I heard that burp from upstairs. That's my girl." Dean takes Sookie from me and swings her up in the air.
"Careful, she just ate. She could throw up right in your face."

I would also laugh and not do anything other than say, I told you so.

"I know this is super random but have you heard from Jackie? I thought she would want to help out with Sookie."

"No, the last time we texted was before the baby shower in June. I haven't texted her recently." I've been thinking of her but don't know how to text someone who stopped talking to me randomly.

"I just find it weird as she always joked about living here once Sookie was born to help out."

"Yeah, she works a lot and does her races. I will reach out to her today and see how she's doing."

I am so bad at communicating with others. I can be attached to my phone and not talk to any of my friends. Lately, I have been talking to my friends on my book account. I feel more myself there and not judged. I post whatever and people love Sookie. I get a lot of other moms telling me I'm doing a good job and how strong I am. That is the encouragement I need and I don't think my other friends, except Rita, get that. Ellie gets it but also has her hands full with my nephew.

"Okay. I haven't heard you talk about her recently, just Ellie and Rita."

"Ellie has been a blessing by helping me with so much and Rita makes me feel like a human. Sadly, our other friends haven't reached out but I

figured it would happen. Babies change relationships. Our friends from college still party and start hanging out at nine. I prefer to sleep."
Dean chuckles. "I know. I get that babies change relationships but don't shut people out. I know you love reading and Sookie, but don't forget the outside world."

I sometimes don't like the outside world. Isn't that why people read? To escape to another world and have that time spent in Neverland or on a cruise with a lover. That is what I like but I get what Dean is saying.

"I know. Get going so you aren't late. Meg will be here in an hour."

Sookie is just staring at both of us while we talk. Dean gives her back to me but kisses her on the head one more time. There are not enough kisses in the world for me to show Sookie how much I love her and I can tell Dean feels the same way.

"Have a good day. Text me if you need me." Dean always parts with this line.

I smile after him and look down at Sookie. "And what do you want to do today?"

She looks at me and reaches toward me. Her lips purse forward into a pout and I'm hoping she will smile soon. Sookie has been playing with her mouth a lot so hopefully if I make faces, she will mimic me.

I lay her down and make faces toward her. I give her toys to grasp which she will hold for a few seconds and drop. My phone is always on camera mode as I snap pictures of her and send a couple to Dean. He told me how he shows his students Sookie and how a lot of them want to meet her. I don't blame them. Sookie is a doll.

Soon Meg is here as I see her car in our driveway.
"Sookie! Your Auntie Meg is here." We walk toward the door and open it to reveal Meg.

"Hello! Hold on, let me wash my hands before touching Sookie. I do this before touching my Rylee too. My COVID test came back negative yesterday so I'm good!"

Meg takes more COVID tests than anyone I know but I appreciate her effort. I wouldn't want Sookie getting sick before her surgery.

"Thank you." I don't know what else to say after that.

"How are you? How are you feeling?"

"I'm feeling okay. My incision still gives me some pain but not as much as a couple weeks ago."

"That's right, you had a C-section."

"Yea, did you have that with Rylee?"

"No, Rylee came super fast. My water broke and it took me a while to get to the hospital and once I was there, I started pushing."

"That's crazy." I look at her and she seems a little chunkier than when I saw her at the hospital when she stopped by with donuts. I don't want to ask but I can tell she sees me looking.

"Don't tell anyone but I tested positive a couple days ago. I'm expecting."

She had mentioned she wanted another baby when she took pictures of Dean and me for our one year anniversary. Meg takes exquisite pictures and she is my go-to photographer.

"Congratulations! That's so exciting. Are you going to find out the gender?"

"No. I like it to be a surprise."

I have no clue how she can do that since she is a planner like me. "Good for you. I could never do that."

"Anyway. Tell me where things are and the Princess's schedule."

"She should go down for a nap soon, as she got up a little after six. Her milk is in the fridge."

Meg interrupts me as I'm about to say more. "No water and formula?"

"No. I pump every three hours, sometimes four. We add formula into my breastmilk so she gains weight for her surgery."

"That makes sense. How much formula?"

"Just one scoop." I grab the formula as I take it out of the cabinet. "This is the cabinet with her bottles but the milk is in here." I walk toward the fridge that has a plastic container of my milk in the fridge.

"Okay. Warm it up in the sink?"

I go back over to the cabinet as the bottle warmer is on that counter so it's all easy access. "This is the bottle warmer. You plop it in, close the lid and hit the right button twice." I do it so she knows.

"That's super easy! I just heat water up and do it the old-fashioned way." "The NICU had this and it's way easier for us. Our faucets take forever to give hot water and having it warm that way takes longer. I prefer the bottle warmer but you can use whatever method you want."

"Okay. Well, you get going. Oh wait! Her nursery and diapers and whatnot."

I asked her to get here early so I could show her where things are and because she normally runs late. She got here earlier than I expected so I'm not worried about time, oddly.

Sookie and I lead the way up the stairs as Meg follows us to the nursery. We go toward the nursery and I realize Meg hasn't seen it since she was unable to come to the baby shower. We go into the nursery and I flick on the light.

"This is beautiful!"

I bought decals from Target and had Dean put them on the wall. I love the forest feel in her room. I want Sookie to love and appreciate nature as much as Dean and I. The decals range from trees to moons, to bears and deer. I'm glad Meg likes it as Dean and I put a lot of effort into this room.

I show Meg where her clothes, diapers, cream and toys are . We don't do anything abnormal with changes as I have had odd requests while working in preschool. One of the parents told me to not use a wipe but to take another diaper to fan dry her baby's butt.

"Cool, cool. Get going so you aren't late."

I look at the time and see I still have a bit of time but I do need more vitamins. It takes me a few minutes to say bye to Sookie. I hate leaving her even though I know she's in good hands.

"Bye sweet pea. Mama loves you."

I give her a butterfly kiss and leave.

I head to the store before heading toward Worcester. I feel good. I'm out of the house and am not feeling bad for leaving Sookie behind. I hate leaving her but I know I need a break from her once in a while. I try to keep my mind blank which isn't that hard for me to do especially when I'm walking. When I'm driving, I'm creative. This is where I feel more myself by singing and dancing.

The drive isn't too bad. I park and head in. I don't know what to expect at this appointment as my first one was telehealth. They seemed concerned about my mental wellbeing. Postpartum depression and anxiety are real. I know I have anxiety as we went over it during my last visit. My doctor said my emotions are valid as Sookie leads a life that's different from others. It has been hard to cope but now that Sookie has fewer appointments than her first week home, it's more bearable. I try to think of the positives as I walk toward the office.

Once I'm in, I don't wait long. I see the nurse practitioner right away. She asks me questions about the bleeding and how I'm feeling. I tell her everything. I never hold back, especially since she can help me if I truly need it. Once she starts inspecting my cervix, things get weird. She pokes around more than normal and keeps the tools in for a while longer.

"Everything seems fine. I just want to get the doctor real quick as I have a question for her. I will be back in a few minutes."

I don't wait long. She comes back with the doctor.

"Hi Jackie, good to see you again. Christine was telling me you are having heavy bleeding. I'm going to take a look at your cervix so you will feel probing."

I do feel it and just try to relax. I have no clue what's going on but I try to stay positive.

"Your cervix is soft and low which indicates you're having your period. This can happen early, but it's rare since you are breastfeeding."

This calms me down as I thought something ruptured or some sort of needle was inside me scraping me up.

They must see my sigh of relief as the doctor smiles. "Is there anything else you are concerned about?"

I think for a moment. "I still have pain when I move but it's mostly on my right side. I thought the pain would be gone by now."

"Your delivery was quite intense. Having read your file, you shouldn't have started pushing at seven centimeters dilated. You put your body through the wringer so you might feel it longer. With how Sookie was positioned, you feel it more on your right side. You were pushing when she was still sunny side up. I'm going to talk to the team as one, you shouldn't have started pushing at seven centimeters and two, you shouldn't have tried to push when your baby wasn't positioned correctly. I am sorry for that but it seems you and Sookie are true superwomen."

Knowing that I shouldn't have pushed that soon makes me feel better. It actually makes me feel badass since I could be in more pain right now due to it, but I am not. I know I could sue for malpractice due to what she told me but my concerns are Sookie's health; not mine especially since there is nothing wrong with me. Other than some pain on my right side I feel great. My body isn't damaged and if I want another baby now, I know to save myself the time and effort of pushing until my baby is ready. I feel a weight lift off my shoulders.

"We should talk about birth control and if you want another baby. If you do, we always encourage you to wait at least fifteen months after your first child but we know things happen."

I do think about Sookie having a sibling and I want that but I know that we aren't out of the woods with her health. Her surgery will be costly and we don't know what her future will look like health wise. As much as I want three kids, financially I can't see Dean and I making it work. Not unless we become millionaires. I don't know how other families make it work with a parent staying home as that's what I want. I don't want to go down so many rabbit holes about parenting in front of my doctor, so I look up at them and see them looking at me.

"We have talked about having more than one kid but I'm not sure at the moment."

"Okay, well, looking at your questionnaire your anxiety seems better from your previous appointment. If you have any other feelings and need help let us know. Postpartum depression and anxiety are real and if it's starting to control your life let us know."

I look at them and nod. "Okay. If anything, I'm just always worried about Sookie's heart condition. I don't know what to expect and if there is anything I can do to help her. I also feel like I can do more to better help her but I don't even know how I could do that. I just want her to be alive and thriving."

"That is completely normal for a mom like you in your situation. The best you can do is make sure you are happy and healthy and everything else falls into place. You are doing everything you can and Sookie is really lucky to have you as a mom. Keep doing what you're doing, which is love her unconditionally."

I know this is true and I do love Sookie unconditionally. I would take all her pain away so she doesn't know what pain feels like. I would go on the operating table for her so her heart doesn't have to stop and somehow not start again. I would do anything for Sookie as she is my one and only.

"Well, if that's all we won't keep you from her much longer. You are fit as a fiddle but if you need anything let us know."

I nod as we all walk out of the room. I do need to remind myself that I need to take care of myself first. Lately, I've been stressed about everything. Keeping the house clean, making sure something is out for dinner, pumping on time, making sure Sookie is happy and fed, and Lance is happy by not meowing at three in the morning and wanting to play. Life has been challenging but I'm starting to feel hopeful again that life will be brighter.

Chapter 24

I wake up after having the same dream with that creepy man but this time he doesn't stab me. He stands there and then acts like Dr. Strange as he opens a door that goes from Susan's parents' house to another world. It was very odd as he kept telling me we were saving Sookie. All I want to do is save Sookie so I followed him. He showed me people who were enclosed in bubbles who wanted to hurt Sookie. I woke up when one of the bad guys got out of his bubble and I thought how odd my dreams are becoming. I know my dreams are my subconscious telling me something but this is just bonkers. I have no clue what this dream is telling me. Once Jared bought me a book that interprets dreams but I know I don't have time to find the dream book and figure out what my mind is telling me.

I walk into the kitchen at four A.M. and get my pumping stuff together. I've been in a groove where Sookie has been taking naps while I pump which makes me happy. I know this won't last forever but I'm taking it while I can. I know that she is only sleeping this much because of her heart condition, so I'm trying to get as much reading done as possible while I pump.

Dean and I haven't been talking as much as he has been so busy with work. He finally applied to get his master's degree which I've been on him to do for at least two years. We haven't been having issues but I do have a bit of resentment toward him at times. Mostly, he has been talking about sex a lot and after my six-week appointment I learned how vile I am. My doctor explained to me how everyone in the house has HPV as I have it. However, I feel disgusted with myself. Luckily, it isn't a strand that is fatal and I don't have warts but I don't even want to touch myself anymore. How can I when I have a sexually transmitted disease?

I only told Ellie about my HPV and she has been a good friend. I wouldn't want to tell anyone else about it, not even my sister. Dean knows as I'm not going to keep that from him. I want him to know why we won't have sex any more. No more kids if we won't have sex. I know Dean is patient and loyal but I know he won't like no sex forever. I just don't know how to love myself with a disease like this. I was able to start working out and was feeling myself again but once I found out about HPV...I just felt like I spiraled down into anxiety again.

I feel alone, again. My friends won't understand what I'm going through as only Meg has kids but she and I aren't very close, and she works a lot. I sigh and try to relax. Dean does know when I'm stressed and I don't want to worry him. I remember what the doctor told me about taking care of myself. I need to do things that make me happy other than reading and working out.

Working out also puts me in moods too. My incision burns when I do any core workout. Jackie and I shared a beachbody account but she must have changed her password as I can't do any postpartum workouts there like I intended to. I could buy it for myself but I want that money to go toward Sookie's surgery. I know my incision is just healing but it still feels extremely tight.

Today, Sookie has her first Early Intervention appointment. I'm not sure what to expect but Meg told me how Rylee had early intervention too up till she turned three and then it just stopped. She told me how no one reached out to her and it was sudden too. I'm apprehensive about it because I don't like having it as a reminder that she has Down syndrome. Sookie doesn't have any indications that she has it other than a pompous doctor giving us random facts you can find from Google that Sookie "supposedly" has. I don't want verbal nonsense. I want tests that prove she has it other than my amniocentesis, which hurt like a bitch, but I don't want to put Sookie through more testing.
I don't want doctors to probe and prick Sookie multiple times just to satisfy my desires. What I want with regard to her "diagnosis" of Down syndrome would only appease Dean and me. I know I could do it before she turns four, but how will I know if she remembers it later on in life? I remember getting tested for my learning disability. It made me mentally shove the middle finger toward the doctor and say, challenge accepted. It took me a while to accept what the doctor told my mother and me, but eventually I decided to do what makes me happy. I want Sookie to do the same.

I feel eyes on me as I take the pumping parts off of me. Lance is curled up on top of the couch cushion behind me. He has been waking me up early making me fear that he will wake Sookie. I know Sookie is a heavy sleeper as once Dean set off the fire alarm when cooking and she slept through it. I also have vacuumed while she sleeps too so I know Lance meowing shouldn't wake her.

Lately, I have been feeling down. I know I could talk to my doctors about this but I feel like my mood will improve after Sookie's open-heart surgery. I have faith that everything will work out and I feel like depressed people don't have faith or hope. Dean sometimes says he is worried about me but I know I'm okay. There are days when I'm overwhelmed but I didn't realize how much emotions are put into parenting plus breastfeeding. I never really thought of the emotional aspects of parenting and just thought that Sookie and I would be best friends.

I'm washing my pumping parts at the sink as I'm thinking all this when Dean slips his arms around my waist. He startled me but I somehow didn't jump.

"Hey, babe. You sleep okay?"

I try to finish washing my parts but it's difficult with his arms around me. I like finishing what I'm doing and he is distracting me.

"Yea. Lance just woke me up with his meowing again. I wish he could be like Sookie and sleep while we slept."

"Cats are nocturnal Jackie, you know this. He is adjusting to Sookie as much as Sookie is adjusting to him. He will get there."

I know Dean is right. Lance has also done this before. When we lived in an apartment, Lance would meow incessantly and we closed our door but it became worse. He became better once we bought a house and he has new hiding spots. I do worry about him as he has been pooping near his litter box but not in it. Dean has sworn at him and threatened to get rid of him but I don't believe him. We both love Lance too much to give up on him.

"How did you sleep?" I turn around as he slips his arms away.

"I slept okay. I went to bed at eleven so I didn't get much sleep. Sookie ate well at her nine o'clock feeding."

Dean has been amazing by doing her nightly feed so I can sleep till her midnight feed. Sookie however, could care less about eating at midnight and would rather sleep on me. I'm glad her two-month appointment is in a few days because I think Sookie could sleep through the night as she hates it when I wake her to eat. I don't blame her. I would hate it if someone woke me up to eat at night if I wasn't hungry. I just hate that I waste a good three to four ounces of my milk that she doesn't drink.

"She doesn't eat for me at night. I just pump and go to bed. My watch tells me I'm up for only thirty minutes since she doesn't eat."

Dean shifts as we stand in the kitchen talking. "Shouldn't she be eating though? She needs to gain weight."

"You can't force someone to eat Dean. If I force eggs down your throat when you aren't hungry you won't like it or if you eat it, you will feel sick."

He nods in agreement. "I see your point. I just want her to be big and strong for her upcoming open-heart surgery."

"I know. Her early intervention appointment starts today and the therapist will be coming weekly to help Sookie get stronger."

"That's right. What time is that?"

"I said eleven so Sookie isn't eating since they will want her moving. I don't think it matters if she is eating but still."

"Let me know how it goes as I'm interested to know what the first session is all about."

We met with the program coordinator a week ago and set this appointment. The therapist will be evaluating Sookie to see if she qualifies for early intervention.

"I'm going to go workout. Yell down if you need me." Dean gives me a chaste kiss on the lips. Dean has been working out in the morning a lot recently and I have just been sleeping.

"Sounds good. I'm going to go back to bed for a bit. If I'm not awake before Sookie, can you wake me?"

"Of course."

He envelopes me into a bear hug and we part ways. I head upstairs as he heads downstairs. I will never understand how he can get little sleep and still do all the things he does. He truly inspires me to be the best I can. I shake my head in wonder as Dean embodies a compassionate human with vast amounts of love for everyone.

Dean wakes me with a kiss to the cheek. I open my eyes and love this.

"Jackie. It's almost six. Sookie will be up soon."

I roll to my left and open my eyes to see his face. He really needs to shave but I know how much he loves having facial hair.

"Thanks, honey."

I don't want to get up but it's closer to the time of Sookie's first early intervention session and I'm excited and nervous. I have been working with Sookie to do things but she's only a month old.

"You okay?" Dean looks at me with a worried face.

"I'm just nervous for Sookie's first session as I don't know what to expect."

"She will rock it. Don't worry about it."

I have been worrying about it a lot lately and I can't help it. Before Sookie, I rarely worried about much. The only thing I worried about was when Dean rode his motorcycle. Now, I worry about everything and anything. I worry about what I will do for a job, Sookie's health, the house that seems to fall apart, Lance, and my boobs. My boobs still feel weird. I know I need to adjust to producing milk but I've never had my boobs this big before.
"What are you doing?"

I realize I'm fondling my boobs as I'm thinking about them. I chuckle and say, "I was thinking of how big my boobs have become. It's a little awkward as I can't even sleep on my stomach anymore."

"I can only imagine. They look amazing though." Dean looks at me suggestively and I know what he wants. I know sex is going to be an issue between us because even before Sookie we didn't have sex a lot. Now with my body feeling foreign to me I can't see it happening any time soon.

I roll out of bed and brush my hair. It feels gross as I haven't washed it in a couple days. It feels limp and too long. Dean is on his side of the room getting dressed for work.

I look over wondering why he is getting dressed now. "Don't you leave around seven?"

"Yea, but I figured I could get ready and help you."

This is why I love him. He rarely thinks of himself and does things to help me. I wonder how I got so lucky to have him in my life. He stays up at night to feed Sookie, does his work for his students even though he doesn't know the subject he is teaching, cooks, and helps out around the house. The man is a saint.

I love watching Dean with Sookie because of how he interacts with her. He coos and ahhs at all the right times. Sookie's eyes widened in delight at him. She still hasn't smiled but I know once she does, she will mean it. Sookie seems to be like me in that respect as I don't smile at everything. I have to genuinely be happy with whatever is in front of me. A joke has to be funny or I won't laugh. Sookie seems to be taking after me in that regard. I don't mind her being quiet and contemplative like her mommy.

"I have to get to work. You two have fun." Dean hands me Sookie as he stands from the floor.

I'm sitting on the couch in my designated spot on the left side. I take Sookie and love her cute round face. We dressed her in her Hogwarts outfit with the Hogwarts crest of gold and red on the onesie and red pants. It looks adorable on her despite her red hair. Her hair is starting to get lighter and I hope it stays red. I've always wanted red hair and it would be fun to have a ginger in the house.

I look at my watch and realize we won't have long to wait. Sookie is starting to fall asleep in my arms so I let her rest as I read on my Kindle.

Sookie stirs in my arms making me look down at her from my Kindle. I realize it's time for a bottle for her so I carry her to the kitchen. I walk around the kitchen holding her getting in my exercise. This has become a daily occurrence and I can tell Sookie enjoys it.

As I'm feeding her, I think of what we can do so I don't tire her out before her session. I want her to wow these people. We end up listening to music as she lies on her boppy. I must have picked the wrong time for the session as Sookie starts falling asleep close to the appointed time for her session. I don't want to keep her up and hope it's okay for her to be sleeping in the beginning.

I put her down in her room and pace the living room while waiting. Some people think this is a nervous habit but it's how I think. I am able to compartmentalize everything by moving my body. Lately, I have been going down the rabbit hole of things that shall not be named.

I look out the window and see two women standing in my driveway. I don't want to seem nosey but I assume it's for Sookie's session. I don't know how many are going to show but they seem to be waiting for someone else. It's a little past our appointment but if everyone is arriving separately then it's hard to coordinate. I step away from the window and wait for a knock.

Once I hear the knock I go to the front door. I don't want them to wake Sookie even though I know she's a heavy sleeper.

"Hello. You must be Jackie. Nice to meet you." One of the ladies puts her hand out for a shake.

I take it and say hello back.

"Is there a big space for us all to sit? We will need Sookie near the end so there is enough room for her to play too."

I was thinking of the dining room but realize that is not the right room for Sookie to play in. I lead them to the living room. They all sit on the floor and pull out laptops and notepads.

The person who asked me the question must be in charge. It's hard to distinguish facial features since we are all wearing masks. Looks can be deceiving so I wait for someone to speak.

The heavy-set woman who spoke earlier pipes up again. "So, we have a checklist that we will go through of adaptive, personal-social, communication, motor, and cognitive skills that we will be looking for. We will be scoring based on your answers as well as what Sookie shows us too."

I nod my head in understanding. She starts asking me questions about our routine, how Sookie likes bath time, what she does while eating, and so on. I'm not sure what this has to do with anything so I try to be honest with some of them even though I don't bathe her. Dean loves having that as his thing and I also can't do it as I cannot bend over. Bending over pulls on my incision and the tightness can be painful at times.

"Perfect! Is Sookie sleeping? Is it near the end of her nap so we can see how she tests for the other skills?"

I'm glad they can't see my face as I grimace. I don't like waking her but we have been waiting for this. I go upstairs to gently wake her. She has been sleeping for almost an hour which is how long she sleeps for each nap during the day.

"Hey sweet pea, the therapists are here to see how strong you are. Are you ready?"

I sniff her bottom first before bringing her downstairs. She smells clean so I go downstairs with her. I touch the wall for balance as I would hate myself if I somehow fell down the stairs with Sookie in my arms. Our stairs are narrow and my feet are so humongous that I always hurt them on the stairs going up. I'm always so worried that I will trip and fall going down.

Once we are downstairs, I plop Sookie on the blanket I left out and one of the therapists with long red hair comes over. We do a variety of things but the one thing that melts my heart is when they ask me to stand in the doorway of the room away from Sookie and call for her. Sookie's head moves to find me and she does. I smile at her even though she can't see it through the mask.

Everyone gushes over how Sookie always tries to find me when I'm not next to her. They also love her red hair and silver eyes. Her eyes are turning more aqua which is stunning. I would gush over her looks as well too.

At the end they tally up Sookie's points and go over it with me. Nothing really makes sense as I'm a visual person. I need to be looking at what they are describing to me. This is why I hate being the only one at Sookie's appointments as Dean is better at understanding things being explained verbally.

Finally, they show me the piece of paper. I see that Sookie did extremely well in personal-social skills and scored poorly in the cognitive aspect. I view this as a goal for Sookie and me to achieve together. A part of me is upset that she didn't score higher in some categories but at her age I'm proud of what she can do with her setback.

I've always taken negatives and let them get the best of me but now with Sookie I need to be positive. I need to take these situations and be constructive, so I don't linger on the bad. Nothing is wrong unless I fester on it and not do anything about it. I need to be a good role model for Sookie so she can learn and grow. I won't tell her what to do so she can make her own mistakes and I'm going to try and not do things for her. I have tried my best in things and failed. My failures made me become who I am today.

I'm going to take this piece of paper and use it as a guide to help her grow. I know Sookie has to work harder but I can tell how determined she is already.

As Sookie is in my lap, I stand up with her to walk the ladies to the front door. I can tell Sookie loved the interactions with the grown-ups and can't wait for her to play with babies her own age. She is going to become such an amazing woman and I'm excited to watch her grow.

Chapter 25

Tears spring to my eyes for more than one reason. My right boob feels massive and not in a good way. It feels hard and whenever I touch it, it hurts like hell. When I pumped, I barely got anything out from that side whereas I pumped five ounces from the other. I know something isn't right and Google is telling me I have a clogged duct. The other reason I'm about to cry is that Sookie is two months old today. I can't believe how time is flying with her.

Her cardiologist mentioned how her surgery will be at three months of age which terrifies me. It is dependent on the team from Boston Children's Hospital so we shall see. That is next month and I don't feel ready at all. I play with my hands due to my nerves. Her surgery needs to happen and my clogged duct will get better in time according to Google.

This clogged duct can go to hell. I have tried massaging it. I tried soaking it in epsom salt in my haaka which I forgot I had till I read an article on ways to relieve clogged ducts. One of them made me laugh as it said to have your spouse suck it out. That would be funny but also weird. Dean has mentioned how he would suck it but I find that wrong. My milk is for Sookie, not Dean.

Right now, I am heating my boob while Sookie is on her quilt that Grandma made her. She is trying to reach for the cords but I keep telling her it isn't safe. I'm trying my hardest not to say the word no in front of her so it's not her first word. It's quite challenging.

Sookie has been trying to roll over in her sessions and I'm trying to encourage her to do that. I know it will happen but I know it can be difficult. I just want her to be strong for her surgery.

I sigh and realize I could have a clog due to being stressed. Sookie's heart has been making me nervous. When I wake at night, I check on her to make sure she is breathing. My dreams have become more intense; in them she looks like a skeleton which scares me. It makes me feel like something bad is going to happen. I know I need to stay positive, especially in front of Sookie.

Sookie has been making some cute sounds lately and moving her lips. It's making me think she will smile soon but so far nothing.

"Baby girl, your two-month appointment is in a little over an hour. Shall we walk there? It's so nice outside."

It's almost October which is the best time of year. It's becoming fall which is my favorite season. It's a little brisk but it's not too chilly or hot. To me it's the perfect temperature. I'm still wearing maternity clothes and love them. Maternity wear is so comfortable and I wish I wore it before I was pregnant. Some of the clothes are becoming too loose though. My real clothes are kind of fitting but my stomach is just in the way.

I try not to think about my body and weight as I can't change it by thinking about it. As a personal trainer I know I need to work out which I have begun. Sookie sleeps well so I've been doing a workout regimen to feel better about my body. I know I shouldn't bash my body. I just wish my stomach looked a little flatter. I could care less about having six pack abs. I just want my stomach to not protrude.

Sookie slams her feet down on the ground and I look at her. "Oh really?" I laugh at her. "You are so strong. When are you going to roll? Tomorrow? The day before your surgery?"
She looks up at me with those blueish-silver eyes and I melt. I'm a goner. This girl has me whipped. Whatever she asks from me later in life, I'm probably going to say yes. She slams her legs down again and makes a raspberry. She has started making that sound occasionally, especially when she wakes. She still doesn't cry when she wakes so I have no clue if she's awake unless I look at the baby monitor.

I look at the clock and stop heating my boob. I was texting Meg about my clog and she told me how her husband sucked out her clog once. I could see those two doing that. They are a tight unit and an adorable couple.

"Okay sweetpea. Let's head upstairs to get you changed into warmer clothes and so Mama can do her hair. Are you ready?"

She looks up at me and I wish she would smile. Do moms obsess over what they want their babies to do? I really hope I'm not alone in this but I also know Sookie is special. If she has early intervention, it makes me think she's going to be behind. With her heart defect it is harder for her to do a lot as well.

I wish things were different. I wish Sookie didn't have a heart defect. I always prayed for a miracle while I was pregnant with her as I want her to be normal. I want her to grow old and do whatever she wants. Currently, she has to work ten times harder to roll over.

I get her dressed and go into my room. I place Sookie on the bed and she moves around. I giggle at her antics and get dressed. I have so many black leggings that I just grab a pair and a shirt so that it takes me less than a minute to dress. I grab a sweatshirt so I don't get too cold and start heading outside.

The hospital isn't a far walk as it's only a mile away. It normally takes me twenty minutes to walk there but I know it may take me a couple more minutes plus they require a COVID test before going in to appointments which is annoying.

I get there in record time despite road work being done on the back road I took. Sookie fell asleep about halfway there, so I'm happy she took a ten minute cat nap. I check us in and fill out the necessary paperwork. The paperwork is about if I'm worried about her not meeting a milestone but I also know she may not meet them due to her heart defect. A part of me hates that but I know every child is different. So far Sookie has been my ray of sunshine.

"Sookie?"

I stand up once I hear our name. The nurse leads us to room one and I get Sookie out of her car seat from the stroller. I feel like I'm finally acting more independently and am not scared to bring Sookie to her appointments. At first, I was terrified that I would do something wrong or hurt one of us. For her EKG, I had to hold her arms down so we could get a reading. I give a lot of credit to moms who have more appointments for their kids than we do.

I undress Sookie so we can get a weight and height. I wish Sookie was in a higher percentile for her measurements but I also love how tiny she is. We were both born the same weight and height. I just had a few more ounces, so she is following in her mama's footsteps. Sookie makes me proud.

"Hello, I'm Dr.Oh."

I remember meeting her for one of Sookie's weight checks. Her accent made it hard to decipher certain words she said. When Dean was with us, he guessed she was Armenian and predicted correctly as she was impressed with his knowledge. This whole time Dean has made an impression on doctors. He makes me feel like an imbecile even though I know I'm smart in my own ways. I'm trying to be better at not bringing myself down as I wouldn't want Sookie doing that.

"I see Sookie is here for her two-month check-up. Do you have any questions or concerns to bring up first?"

"Not that I can think of at the moment." I'm not sure if I should mention my clogged duct as this is Sookie's appointment. My hesitation goes unnoticed by Dr.Oh and listen to what she has to say.

"Sookie is doing well with her weight gain. Are you breastfeeding?"

"Yes, I am pumping and I put formula in her bottle."

"Excellent. How much formula do you put in?"

"I believe it's a tablespoon; one serving of Similac. Now that I'm thinking about her feeding, I wanted to know if I have to wake her at night to feed her. We give her three to four ounces at nine P.M. which she takes but when I wake her at midnight, she barely eats anything; same thing at three. When she gets up at six, she takes a good six ounces. Can I let her sleep since she could care less about her bottles?"

"If she is not drinking it then yes, don't bother waking her. She is at a good weight. As long as her cardiologist is okay with her weight as well. Will you see her soon?"

"Yes, we will see her next week actually."

"Excellent. Have you been to the Down syndrome Clinic yet?"

"No." I got this question at her one-month appointment and mentioned how I don't have the time.
"I highly recommend it as it serves a purpose for you and her. With her diagnosis she has a higher chance of getting diseases such as leukemia. The resources the clinic has will be beneficial for you."
With it being in Boston, I really don't want to go. If we really have a need for it then I will. I looked into the website when it was mentioned at her one-month appointment and it is nice. It supports families and the individual with Down syndrome. I wonder if my mom used it with me.

"When is Sookie's heart surgery?"

"We don't know yet. Her cardiologist is saying if her weight keeps going up then it will be at three months of age."

"That is excellent news!" I nod my agreement. "I strongly urge you to use the Down syndrome Clinic beforehand. Is Sookie also using Early Intervention?"

Her questions are starting to irritate me as she keeps mentioning Down syndrome. I know she is trying to guide me but every time we are here it feels like the same questions. All the time. "Yes, once a week. She started a couple weeks ago." I hope my frustration isn't heard in my voice.

"Good. I will have the nurse come in to administer Sookie's shots. These are to protect her from Hepatitis B, Diphtheria, tetanus, whooping cough, and ear infections. Have a good day."

Dr. Oh is very curt. I haven't met a doctor like her before and really hope we don't have her again. I have no clue why the practice has her even though she does seem efficient. I just hate how Dr. Oh kept labeling Sookie with Down syndrome. I just want Sookie treated like any other baby coming in here.

Two nurses come in with two needles and a little cup. They give Sookie the dose by mouth first and both take a leg. I stand over Sookie so she can look at me. I grab her hands and hum. I picked a Queen song to hum as I noticed how Sookie loves Queen. Once the shots are administered, she cries. I don't blame her as I hate needles myself. I tend to look away once they inject me.

"Take all the time you need to calm her down before you leave."

I thank them and rock Sookie in my arms.

"I know honey. Shots hurt. No one likes them but they are necessary to prevent diseases."

She continues to cry and I dress her hoping that calms her down a bit. I hate hearing her cry as she rarely does it. My heart goes out to her hoping I can take any worries away from her. Sookie continues to cry and I'm at a loss of how to console her. Rocking her and humming is not working. I'm feeling frazzled and hope no one can hear her cries outside the door. Sookie seems to settle so I place her in the car seat. At least, all her appointments until she is six months old are booked so I can skedaddle out of here.

Once she is secured, I run. Not flat out run but speed walk. I feel like one of those women who uses light weights during their power walks, just with Sookie. It's starting to hurt my incision making the burning sensation crawl up toward my chest but I ignore it. Sookie is in pain and I want her home where I know she will be happy. She is making a whimper cry which makes me want to get home as soon as possible.

Since I have the stroller, I have to wait for the elevator to get to the ground floor which is insanely slow right now. I urge the elevator to hurry up as Sookie is still crying. I try to calm her by humming but I know it won't work. I know I'm the kind of person who hates to hear a baby cry in public and now I'm being that person. Yet, now I know how the mother feels. Frazzled. Distraught. At a loss of what the fuck to do to get her to stop crying.

The elevator is finally here as I hear it ding and I thank the Lord. An elderly couple slowly gets off and I hurry in and press the button. Another person snakes their arm in to catch the door when the stairs are right next to it. They have capable legs to bring them a flight down. The man only looks to be in his forties and ran to catch the elevator. If you can run then you can take the stairs. People like him annoy the piss out of me. I try not to glare at him as Sookie cries as the doors finally close.

"It's okay, baby. Mama will run home despite the pain I'm in."

I make sure the man hears me so he knows that elevators are for people who need them. Not capable people who can use a staircase just mere inches away from the elevator.

Once the doors open, I hustle us outside the hospital and toward home. I have run a ten-minute mile before so I start at a jog. I'm glad I'm wearing running sneakers as I did not think I would be running but here I am. Sookie's wails are starting to go into whimpers but I still run. I need exercise which is why I walked so I'm committing to doing this.

My breathing hitches and I wonder why I got into running in the first place. I remember when COVID struck and everyone was forced indoors.

That's when I started running and realized I'm not bad when I'm by myself. If I have the right music and attitude, I can do great. I did 5ks and 10ks during the shutdown and was proud of myself. Before I got pregnant, I did a half marathon which shocked me as I haven't run that far. Dean and Jackie did it with me but Dean was ahead the whole time and I somehow ended up in front of Jackie until I got lost. Running has been a great sport but it's hard to get into.

The burning starts just a couple minutes after I start to walk. My breathing is elevated as I was not breathing correctly giving me this a stitch in my side plus the pain from my incision. I start to wonder how many words there are to describe pain based on what I'm feeling. Before I even think about that I realize Sookie has stopped crying. I am at the rotary which is just five minutes away from my house and wonder if I should keep walking to let her calm down. She loves being outside so I take a peek and see her eyes starting to drift. I could try to walk more despite the discomfort on my right side.

As I near my house getting ready to walk past it, Sookie cries out. My plan to keep walking flies out the door so I head toward our main entrance. I don't bother trying to lift the stroller up the stairs to the porch and leave it in front of my car so it's hidden from the street. I unbuckle Sookie and grab her. She calms instantly in my arms.

I look down at her and see how her eyes are a little puffy from her tantrum. I hate seeing her this way and skim my finger across her cheek. Holding her against my left boob begins to hurt due to the clog, so I unlock the front door and settle her into her swing. She loves her swing when the motion and vibration are on at the same time.

Once Sookie is calm, I start to get everything ready so I can pump to relieve the pressure I'm in. I'm more than fine to pump a little more due to my clog. I wonder if it's clogged because a week ago I decided to stop pumping in the middle of the night. It was getting to be too much for me with feeding Sookie. I wanted to focus on Sookie and not my boobs. It was weird waking up and having my boobs engorged but worth it to sleep more. Now that Dr. Oh said I don't have to wake her at night for her feeding I can sleep straight through. The thought makes me smile as I pump. I've noticed when I'm happy I pump more milk so I grab my Kindle while Sookie sleeps in her swing and hope pumping every two hours instead of three will help my clog.

Chapter 26

"Faster." I hear myself say even though I'm not remotely into what we are doing anymore.

I had been reading a book that had a lot of sex scenes in it making me feel frisky. I put on some nice clothes; including lingerie. Dean and I haven't been having sex ever since I learned about my sexually transmitted disease. I try not to think about that right now though.

Dean is amazing in bed but right now I am over it. It is starting to hurt and I have no idea why. I know he is in the moment and am glad we are in the doggy position so he can't see my face. I'm grimacing even though I'm moaning. Technically my moans are pleasure and pain.

"That's it." Dean says and I hope he is about to come as I don't want to continue.

How can I tell him nicely that it's hurting? He would just want to use more lube and I would want to stop.

"Babe." I try to get his attention. "Honey." He is still riding me as I'm talking. "Dean!"

He stops and I wiggle away from him. I'm currently just in a bra as my boobs feel too weird for me. The way they jiggle is awkward and annoying.

"What? What's wrong?" He looks bewildered.

He has no idea what I'm about to say even though this has happened before.

"It's starting to hurt. I just want to stop." I start to sit up but Dean lays me down on the bed.

"We can still continue. I can put more lube on to make you more comfortable."

My mind isn't in it and it's different. Having sex with a baby in the house is new. I can't wrap my head around it and it's confusing me.

"I don't want to. I'm sorry." I truly am sorry as I did initiate it and am now ending it. I know what he is going to say as it's my first time ending it before either of us comes.

"What can I do to make you feel better? We haven't done this in ages and I miss it."

I wasn't expecting that and he is right. It's why I started it in the first place as when we are both stressed, sex seems to make us feel better.

"Honestly? Nothing. It's me, Dean. I'm starting to think of Sookie which is not going to get me in the mood."

"Don't you want to give her a sibling?"

I go back and forth with that. I have always wanted three kids but to go through all of this? I'm still not used to my boobs and breastfeeding is a pain. A literal pain. My labor was not fun either. I exhale loudly. I don't know what to say or do anymore.

"Dean." I'm emotionally drained right now and don't know what to say or do. "I just. Ugh. Where do I start?"

Dean lays there on the bed as he holds me. This is nice just laying next to each other, almost naked. I can tell Dean would rather be fully naked but I'm not used to my boobs and don't think I ever will be.

"From the beginning or wherever you feel comfortable starting."

Dean is going to make me feel horrible no matter what I say. I feel like I'm always the bad guy in our relationship when it comes to sex.

I sigh. "Don't interrupt me so I don't lose my train of focus. I don't feel sexy anymore and initiating this was hard. Sometimes I feel like I have to so there is no animosity between us. If we don't have sex then I feel like you use it against me when we fight about something. I love you. I'm attracted to you. But things are different and I need to get through things first."

Dean starts standing up and dressing. I can tell I upset him and hate myself for it. I am the bad guy once again and I hate myself for it. I stand up too as I don't want to be the only one with barely no clothes on. I start dressing again.

There is a heavy silence in the air and I instantly regret saying anything. If only I had just kept going, we wouldn't be like this right now.

Dean harrumphs and turns around. He stares at me and I can tell he is sad, not mad. "I want you to be ready Jackie and I hate how you thought you had to initiate this. Sex shouldn't be forced even from you. I want you to want me. I need you to need me."

I chuckle as I love that song. "I know and I'm sorry. I just hate how things are between us. I feel like we are both living in this house but barely say or do anything. We don't do anything together, even sex. I just don't want us becoming stagnant."

"We won't but you shouldn't be forcing this if it's not what you want. I don't want us fighting over sex even though it's normally me who gets upset. I promise not to do that anymore."

I can tell he means it and am glad this happened. I needed to hear that as I don't want him to get upset that nothing happened, or that we had sex but did not finish. I always feel like one of us has to finish and if we don't then the act was wasted. I hate how I feel this way as sex shouldn't be that way. I should know it's about feeling attracted to one another. Sex is about loving one another.

"Can you come here?" I love him for who he is and want to show him that.

He comes toward me and we hug. I pull his shirt over his head and see his scar on his left shoulder from where he tore it. I run my finger over it and kiss it. I feel him shiver against me and lean my head against his chest.

I realize it's the contact I crave. I need to be in Dean's arms and know we need to hug more. I may have started something but we have connected on another level through this and am glad it happened. I hate how I feel sometimes but now I know how Dean feels.

Chapter 27

Sookie's surgery is in a week as her cardiologist thought we shouldn't wait and her weight is good. When I got the call from Boston Children's I was surprised. I was asked if November third was okay for her surgery and the first of November for her COVID test. Since it's our wedding anniversary, I thought why not. I'm not superstitious but I could use it by telling the doctors how the day is special to us and not to ruin it. I don't think they will as when I mentioned the surgeon to Ellie, she knew the doctor. One of her friend's did their fellowship with Sookie's surgeon which makes me feel better.

Thinking of how small the world is comforts me. I had posted on a support page for parents with kids who have Down syndrome about what I should bring for her surgery and so many people responded. A few even took the time to personally message me and tell me not to worry. It was nice that these strangers took the time to let me know what to bring and if I needed to vent, I could go to them.

Right now, I'm freaking out about it. I don't want to lose my only child. Sookie is my world and my light. When I feel down, I look at her and feel better. She still isn't smiling but she is making sounds. Not any baby talk but raspberries. Sookie loves to wake up making them as it's her way of letting me know she is awake and ready to play. She is just like me and wakes up at six every morning. If she has a difficult night falling asleep which does happen, she sleeps till six thirty. She snores and makes other adorable noises that make me smile at night. I know I am lucky.

Now that I'm happy I realize her early intervention session is going to start soon. I find a mask so I can grab it before opening the door.

Sookie is on the floor moving side to side. We have been working on having her roll onto her stomach and onto her back. She almost has it as I nudge her side to prompt her to do the work instead of me doing it. Her occupational therapist is happy with Sookie's progress and so am I. I can tell Sookie would rather we do the work for her and I don't blame her. I wish I didn't have to do half the stuff at work as well. Sometimes I wish I didn't have to clean even though I like cleaning.

The doorbell rings and I go answer it. We ended up with the redheaded therapist, Holly, whom I love. She is gentle but also knows when and how to push Sookie.

"Hello, how are you?"

We always do the casual talk of, how are you and how is Sookie. I always say good even if it isn't. Mostly it's just how I feel so it's not like I'm lying. She is here for Sookie, not for me.

I lead her to where Sookie is lying down on her quilt and have her boppy out for the session. I bought some toys for Sookie to know where her feet are; they have rattles on them. Holly loves them and begins to put them on Sookie. Sookie doesn't get it but looks up and starts reaching for her hair.

"That's good! How long has she been reaching up for things?"

"Ever since our last session." I'm proud of this as once I'm told to work on something with Sookie I do it.

"That's awesome! How long does she hold onto her toys?"

"It depends on the toy. Some toys can be minutes. She has been grabbing her bottles too! She has stopped whacking me in the face with her arms and her hands wrap around it. It's so cute."
"That's amazing! I can't wait to see all this. You are doing so well, Sookie."

Sookie looks up at Holly with her gorgeous eyes that look blue today. Her eyes tend to change every week and I love looking into them and seeing what color they are. I've asked Dean if I am the only one that sees her eyes change color and he notices it as well.

"You know, I've never seen a ginger with silver eyes before. You are quite beautiful, Sookie."

Sookie and I both beam. I did help make her and she is a replica of me. She is more pretty than me as her nose is so cute. The saying cute as a button is weird but Sookie really is cute as a button when you talk about her nose.

"Say thank you to Holly."

Sookie just stares and we both just melt.

Holly guides me to help Sookie roll from one side of the quilt to the other. I can tell Sookie is getting annoyed so I try helping her a little bit more. Sookie better appreciate this in the moment as Holly could challenge her, herself. I try to be the one to touch Sookie.

"So, this is the last time we will meet until after Christmas, correct?"

"Yes. After her surgery she isn't allowed to do much of anything for two months. She isn't even allowed to reach for things."

"That's going to be rough. How are you handling it?"

I'm surprised she is asking. However, Holly is nice. She has three boys and is always telling me about them.
"It hits me at certain moments. I have to be thinking about her surgery to feel nervous, anxious, or even sad. I hate how Sookie will have to go through this. I don't know what to expect afterwards."

"Yea, I can only imagine. You both are so strong."

I blush with the praise and appreciate it. Holly is the only human I interact with face to face other than my mom. I only see others if they are coming to watch Sookie. Now that her surgery is so close, we have to quarantine for a week. Technically it's Sookie who has to quarantine, but I will as well. I had to tell both grandmas who understood but hated it. My mom has seen Sookie the most and also gets to see her before her surgery since she lives so close to Boston.

"Sookie, let's try rolling."

Sookie starts crying as she doesn't want to do it anymore. I try to console her by telling her it's okay when Holly tells me to pick her up. Sometimes putting Queen on helps so I ask Alexa to play it. Unfortunately, it doesn't help so I shut Alexa off after a song. I bounce Sookie in my arms and hum. I always pick this one song to hum that helps her fall asleep. She is starting to drift in my arms.

"It's only been thirty minutes but she seems to be falling asleep in your arms. We can call it quits. Let me just double check the calendar as we won't see each other for at least two months." She grabs her phone and scrolls through. "I have January ninth down at eleven. That gives her two months of recovery plus extra time due to holidays. Sound good to you?"

I look at her phone and nod. "Looks right to me."

"Perfect. You put her to bed and I wish her a speedy recovery. If you need anything you have my cell."

"Thank you." I mean it as she has been amazing for my sanity and has benefitted Sookie as well.

I bring Sookie into her room and swaddle her the best I can without waking her. Surprisingly I don't wake her as I put her in her crib and then I walk downstairs. I grab my Kindle and get comfortable. Lance nestles in my lap as I read. He does this occasionally when Sookie isn't around. I hope he grows more comfortable with her.

All of a sudden Lance's ears go back. His face looks toward the stairs and I look at him. "What? Is Sookie up? Are you my baby monitor?"

I look at my phone and sure enough she is up. Her arms and legs are whacking against her bassinet making it move slightly. Sookie is strong and also sassy today. She must have pretended to sleep to get out of her session since I put her down not even ten minutes ago.

I laugh. "Oh Sookie. Why do I have a feeling you are going to run this house?"

I have noticed myself talking out loud more often. Dean always thinks I talk to him when I talk to Sookie or Lance. It's funny as I always tell him he isn't the only one in the house that I talk to.

I heave myself off the couch and go upstairs to Sookie. She has been starting to sleep more on her left side and Holly is worried she could get a flat head from it. I'm thankful for the information as her head has started looking off a bit. I've been doing more tummy time and wearing Sookie to prevent a flat head. Ellie and Matt bought me this cool Harry Potter baby wearer that Sookie loves. Positioning her in it also helps prevent flat head.

"I'm coming, Sookie baby."

I walk up the stairs as she cries out. This girl is one sassy pants who didn't want to do her session before her surgery next week. She truly is like her mama.

I walk into her room saying, "What's going on? I was curious if you were really tired as it isn't your naptime. You're pretty good at staying up for about two hours." I heave her out of her bassinet and pretend to grunt. "You are getting bigger and stronger every day." I hope for a smile but don't get one. I guess I need to earn it.

I smell her butt and don't smell any pee or poop so I bring her back downstairs. "I can't believe you faked sleep to get out of your session. You really must not want to share your toys."

Lately, I have been on social media and a lot of my friends have had babies. Some of them have been smiling and laughing but not Sookie. That is one of the reasons why I'm concerned as other kids her age, or younger, have smiled. I know I shouldn't compare but it's hard not to. I have texted Ellie about it and she says not to worry. I can't help but compare. It's a bad habit that I haven't been able to get myself out of.

I wonder if I should pack for her surgery as we are leaving for my mom's this Monday. Sookie's COVID testing is on Monday early in the morning and her surgery is Wednesday. Our plan is to get her test done and go to my mom's afterward. Dean and I are staying at my mom's while Sookie recovers so we aren't driving more than an hour every day to see her. I always say everything happens for a reason and I'm glad my mom bought her condo near Boston.

Since Sookie only has so many clothes, I decide to wait to pack her clothes until this weekend. I hate waiting but I can't wrap my head around what to bring and how much to bring. The paperwork we received about what to expect told us Sookie would be in just a diaper for the first two days after surgery. I try not to think what she will look like afterwards but can't imagine anything other than something grotesque. My mind can get very dark and morbid.

Sookie is currently on her stomach just lounging. If I don't push her and tell her what to do, she is content on her tummy. If I put toys in front of her and tell her or prod her to reach, she will cry. She is one tough nugget.

I decide to text Dean as it is finally afternoon and I sometimes get a response back. I get bored after a while staying inside with Sookie having her do tummy time. I know I shouldn't wish for her to be bigger but I can't wait until she can talk and walk. The conversations we will have will be epic. Plus, we can do more activities once she walks and sits up. I also text Ellie to see who will respond. I have no clue how to entertain myself when she is up but even when she naps, I find myself bored of doing the same things over and over.

Ellie: I find myself bored too. It's hard staying motivated with a baby.

Thank goodness Ellie agrees. I would be worried if it was just me that felt this way.

Me: I find myself on my phone a lot just scrolling social media which puts me on a spiral of comparing Sookie to other babies. What has Roland been doing?

Ellie: Ro does tummy time and reaches for toys above him. We also have a bouncer that I put him in with toys in front of him as well. I go outside with him too to break up the day. It gets repetitive but being outside is fun.

Now that I know Sookie does the same thing as her cousin, I feel better. I try to enjoy my time with Sookie while I can. I know I won't be able to stay home forever even though I would love to not have to work. If Dean wasn't a teacher and had another job that paid better, I might have had a chance at being a stay-at-home mom. I wouldn't want to stay home forever but just for a couple years before preschool starts. I love the first couple years where she does things for the first time. Working at a preschool I tended to see the first moments instead of the parents and I wouldn't want that. I also let the parents think their kid did it first at home instead of at school as I didn't want to take that joy away from them.

I look at Sookie and my feelings of boredom dissipate. Sookie is actually trying to turn around on her boppy which makes me chuckle. This girl is a spitfire who makes me roar with laughter. Her face brightens up when she hears me laugh.

I get on all fours and we stare at each other as I make faces at her. At the moment, I'm okay with her not smiling. She is currently smiling with her eyes which is better than nothing. I try to take the little victories as they come.

Chapter 28

Sookie and I are in the nursery as I'm packing her bags. I butchered up when all the appointments were as Sookie is getting her COVID test tomorrow, Sunday, instead of Monday. Monday morning, we are meeting with the surgeon to go over what will happen and ask any questions. Traffic in Boston is horrendous and I'm not looking forward to it even though I won't be driving.

I woke up this Saturday morning in a panic due to another terrifying dream of losing Sookie so I've been in a mood. Dean is currently outside as we ordered a dumpster to get rid of a lot of junk in our house to make room for all the presents Sookie is still receiving. A lot of these gifts are things she won't be able to use until she is older so we have to rearrange some rooms. Our house is starting to get messy. When I look at a closet full of our stuff I feel overwhelmed with where to start organizing. I normally love organizing but with having more things come into our house unannounced, it's overwhelming.

I hear Sookie make a little noise in her crib as I'm pulling her clothes out. I'm looking for clothes that she can wear with wires all over her body, so buttons on the side or in the middle. Sookie seems to be enjoying her crib. It's her first time there and I wanted her to move around. Her room has hardwood floors and we still don't have a carpet for it yet so I'm not sure how she will like the hardwood floor.

Thwonk. Startled, I look over at Sookie and can't tell where she is. I laid her on her back to look up at the ceiling near the right corner and she isn't there. Confused, and a little panicked, I stand. What the hell, I think to myself.

"Oh my God! You rolled over!" I start dancing and do a happy dance. Sookie looks up at me startled. She isn't used to seeing me this happy.

I grab her and run downstairs to tell Dean. I put Sookie on the floor and dash to the door. It's drizzling outside so I poke my head out. "Dean! Come quick! I need you!"

I realize that he might think something is wrong but I can't take back what I said now. I'm just so happy and proud of Sookie for rolling over all by herself.

Dean comes running in. "What? What's wrong? Is Sookie okay?"

I bring him to the living room where I laid Sookie down. "Sookie rolled over! I put her in her crib on her back toward the right corner and I heard a sound. When I looked over, she was on her stomach!"

"Geez, Jackie. With how you sounded I thought someone got hurt. Don't scare me like that."

"Sorry but it was her first time rolling and I got super excited."

"Yea, I can tell." Dean chuckles. "You are going to be the death of me, aren't you?"

"Hey. When we look back at this moment we are going to laugh."

Dean shakes his head in amusement. "I need to go finish as the mattress needs to be on top, not the bottom. I'm almost done and then I will be in."

"Okay. Take your time. I'm going to see if Sookie can roll over again!" I clap my hands in excitement and bounce a little.
Sookie is on her quilt. We have a foam mat that I could put together which will give her more grip but the quilt is easier for me. Sookie also seems to love it as well.

"Okay, baby girl. Mama wants to see you roll over again. Do you think you can do that?"

She just stares at me but I take it as a yes. I can't get over how cute she is. Her eyes have become more blue instead of silver. I find it interesting how babies' features change over time. Sookie's looks have been changing in just a span of three months.

I try to imitate the rolling motion by doing it myself. Dean does this with Sookie all the time by grabbing her hands so they do it together. She doesn't smile but makes a cute sound that sounds like a squeal.

Sookie starts crying. "Hey, hey, hey. No Sookie, no cry." Lately I've been singing this when she gets frustrated. It seems to work as she calms down instantly.

Music makes her feel better. Dean loves that and plays his guitar for her. I bought him a mandolin for Christmas so he has another instrument to play with Sookie. I have tried playing Baby Shark or Kidz Bop but she seems to not like it as much as rock music. She is truly Dean's daughter in that regard.

"Okay, love bug. How about we try to reach for some toys? You won't be able to do that after your surgery. Let's show those doctors who's boss!"

I want Sookie to know she is the boss and that she shouldn't have someone tell her what she can and cannot do, except mom and dad of course. I remember getting tested for my learning disabilities and the doctor telling my mom and I how I "most likely" wouldn't go to college or graduate college due to my disability. This one memory is still with me but I take it with me and use it a lot because I took it as motivation.

Sookie is not rolling but I also am not rolling either. Now that she rolled, I don't want her to forget how it's done.

"Sookie. Can you roll again? Like this?" I show her how she rolls and keep my core tight. If I keep it tight it doesn't hurt my incision as much.

Sookie just stares at me and I laugh. My efforts are futile at this point so I let her be. I finished packing for her and mostly for me. Tomorrow morning, I will finish packing.

I'm surprised I'm not nervous. Anxious, yes, but not nervous. The unknown has always made me anxious about what to expect. I know nothing about open heart surgery and complete AV Canal Defects. I have read up on it but science is hard for me to remember. I did well in science in high school, but I just can't wrap my head around the terminology.

The front door opens and slams. Our front door doesn't close all the way unless you slam it. This old house is starting to show its age more and more. Dean did some work to make the floors more even but it resulted in some walls having cracks in it. The work of fixing things in the house seems to pile up and I wish I was able to help. I love painting but know I can't do that with Sookie around nor would I want her smelling the fumes.

Dean walks into the room and squats next to Sookie. "Hi baby girl. Are you having fun with mama?"

"Yeah. We tried rolling but I think I scared her or something."

"Well, let's do it our way, shall we pumpkin?"

Dean takes Sookie's hands as they roll with their heads facing each other. It's adorable to watch. Dean is amazing. He puts in so much effort when he doesn't need to. I knew he would be an excellent father.

It's finally Sunday and I oddly feel…nothing. I've noticed my way of coping with difficult situations is shutting off. The only thing I keep thinking about is what else I need to pack at the last minute. I tried doing a list on our chalkboard last night to help but I keep thinking I'm forgetting something. I forgot to ask Dean if he wanted me to wake him this early so I hope he either wakes soon or Sookie wakes him up. Come to think of it, he never wakes when Sookie wakes. The guy sleeps through anything. I bet if I found a bullhorn and held it in front of his face he wouldn't wake. I'm tempted to buy one to try it out. I smile at the thought.

As I finish pumping Dean is coming downstairs and I feel aroused. This is my first time feeling this way after having Sookie. I was wondering if something was wrong with me as Dean is very attractive and we used to go at it like bunnies in college. I'm glad I am feeling this way but don't say anything to Dean so we can leave on time since we need to be in Boston for a nine o'clock appointment.

"Mornin'." Dean is not much of a morning person at first. He needs coffee and at least an hour to be slightly awake.

I have always been a morning person and remember conversations better at this time of day. Dean is not, especially since it is four A.M. I know not to talk about anything too serious yet.

"Good morning. Sleep well?" I know not to ask too many questions.

"Yea. Just couldn't fall asleep right away."

"Thinking of Sookie's surgery?" I know I was last night. My dream was horrible. Grotesque. Something I'm trying to forget as I don't want to think of Sookie ending up that way.

"Yea, a bit."

"I made coffee so it's hot. When were you thinking of leaving?"

I've been thinking of this myself as I would like to leave as soon as possible. We have to pack Sookie's bassinet so our car is going to be packed. One of us has to be sitting with her for her COVID shot too.

"I was thinking of leaving at six, six thirty?"

"Okay. Did you want to stop at my mom's to drop anything off?"

"No, we should be fine."

I listen to him as he is better about knowing how long it takes to get to places plus traffic. I have been monitoring it as well at different times this week and it's been different every day. Boston is one place I would never live.

I take my pumping parts with me to the kitchen so I can wash them, dry them and pack them. We also have to pack some of my milk at the last minute, so it doesn't melt, to bring to my mom's too. I had to tell my mom

I would need quite a bit of room in the freezer as I seem to be an oversupplier. It's a good thing but annoying as we don't have freezer space. I wish our in-laws would give us their deep freezer but I know they use it.

I try to think but can't. I look at the chalkboard for guidance and go through the list of things to pack while not waking Sookie as some of my things are in our room where she still sleeps. I'm glad I wrote it last night as I would be lost without the list. My type A personality comes in handy at times.

Once I'm done packing, it's close to when Sookie should get up for her bottle and for us to leave. I hope I packed enough books and the right books. I'm a mood reader. If I'm anxious or depressed, I need romance. Yet if I'm happy, I read thrillers or historical fiction. That part I don't get but I'm also not normal.

"I should wake Sookie if we're leaving at six. Can you pack her milk and any perishables while I wake her and feed her?"

"Yea. Is everything else packed?" I nod. "Okay, I'm going to go up with you to take apart her bassinet first."

If we didn't communicate as much as we do we would fight. There are times when Dean doesn't tell me things that make me upset. I wouldn't say we fight but I get annoyed. I don't hold it against him but I tell him not to keep things from me so we don't fight. I don't want Sookie remembering her parent's having raised voices, so I'm thankful Dean is so open with me.

As we both go upstairs, I feel…weird. I feel like what's about to happen isn't real. Should any baby at three months of age go through open heart surgery? I try not to cry and paste a smile on my face to wake Sookie. Once I peek in, it's hard to fake the smile. She sleeps so peacefully with her mouth slightly open.

"Sookie." I place my hand on her belly to gently rouse her. "Sookie, baby. It's time to wake."

She stirs a bit but doesn't wake. I hate waking her but know she can sleep in the car.

Dean intervenes. "Sookie, time to get up. Mama made fresh milk."

My hand is still on her and Dean's hand goes to her head. Her eyes flutter open and I pick her up.

"Hey baby girl. Today is the day we drive to Boston and Grandma's house. I'm going to change your diaper and outfit first, okay? I already started warming your bottle."

I always start her bottle first before coming to get her. I know when I wake up, I'm hungry and always want food. It's why I get hangry in the morning. I'm first up but hate eating by myself. If I have a snack then I won't want breakfast. It's a catch twenty-two.

I've gotten good at changing Sookie within the four minutes it takes for her bottle to warm up. I grab a burp cloth from under her table and bring us downstairs. Where I place her is always the same: the floor but with her on top of something. I haven't followed my routine with her this morning so it's slightly off. Sookie is used to her schedule changing with all her appointments but I don't like schedule changes.

After I feed her and the car is packed, we are off. Our first road trip and it's for something I probably won't want to remember. All I can do is hope for the best.

"You okay?"

I look at Dean. How could he be okay? "I don't know. I just keep thinking of everything. Also, how am I going to fit back there for her COVID test?"

"What?"

How could he not hear me? "One of us needs to be with her for her COVID test and her bassinet is there."

"You never told me this."

"Yes I did…or I thought I did."

"I wish I knew this sooner as now we need to stop at your mom's before the hospital."

"We have enough time, right?"

"Just barely. We can't make any stops though so if you need to pee you have to hold it."

I sigh. That's hard for me to do but I guess I can at least wait till we're at my moms. Hopefully I can go there before the test. Obviously, we didn't share everything and I'm feeling the stress. I swear, I told him everything but whether he heard me is another thing.

I don't want to fight so I keep my reply simple. "Okay."

We are silent as we drive toward Boston. Sookie is sleeping in the back like I anticipated. It took her a while as she wasn't awake for long but the motion and sound lulls her to lalaland. I think I'm about to join her.

"You can always talk to me, Jackie. You aren't alone in this."
I have no clue what he is talking about. "I know."

"I feel like you have to be strong during her surgery but you don't. I'm nervous too. In fact, I would be worried if you weren't."

I don't feel nervous but I'm not happy about it. Right now, I'm annoyed. I feel like Dean is cornering me and I think it's because I was crying a couple weeks ago about having a few more clogs. They are painful and I don't know why I keep getting them. When I talked to Dean about it, he suggested using the massage gun and heating pad which has been helping tremendously when I get them. In fact, it was therapeutic talking with him about pumping as I feel like I have to pump for Sookie's health.

Originally, I thought I would be breastfeeding and would do it till she was one or after her surgery. I never knew anything about clogged ducts or mastitis. I hope I don't get mastitis but knowing my luck, I most likely will get it. I've already had three clogs on the same boob since Sookie turned two months old. I want to stop but know I can't. Sookie's health depends on my milk and attitude.

"Jackie?"

"Yea?" I know I spaced out a bit but we weren't really talking.

"I just want you to know I'm here for you."

"I know. I've talked to you about how I feel all the time Dean. Other than feeling annoyed, I'm fine."

"Okay. Sorry." He pauses which he rarely does when he has a lot to say. His ADD makes it difficult for him to break. "I just feel like everything is different since Sookie has been born."

"It is different. Vastly different. Having a baby changes your life but one with health problems makes your life revolve around it."

"But does it? Should our lives revolve around it? There should always be a balance."

He makes a point. Right now, I don't know what that balance is. "Maybe that comes after her surgery. How are we supposed to know? This is our first rodeo."

"True. There is no book that talks about it?"

I laugh. I honestly wish there was a book that tells you how many appointments there are for a baby with a congenital heart defect who also has Down syndrome. Sookie could have a plethora of other diseases lying ahead of her – who knows? Books are what I'm good at as well as reading and writing. He makes me wonder if I should write my own guideline for mothers about what to expect for Down syndrome babies who have a congenital heart defect. Yet, for me, it's been more emotional than anything. How could you even begin something like that? Sometimes I can't wrap my head around her having a heart defect. I still push it out of my mind and think she's healthy. That's why I sometimes think this is all a dream and I'm going to wake up.

I look at Dean who is watching me from the side. "I wish."

"It took you a while to respond."

"You made me think I should write something about it."

"You should. You are a great writer. Why do you think I always go to you to proofread everything?"

"Because I am awesome."
Dean chuckles. "I miss your confidence. I haven't seen it in a while."

"It's been hiding for a while but it peeks out once or twice."

"Let's go out on a date this week. There is a brewery I want to go to that's close to Children's Hospital."

That would be nice. I saw Ellie and Matt do that recently and I was jealous. I've been jealous a lot recently and hate it.

"I would love that."

"Good, I think we need it. I feel like we both have been stressed with what's going on and I know I need time out."

"Yea." I don't know if this is Dean trying to get us to talk but I know it's going to be a long drive regardless. "I know I've been down a bit…okay, a lot. I just see my friends who have given birth around the same time as me and it's hard. It's been hard for me to grapple with everything. I feel like I'm drowning in my emotions as sometimes I'm happy but the next I'm sad.

"I know my emotions are legitimate but I just wish our lives weren't like this but I know it is. I hate how I can't do anything to help Sookie. I hate how you come home stressed from work and go right to your office to do lesson plans, grading, and work for your masters. I hate how I still feel pain from my incision and can't do certain exercises. I hate how Sookie won't have a normal life."

I find myself crying and I dab at my eyes. I hate crying. I sniffle and try to be quiet for Sookie's sake.

"Jackie. I know you are going through a lot and I hate it. I try my hardest to do the best I can for you and Sookie. I too hate how your labor wasn't the best. I wish I had told you not to push as soon as you did. I can't change the past but I can control the now. Right now, I'm trying to be strong for this upcoming surgery because it's vital for Sookie to lead a normal life. This surgery will give us that normal we all crave and want.

"We were dealt with shitty cards. You had such an emotionally hard pregnancy learning about potential health issues that Sookie might have. Just learning that Sookie has Down syndrome was tough to absorb. I have never seen you so adamant till that pregnancy. You changed your lifestyle just for Sookie's health. You have been an amazing mother since day one.

"I still applaud you for not drinking coffee for six months. But Jackie. Know this, you are not alone. You have me, your family, and your bookstagrammer friends."

I laugh as he mentions the last people. I have met amazing people through social media despite how that platform also makes me depressed.

"You are right." My voice is wobbly from crying. "I try my hardest to always be there for Sookie and want the best for her. I hate what's about to happen as I have no control over anything. I don't know what to expect."

"Did you talk with Ellie about questions to ask?"

"I did. I screenshotted the text so I could just pull it up in pictures since we text so often."

I can tell he is impressed. It takes me longer to learn things and remember things but one thing I try to be is one step ahead.

"We will learn more about her surgery tomorrow from the doctor and the good thing is that we have an in with him. That gives me more peace of mind."

"It does for me too."

I feel lighter. I haven't been this open with Dean about my feelings in a while. I always think about it and sometimes will voice my thoughts to Sookie but I don't want to burden her with all my thoughts. She is only a baby, and she is my baby.

Chapter 29

"Do you remember going to Boston Children's Hospital with me when you were screened for your learning disability?" my mom asks me.

It is the night before Sookie's surgery and my mom, Dean and I are sitting in her living area. Her condo has an open floor plan as her living room is open to the kitchen and dining area. Down the hall are two bedrooms with two full baths and an office. It's a nice size for her.

I have no clue what she's going to say as I know we remember things differently. "No." I'm a bit hesitant to know but also intrigued.

"I had looked up the directions to Boston the night before so I stopped to get coffee before your appointment. Driving into Boston was horrific. We ended up late due to me taking the wrong street and there being so many one way streets. Once we met the doctor, I apologized for being late. You interrupted by saying 'if you didn't stop for coffee, we wouldn't be late'. I was mortified."

I don't remember this but it's totally me. I'm very blunt and used to say what was on my mind. I had no filter as a kid.

Dean laughs. I look over at him and smile. It's been a bit tense but Dean and I are better than before. Our talk in the car was much needed yet this surgery has a lot riding on it.

My mom was sweet and gave us an anniversary card and some chocolate. She knows me well when it comes to what I want. Chocolate or wine is the way to my heart. I look at the time and realize it's time for me to pump and go to bed. We have to be at the hospital early as her surgery starts at eight. We plan to get there at seven thirty.
When we went to meet the doctor, we asked about parking and were able to get tomorrow and the rest of her stay vouched for. We only paid for a meeting with the doctor on Monday but it was expensive. I will never understand why hospitals expect you to pay to go there when you're in

need of medical care. The cost of healthcare in this country sometimes makes no sense to me.

I decide to stop thinking and stand up. "I'm going to go pump and head to bed. I plan on having an alarm for two for her last bottle."

"Remember it's just breastmilk, no formula."

"I know. I also plan to give her the Pedialyte at six too as that's the last time she can have anything."

"Okay." Dean stands up and gives me a kiss. "Text me if you need help."

I had to text him yesterday when I was pumping in my mom's office as I had a massive clog that made me cry. I still wish people would tell you all the things that happen during breastfeeding. It may not have changed what I did but knowing about clogs would have been nice. The class I took for labor and delivery could have mentioned it, as we learned about things that happen after you are discharged from the hospital.

I see a notification from Facebook messenger pop up. It's Dean.

Dean: You Okay?

Me: No.

Dean: Want to talk? Your mom is watching Animal Planet.

I laugh. My mom does love animals.
Me: Talking about it will only do so much. But...I sometimes am jealous of Ellie and Matt. I don't know if jealousy is the right word as having Sookie is amazing and I love her so much that words cannot describe it.

Dean: But...

Me: I still wonder what would have happened if I didn't have the amniocentesis. I know I shouldn't wonder about what if's but I do. It's a bad habit of mine.

Dean: It is and you need to get over it. Sookie rolled over. Dr. Oh even mentioned how she would be delayed yet Sookie ROLLED OVER.

Me: I know. When I work with her, I see how hard she works. She has more perseverance than I do. The dedication Sookie puts in is amazing.

Dean: Exactly. Don't stress. She is OUR daughter. She is going to be the most bull headed, independent, stubborn, and adorable girl.

I giggle. She already has shown that and it is adorable. I'm amazed with how far Sookie has already come. My daughter is already showing a doctor that their "predictions" are wrong. She truly amazes me and I know Dean is right.

Dean: Why do I feel like there is more?

Me: Well… do you really want to know? It's about you.

Dean: …now I have to know

Me: We've talked about this before so I'm just going to say please stop being on your phone so much around Sookie. I don't want her to be absorbed in technology when she is older. I want her to be absorbed in books or nature.

Dean: Ok.

I sigh in exasperation. This is why I sometimes dislike talking with him about this as his short answers infuriate me. He knows how to get under my skin but I also know he is trying to play with me to lighten the mood.

Me: I'm almost done pumping. Could you come get my pumping stuff so I can get ready for bed?

I don't get a response but I hear steps outside the door. Dean comes with his phone in his hand.

Dean: Yes.

"Really?" I roll my eyes at him. He has been doing this recently and it's annoying yet cute. I can't decide which one.

"Yes, really." Dean picks up my pumps and heads out as I get dressed. I don't want to be walking around my mom's place naked. I may do it at home but I won't do it here.

I walk into the kitchen and see Dean cleaning my pumping parts. "Thanks, honey." Lately, he has been cleaning them and it's been helpful. Washing the parts is starting to destroy my hands.

"Of course. Is the Momcozy all set to use tomorrow?"

"Yea. It's still in my bag."

Dean was amazing and bought me the Momcozy so I could pump in Sookie's room after her surgery and not have to worry about where to pump and having to undress in public. I used it a few times and love it. I just need to be careful as I thought I could lean over. When I first tried it, I was pumping while Sookie was playing and I leaned in to kiss her and my milk spilled out. My milk went all over her but she screamed in delight and started licking herself. The girl is definitely like me.

"Goodnight." I say it to Dean and my mom who say it back. I can tell my mom wants to say more but I'm so emotionally drained that I head to my room. I don't mean to be rude but I need to start taking care of myself which means sleep.

Today is the day. The day we have all been waiting for. Talking with the surgeon on Monday put my mind at ease as this surgery should be the only surgery Sookie needs. Of course, there are always risks but I try not to think of them. If I think of the risks then I won't stay positive. It's a horrible flaw of mine but if I don't think of everything I can have my mind at ease. That's what I'm telling myself at least.

"Dean." I try to talk softly as Sookie sleeps next to us. I nudge him with my hand.

He mumbles and starts sitting up. Once he does that, he should stay up. Lately, he will go back to sleep but parenting is exhausting. Sookie is a good sleeper but she has her moments of taking forever to go down.

"I'm going to pump."

I hope he hears me. He surprised me by waking up at two when I fed Sookie. She took the whole bottle which surprised me. I think she knows what's going to happen as she is smart. Lately, whenever I feel down, she copies me. She probably feels a mixture of emotions. Fear. Nervousness. Anxiety.

Sookie can have Pedialyte when she wakes but after that she can't have anything. I worry that she will be hungry but I plan to bring some of my milk tomorrow. For twenty-four hours after the surgery, she can't have my milk. I have a great stash with me and think I brought too much milk to my mom's. I have to remind myself how much I make.

"Good morning." Dean comes into the office where I'm pumping to kiss me on the forehead. "How did you sleep?"

"Okay." I slept fine despite waking up at two. I did toss and turn a bit but the bed my mom has is very soft. My back is aching a bit from it as I'm not used to it.

"Want me to make you breakfast?"

I'm not sure I can eat but I know I should. I won't want to leave once Sookie goes into her surgery. "I should eat. Cheesy eggs?"

Dean makes some amazing cheesy eggs. When I used to drink too much in college, my breakfast would be cheesy eggs with toast. It was the best then and still is.

"Sounds good."

He leaves me so I can finish pumping and to my thoughts. I feel like my life has revolved around pumping. I think I want to start weaning after her surgery. Having so many clogs within a month has taken a toll and I don't know if I can keep doing it. I never knew how emotionally draining breastfeeding is. I know my well-being affects the amount of milk I make and I can tell the difference. I need to change something because I can't keep living like this.

My life is Sookie. Spending time with her is my number one priority. I could care less about work but I do want to be able to provide for her. Her happiness and health are what I want to ensure stays at the top of my list. I know my well-being should be first but seeing her happy makes me happy. I'm simple. If she is happy, then I am. If you had told me two years ago that I would put someone else first I would have laughed at you. I have always taken care of myself first but now my happiness is Sookie.

After her surgery, I plan to change things for Sookie and me. Right now, though, I need to take care of my milk, eat and feed Sookie.

Dean is cooking eggs and coffee is poured. I love my coffee lukewarm or iced. Hot coffee is not my jam. He takes the eggs and slides them onto a plate.

"Bon appétit."

I kiss him on the lips to show my thanks. I know I also have not been initiating kisses so I'm also going to start doing that. I have become a robot going through the motions and letting everything get to me.

"Thank you."

Dean looks at me surprised that I kissed him. "You're welcome."

Dean goes across the hall to the gym the condo has. I would join him but I stay just in case Sookie wakes. My mom comes out to give me a kiss and tells me how amazing of a mother I am. She has always been my cheerleader. We may have our differences but she is always there supporting me even when I think I don't need it.

It's close to the time to wake Sookie and I go to the pack and play. She looks so peaceful that I don't want to wake her but I know I need to. I nudge her softly so she can try some Pedialyte. Sookie hasn't had it before so I'm not sure she will really take it but it doesn't hurt to try.

"Hey, sweet girl. I want to try to give you some juice. It's the last thing you can have before we go make you into more of a super baby," I whisper as I carry her to the kitchen.

I pour some of the Pedialyte into a bottle and bring it to the couch to give her. I situate myself and her on the couch so she is ramrod straight. I don't want her choking on this as it's not as thick as her formula.

Sookie starts coughing as she tries and looks at me perplexed.

"It's juice, lovebug. If you don't want it, that's okay," I say.

Sookie doesn't drink anymore which makes me weary. I try not to let my emotions get to me now as I know once she is in the surgical room, I will be crazy. Dean comes in as it's time to leave for the hospital. We pack up our belongings and head out. Driving into Boston isn't too bad as it's dark and not many people are on the road. Sookie sleeps till we check in and there are other kids around us waiting for their operations. It's sad seeing other kids needing surgery, even if it's needed.

We are called and go into some sort of triage where more kids are. I have tunnel vision and follow the nurse to where Sookie will be before her surgery. We are asked a few questions but I hold Sookie in arms not wanting to let go. I don't know what will happen and try to make an effort to appear stronger than I am. Once they wheel Sookie away, I turn into Dean's shoulder and let the tears leak.

Waiting is brutal. Sookie was wheeled off just about a half hour ago and I'm trying not to bawl. I can't stop thinking of her laying on the gurney. Cold. Alone. No Mama's hand to hold. I try not to think about it as Dean and I walk to the number we were given to wait for news. I see so many families waiting for their loved ones to come out of surgery. I know I'm not alone in my grief but I feel isolated.

Dean is sitting across from me and I'm trying to read *The Whisper Man*. I also brought a romantic comedy so I have a fluffier read but I started this book before her surgery. Surprisingly I read for a good twenty minutes before I remember what's going on.

I look up and we are in a little secluded area that is blocked off from all the other families but I hear some of them talking. I see a man walking from area to area with a dog and can't wait for the dog to come to us. I look down at my book and become engrossed yet again.

"Good morning." It's the man with the dog!

"Good morning." Dean and I say in unison. We have said the same thing at the same time for years. We sometimes think the same way, it's uncanny.

The man explains how he goes around with his dog to help families pass the time during their child's surgery. I love the idea. We end up talking about hiking and mountains. He only stays for a couple minutes until a woman stands in line to check in. I can't tell if she's a counselor or pastor. Her badge is hidden from me so I can't read her title. All this lasts about ten minutes and we are alone again.

"Are you actually reading?"

I look at Dean. "I was. Now I'm thinking about Sookie. Do you think everything is going well?"

"I think so. No news is good news, remember?"

I nod. He is right. Sookie just needs to survive the bypass. That is the crucial moment in her surgery. They are literally stopping her heart to fix the holes and starting it again. Her surgeon used all the terminology to explain it which Dean got but I didn't. As a past nurse's assistant, you would think I would know but I don't. My memory isn't the greatest.

I sigh. "I feel like I should move my legs."

"There is coffee where we came in and some snacks. We could also go for a little walk."

I look at him with a little grimace. "I don't know if I want to leave."

"We could find the liaison and let her know we are leaving. She also has our number to let us know of any news too."

I remember now that he mentioned it. I don't want to leave as it makes me feel like I'm leaving my baby girl. I hated watching her being wheeled away from me. I also know I wouldn't have left her if she wasn't pushed off.

I look out the window on my left and watch all the people walking. All these people in a rush. They don't stop to say hi or take a second to appreciate their life. Anything could happen and they were going too fast to stay in the moment. Their life could be gone in a blink of an eye and all they were doing was looking down at their phone instead of up. I'm in my head as I become more depressed. I try to stay positive but it's difficult.

I stand up. "We should go on a walk. I'm going into a downward spiral of negative thoughts and the sun would do me some good."

"Let's go to the rooftop garden. We can check it out."

We take the elevators to the top floor and see that the rooftop is just a rooftop. It is nice but nothing fancy. I can see it being nicer in the summertime but it's November and a little chilly up here. I feel like I'm living my life outside of my body right now. I don't feel anything.

Dean finds a corner and turns around. I go into his arms and feel his warm embrace. His arms envelope me and I inhale him. He smells like his deodorant more than anything.

"Hang in there. Sookie is strong. She's got this."

My eyes well with tears but I refuse to cry. I need, no want, to be strong for Sookie. As her mother I need to be strong for her when she's out of surgery. It's going to be a long day.

"Can we just go back? I feel like we are going to get some news soon."

"Okay." I hear Dean sigh. I can tell he is anxious but hiding it well.

We go back down and find our spot with our stuff. We are sitting for a couple of minutes when I get a phone call. I don't know the number but I pick it up.

"Hello?"

"Hi. Is this Jacqueline West, mother of Sookie?"

"Yes, it is." My heart twists into hope but then seizes. This could go in one of two ways and I hope for the best.

"Sookie is doing great. She just went onto bypass so her surgery is halfway done. We will call you when she's out and in the CICU. If you have any questions, you know where to find me."

We hang up and I don't know how to feel. I'm relieved but I also have another feeling I can't pinpoint. Her surgery is almost done so anything is fair game.

Dean looks at me waiting for me to tell him what's going on. "Sookie went on bypass and her surgery is halfway done."

"That's good! It means the blood is flowing through her heart and the surgeon fixed her holes."

I feel like we should celebrate but at the same point it's still early. The doctor did mention there are complications after the surgery that could happen. I don't know why I can't stop these negative thoughts.

"Why do I still feel like crap if she's on bypass?"

"She went through the most difficult thing in her life. She has shown us how strong she is by rolling for her first time. Jackie. Sookie is our daughter. She is superbaby."

"True. She was just brought back to life." That does make me feel a little better.

At least three hours go by and we are able to see Sookie in the CICU. She looks so tiny on the bed with so many wires attached to her. The amount of wires on her makes me almost cry out but it's seeing her that makes me stop. Her body is as puffy as a marshmallow. She must have a lot of fluid retention in her body to look this way. I do not want to know all the details of the surgery she went through to look like this. I am more than happy to stay in the dark.

"Sookie did great! Her vitals are good. Feel free to leave any of your stuff if you want but unfortunately you can't stay here, I'm sure you're aware."

"Yes, we are." I don't know how I was able to talk but I did. Looking at her is difficult but she is sleeping for now. She starts to stir as she must have heard my voice.

I go to her and place my hand on her hand. I squeeze gently. "Hi super baby." I whisper so no one can hear me.

Sookie's eyes flicker open. She looks up at me and I see a look I haven't seen before. She must be in pain. "Is she on pain medicine?"

"Yes. I recently gave her some and she will be highly medicated for a while. We will wean her off of it in two days."

I nod and hope starts filling me. I know Sookie is in pain as I see it in her eyes but I can tell us being here is helping her tremendously. I plan to stay by her every single day, for every waking moment I can.

Chapter 30

Being a parent is hard. I feel like everything I do is wrong. Everything I say is wrong. Last week was difficult as Sookie recovered from her surgery. Her surgeon was so impressed with her despite one hiccup in the beginning. She had a fever and something was going on with her liver. All I know is that they skimmed my breastmilk for Sookie to eat and she was not a fan of it but had it anyway. She really is a super baby.

I am home with Sookie and Dean is at work. I learned that an adult takes five to seven days to recuperate from open heart surgery. It takes two weeks for an infant. It took Sookie seven days. I know I should be happy but it's halfway through the day and I feel like I'm going insane.

I'm thankful Dean bought me the Momcozy as it's making my life ten times easier but Sookie has so much more energy. I never realized how tired she was until she had her surgery. She is running me ragged. I'm near tears in frustration. All I want is Dean back home or someone to tell me what to do or that I'm doing it right.

"Ahhhh."

Sookie also found her voice and many facial expressions while recovering too. My daughter might have a career in theater just like her mom. I expire. That nap only lasted twenty minutes. My 'me time' has dwindled into nothingness today.

"Ahhhhh."

She can't do tummy time or any activity for six weeks. Her head has also started to be extremely flat and I'm trying everything in my power to help her head remold. It's been difficult since she isn't allowed to do tummy time. When she took a nap earlier, I repositioned her head twice. Sookie is one stubborn baby as she kept moving her head back.

"I'm coming, lovebug."

I swear I'm going crazy and it's only the first day back in our house. Dean and I did go out. In fact, we went out twice and it was nice. One of the nights I actually really enjoyed myself and instantly felt regret that Sookie wasn't with us. Parenting is difficult. All these emotions swirl inside me and I don't know what's right or wrong.

I open her door and go toward her bassinet. "Hi Sweetie. How was your nap?"

She looks up at me and her lips twitch. I can tell she is trying to smile. Now that she found her voice, I know I will hear her laugh soon. I can feel it in my soul. Or maybe it's my mother's instinct.

I unwrap her and pick her up. She is starting to get heavier making it difficult to carry her at times. Looking at her after a nap that made her happy, makes me happy. Earlier when I put her down, she was not happy. We both weren't.

"I can tell somebody is feeling better. That makes me feel better."

I check her diaper and don't need to change her. Picking her up is difficult now as I have to remember to scoop her up instead of picking her up under the armpits. I keep reminding myself that I'm picking my ice cream up.

"Aren't you the yummiest ice cream I've scooped?" Sookie looks at me quizzically. I smile and she smiles. Her smile is infectious. It's an open mouth smile and so gosh darn adorable. Once I saw it, I melted. Her smile transports me back to when she smiled for the first time. It was near the end of her stay in the hospital and one of the doctors was talking about her. Of course she smiles when someone is talking about how amazing she is. Like mother, like daughter. We both love it when someone speaks highly of us to our faces.

Sookie is on five different medications so I look at the board that Dean and I made to make sure she doesn't miss anything. Our life is going to revolve around her schedule due to her medications. She also has developed a reflux as she spits up after every bottle. It doesn't seem to faze her as she smiled earlier as it dribbled down her chin. It was actually quite adorable, yet gross. Looking at the board gives me so much anxiety so I look away. For one of her medicines, I have to wake her up which I hate doing.

We meet with her cardiologist this week to follow up. It keeps my mind at ease that we have a good team of doctors for Sookie. I just hate how Sookie now spits up all the time and there are times when it's a fountain of milk coming out of her. I worry that she isn't gaining weight. Dean and I agreed to put formula in her bottle to make sure she is getting her nutrients but I feel it isn't enough.

Why does parenting have to be so difficult? Who would think I'm capable with a tiny human in my hands? Obviously, I suck at it as Sookie is now howling for a reason that I cannot fathom. I stare helplessly at her trying not to rip my hair out of its scalp. I can't help but cry when I am so frustrated. I really wished I spoke baby. If only there was a baby whisperer.

"Sookie, honey. You're okay. What's going on? How can Mama help?"

I wish to all gods that something will give me a clue. I have no clue if she's in pain or not. I remember her crying out in pain when she was in the hospital. It was a day after her surgery and her face scrunched up tight and she wailed. It was ear piercing. Sookie rarely cried but I knew she was in pain. It was the worst sound I have ever heard and I felt so helpless as the nurse was standing there giving her more pain medication. Sookie isn't out of the woods yet. She is only a week post-operative and needs her medications to make sure she doesn't get an infection and her heart doesn't work too much.

She tries to move but I limit her movement so it doesn't pull on her stitches. Sookie can move her arms and legs but has to be careful with pulling her chest muscles. It's going to be a tough six weeks. She is like her dad in many ways and one of them is not being able to sit still. She is always wanting to move.

I feel powerless. Weak. Feeble. All the words that describe how incapable I am of being a mother. If I can't help myself with being happy, how can I help my daughter? I sigh as I stare at Sookie who is banging her arms up and down.

I grab her arms and say, "Careful there honey. I don't want you hurting yourself. Your surgeon did an excellent job with patching you up nicely."

Her scar looks extremely cool but very red. I have to keep an eye on that area to make sure it doesn't get infected. The nurse went over all her medications plus wound care so Sookie could come home. They weren't worried about her, not even her spitting up, and sent her home. I have been nervous ever since. It makes me wonder if Sookie can feel my nervousness so I try to control my emotions. I used to be able to do this but ever since Sookie was born, I forgot how to breathe. I forgot how to destress. I forgot how to have fun with Dean. Until we went to the brewery, it had been months since I had laughed.

"Ahhh."

One thing I do love is that this surgery gave more animation to my daughter. She has been a chatterbox. Her smile makes me the happiest mother in the world.

I know it's going to be difficult but in two weeks it is Thanksgiving. Dean will have a short week and Sookie gets to meet her cousin for the first time. Ellie and Matt are coming here with my mom to celebrate and I'm looking forward to it.

We are also going to Jared's in-laws house which I'm excited but nervous for. Sookie can't be with a lot of people so I'm hoping no one is sick or could potentially have COVID. I know Jared's in-laws work so I'm nervous for Sookie's health. I know I can't control everything and need to loosen my tight reins on Sookie's life, it's just so hard.

Chapter 31

Thanksgiving at Jared's in-laws went interestingly. Dean does not know how to say goodbye and my plan of staying there for a few hours turned into staying there for five hours. It took forever to put Sookie down for bed as she was so overtired due to not having a third nap. She's still recovering and will be, so napping is vital which Dean did not seem to get. I know I shouldn't be frustrated with him but lately I can't let things go.

My mom and I chatted and she mentioned how worried she is for my mental health. It has gotten worse ever since Sookie's surgery since I'm so hyper-focused on Sookie. I don't want her to get sick. I know I can control where she goes and whom Sookie sees so I know I'm trying my hardest to make sure she doesn't get sick. I feel pressured to make sure her scar doesn't get infected. I'm trying my hardest for her not to pull on her stitches. It's difficult. It's stressful. No one seems to get it except Dean.

Dean has been a great listener hearing me talk about my feelings and being there for me. I honestly don't know what I would do without him. I hate burdening him with my thoughts as I know he too has to deal with everything. We cope differently and for me it's talking. I can't talk with Rita about this as she has her own problems to deal with. I can't talk to Meg as she is pregnant and has a toddler. My college friends don't understand and could care less as they are traveling and working. I haven't even talked with them as when I have talked to them in the past, they just say sorry. I tried texting Jackie who I used to go to for everything but she decided to stop talking to me. I feel alone. Either my friends don't get what I'm going through or have abandoned me. I have no one except Ellie who has her own burdens, so I try not to go to her too often.

Ellie, Matt, Roland, and my mom should be coming here shortly to celebrate Thanksgiving. Dean put a meal in the crockpot to make cleaning up easier. I am having a drink of wine while Sookie sleeps. A book is in my hands but I can't read as I'm nervous.

Sookie hasn't met another baby face to face before, nor a dog. Ellie and Matt bring their dog everywhere with them. I don't blame them as he is adorable but Lance will be mad at us. We have been having issues with Lance. He is pooping near his litter box but not in it. I was in the bathroom yesterday and the cat just squatted by his litterbox and pooped on the floor. I yelled at him which made Dean come running. Lance must be going through something and I wish I knew what it was.

I seriously hate being an adult. I loved it when I could just go to school, read, play soccer and tennis, and do what I pleased. Now I worry about everything. Bills, Dean, Sookie, Lance. I worry about everything. I don't even know what I'm going to do for a job once my maternity leave is over. That depresses me too. Sookie can't even be in a daycare setting until February.

"You okay?"

Dean walks in, opening up shades in the windows facing the side street where our visitors park.

"Yea. Just a lot on my mind."

"For now, just relax. Your family should be here any minute and Sookie should be up soon."

Sookie has been moving her arms overhead which she shouldn't do but it doesn't seem to hurt her. I just worry that Matt or Ellie will pick her up wrong and she will start crying. I could hold Sookie myself and make sure no one holds her but everyone loves holding a cute baby.

"I know. I'm worried that someone will pick Sookie up wrong and she will cry out in pain. I can't bear to hear her suffering."

Sookie woke up one night crying out as I slept through a dose of pain medicine for her. I felt horrible and hated myself for doing that to her. Her pain is starting to subside and she now only takes baby Tylenol to help.

"We just tell them how to pick her up and it should be fine."

I have no clue how he can be so casual about it. I'm freaking out.

"How can you be so chill right now?"

"Well, what do I have to worry about?"

He looks at me questioningly. "Everything! I know it's been almost a month post-op for Sookie but anything can happen. What if one of them is sick and doesn't know it? Sookie could end up in the hospital."

He motions for me to stand so I put my book down and stand from the couch. He wraps his arms around my waist but I take his arms and wrap them around my shoulders.

"Jackie. If that happens then it happens. We can't control everything. I know you want to so Sookie can be healthy and safe. I get it. I really do. But for today I want you to get out of your head and have fun. I know Sookie's health is vital to you and it is for me, but you need to let yourself breathe."

A car parks on the side street and I notice it's my mom's car. I need to put my game face on and pretend to be happy. I really just want to be with Dean and Sookie but know family is important. I can't shield Sookie forever.

I pull away from Dean. "I know you're right but I have to feel okay about situations that I put Sookie in. I'm trying my hardest to be happy but it's difficult. Sookie won't be like Roland. I know I'm going to look at him and wish Sookie could do the same things."

"I get that, I do. Sookie will do things when she is ready. Every baby is different. Try not to think that way as they are coming into the yard. I'm going to go help them. Be positive."

Dean goes off to help them as I stand in our living room. Sookie is awake so I go upstairs to get her to meet her cousin, aunt and uncle.

"Hey baby girl." I'm starting to talk to her as I walk through the door. I look into her bassinet and she's staring at me with a grin. "Ah, aren't you the cutest little button? Are you ready to meet your cousin, aunt and uncle?"

I grab her and walk downstairs as I hear the front door open and everyone comes in. I walk into the kitchen holding Sookie in my arms.

"Hello!"

Ellie and I embrace and hugs start. Everyone gushes over Sookie and how brave she is from her surgery. Sookie is soaking it up and loving it. This girl loves attention as she also started smiling when nurses and doctors told her how cute she is.

We all walk into the living room and I hold Sookie in my arms.
"May I hold her?" Ellie asks me.

I'm hesitant but Dean told me to stop putting bubble wrap around her. "Yeah, just don't put your hands under her armpits. It will pull on her incision."

Ellie nods and takes Sookie. I stare making sure Sookie is okay. My brother comes over with Roland who is quite big and has very light hair on his head. Roland doesn't have much hair. In fact, Sookie has more hair than he has which surprises me.

"Hi, Roro." I grab his hand to shake it and he grins and laughs. My heart breaks into tiny pieces as I still haven't heard Sookie laugh. Another thing Sookie hasn't done yet.

Matt embraces me with one arm. "How are you doing? Is Sookie doing better?"

I nod. "Sookie is doing better. She doesn't need pain medicine anymore. I'm okay. I'm just trying to handle her medication schedule."

"Yea, I bet that's tough. I can't even imagine."

I don't even know what to say to my own brother. I'm at a loss of what to talk about. I know I should ask about Roland but I can't bear to do it. I know I will compare the babies as I already have. I feel like a horrible mother comparing my girl to her cousin.

Dean comes over and takes Roland from my brother. "How's it going Roro?" They sit on the floor and play with Roland who is sitting up. The baby doesn't even topple over. Sookie can't do that.

I feel tears spring to my eyes so I head to the kitchen for a little more wine. I've decreased a few pumps in my schedule making it slightly better for my well-being. It's still difficult juggling pumping and taking care of Sookie. I don't want to think about adding work into the mix.

"How's it going?" My mom followed me into the kitchen. "Need any help with anything?"

I look around. "No, I'm just looking for some appetizers. I know Dean bought some."

Dean comes in and says, "It's downstairs. I'm going to go get them. How's it going, Allison?"

Dean and Allison hug. "It's going well. It's nice having everyone over at my place."

"I'm glad." With that Dean is off for the appetizers.

I'm standing in the kitchen with my mom and I feel awkward. Why do I feel so awkward? This is my family and I feel so out of place.

"You're doing an amazing job, Jackie. I'm so proud of you. Sookie looks healthy."

My mom is going to make me cry, which I don't want. I'm already hormonal due to my body hating me.

"Thanks, mom."

I grab my wine glass and have a little bit more before I stop so I can pump in three hours. I know I can have a serving as long as it's two hours beforehand. We walk into the living room and I see Roland sitting on the floor with Ellie holding him for support from behind.

I put a smile on my face. I didn't realize how hard it would be to see Roland.

"We have a present for Sookie!" Ellie exclaims in excitement.

"Really? What for?" I'm surprised as Sookie has nothing to celebrate other than being awesome.

"She kicked butt recovering from her surgery."

Hearing that puts tears to my eyes. I know I'm becoming dewy-eyed. I can't control my melancholy for too much longer. I've come to terms that crying doesn't make me weak but I'm not going to ruin this day.

"That's so sweet," I say, hoping my emotions stay at bay.

Matt comes over with a gift bag and hands it to me. I open it to see a book about the ABC's but with amazing women from past and present. It's adorable.

"Thank you." I look at Matt and Ellie and try not to glance at Roland but it's hard. He looks so much like Ellie's dad it's uncanny.

Dean comes in with cheese, crackers and grapes. He places it on his snare drum that he bought a couple weeks ago. Tucker, Matt and Ellie's dog, goes after the food first. We all laugh as Matt reels him in with the leash. Tucker has been on the leash this whole time and once Lance saw him, he ran away.

I grab some cheese and try to think of something to say. "How was the drive here for Roland?"

"It was okay. He slept a little bit and then got a little fussy." Ellie seems to be talking more than Matt but she's always been the talker. "How is Sookie with car rides?"

"She sleeps most of the time. If she isn't sleeping, she gets cranky." I always make sure her appointments are when she isn't sleeping. Sookie doesn't have much of a schedule due to her medicine but she does have a loose one.

"That's good!"

I see it's time for Sookie's bottle so I start her bottle as Grandma holds her. Grandma is asking for pictures with her grandkids so I hurry in once her bottle is in the warmer. Dean is taking pictures with a phone. Looking at Roland and Sookie is quite adorable. They look at each other and don't know what to think of each other.

"How about the mothers with their babies?" My mom would think of that. It would be nice to have more pictures. I'm all about taking pictures of Sookie.

Ellie and Roland sit next to Sookie and me. We sit close and Roland leans in closer to Sookie. I'm not sure what Roland is going to do but I'm interested to find out. Babies are quite entertaining. He ends up placing a hand on her and Sookie doesn't react. They are cute together.

Once Sookie eats, Roland eats. Ellie is breastfeeding which makes me feel like I should have pursued doing that more as she hasn't had any issues. I just got rid of another clogged duct. I'm getting so used to them that I don't even feel the pain anymore. It's just uncomfortable holding Sookie in my arms.

"Where can I put Roland down for his nap?" Ellie comes down the stairs as she breastfed him in the office.

"Oh, we made the crib for him to sleep in. We figured he would be too big for the bassinet that Sookie uses. Is that okay?"

"Yea, that's perfect! He hasn't been in one so I'm interested to see how he likes it."

Ellie is up there for a while putting him to sleep as Matt and my mom talk. Dean interjects once in a while and I just sit on the couch listening. So far, I feel like I'm doing okay. It's a little hard seeing how behind Sookie is but I know how determined she is. She has gone through so much that I know she will do everything when she's ready. I have to keep reminding myself of this.

"The food is ready." Dean announces.

He made pulled pork for sandwiches with coleslaw and salad. My mom brought her brownies and I've already had one. I can't say no to chocolate and I'm a big proponent of dessert first then the meal. Ellie comes down so we all go into the kitchen and grab food. I hear everyone talking behind me but, to avoid crying, I'm chanting my mantra that Sookie will do things when she's ready. I didn't realize how hard it would be to see another baby Sookie's age doing more.

We eat and talk about the babies. I try to be a part of it but it's hard. Talking about Sookie and Roland is difficult. Sookie is still recovering and has a long road ahead of her and lots of catching up to do. I get up and go to the kitchen to not shed a tear in front of them. My mantra is not working. I put my plate down as my mom walks in. I feel the tears coming down so I go up the stairs at the front door. One thing I love about this house is that it can be a maze. We have two staircases. One by the front door and one in the living room.

I open the bathroom upstairs and close myself in it. I let the tears fall and try to be quiet. I know everyone is worried about me. I'm normally more chatty and tried to talk.

I hear a knock on the door. "Hold on." I try to sound chipper for whoever it is.

"Can I come in?"

It's Dean so I open the door. He sees my face and hugs me.

"I know how hard this is for you, it's hard for me too. Your mom just pulled me aside to tell me she saw you come up here about to cry." That makes me cry harder. "Jackie. Hey." He pulls me in tighter. "It's okay. Once Roland is done napping, they plan to leave."

I nod my head letting him know I heard him. "Okay. I'm sorry. I kept telling myself I wouldn't cry and here I am blubbering like a fool for no reason. I know Sookie will do everything Roland is doing just in her own time. I kept telling myself that and here I am." I feel like a hot mess.

"It's okay. They all get it. You are going through a lot and take Sookie's progress seriously. They think it's commendable how strong you have been today."

"I don't feel strong."

"It takes a strong person to show emotion and that's what you're doing."

"In a bathroom though."

"Doesn't matter. You've been showing it all day and wanted privacy. I'm going to go back but come down soon. Apparently, Roland doesn't nap long."

I remember Ellie texting me about that and how she is trying to sleep train him. I wish Sookie could be on a schedule like Roland but her medicine is making it tricky as I have to wake her early for one of them.

I wipe my eyes and look at Dean. He looks at me as if I'm beautiful when I know my face is red. "Let me wash up before coming down."

"Okay. See you downstairs. Hey, before I leave, one more thing. How does a man on the moon cut his hair?" He pauses even though I don't know why. I never respond to his questions when he jokes. "He eclipse it."

"Oh my lanta." I smack my forehead but it was an excellent joke. He finally made me laugh from one of his corny jokes.

Dean leaves and I look at myself in the mirror. My eyes are slightly red and my cheeks are a little inflamed but other than that I look fine. I splash water on my face and take three big breaths. I got this. My family isn't judging, thankfully. I hear a little cry in Sookie's room so I decide to head downstairs. I pass Ellie as she comes up to get Roland. At least it isn't just me who wants to always be with my baby. I hate leaving Sookie with anyone, even Dean sometimes. I love holding her and rocking her. If she cries, I hold her and sing to her. I don't care if I don't sleep. I would rather hold my girl who needs a calming hand.

Sookie is laying on her pink play mat with her toys hanging above her. She just lies there as she is used to one of us telling her to take it easy. It's hard as she wants to move and we also want her to move.

"Here comes Roland." Ellie announces as they walk downstairs. Ellie puts him down next to Sookie with him still in his sleep sack.

"Aw, look at the cousins." I have to say something as I need to get out of my funk. They do look cute together.

Ellie unwraps Roland and he stretches with his arm going overhead. He touches Sookie and he rolls toward her. My heart aches as Sookie isn't allowed to do half the things he is doing. I don't know when I will stop comparing, if I ever will.

Ellie starts taking pictures of them but it's a dark room when it's gray outside. Snow is predicted to fall in about an hour so the weather is matching my mood today.

"Sookie needs to go down for a nap. I'm going to bring her upstairs." I'm about to pick her up but Ellie stops me.

"We are going to head out to beat the snow. Can we let them play for a couple of minutes?"

Sookie needs sleep but it is the first time that the cousins are together. It's hard for me to say no, especially since I didn't realize they were going to leave so early.

"Okay," I exclaim. I hate saying no to my family.

Ellie and I talk to the babies as they lay together and she is snapping pictures of them. Sookie looks over at her cousin and reaches out to him. It looks as if they are trying to hold hands. My heart melts with how cute they are with each other. Seeing them together makes me realize how Sookie's head has lost some roundness to it in front. I vow to myself to wake up every couple hours to position her head so she won't need a helmet. We already spent an arm and a leg on our medical bills from my labor. My cesarean and Sookie's NICU stay were costly. I can only imagine how much more the bill would have been if Sookie stayed longer. Now with her surgery, money will be even tighter.

I hear the front door slam and the guys come in with my mom. Dean is chatting with Matt about something. I can always hear Dean. His voice carries and can be loud. I normally don't mind it but there have been times when I shush him when Sookie sleeps.

"Hey guys. Hi cousins!" Dean says and plops onto all fours. He is quite a character sometimes. He tickles Roland who laughs. I watch. It doesn't make me cringe as it did earlier.

We all hug and say goodbye. Dean walks out with everyone as I bring Sookie upstairs for her nap. I love Sookie and can't wait for her recovery to end. I can see how it's not just me hurting but also Sookie. I saw how she wanted to play with her cousin which is why it was so difficult for me. Sookie and I are eerily alike. Whatever one of us feels, the other feels it too. I have some work I need to do to make myself happy but don't know how. Ever since she was born, I've been on edge and I thought her surgery would have lifted a weight off my shoulders but not completely. Our speedbump is not yet over but I feel we are almost over the hump. I just need a little help.

Chapter 32

"Jackie, you need to stop being a martyr."

"What?" I have no clue what Dean is even talking about.

"You act like you are doing everything in this household when you aren't. When I say how tired I am you act like it's a competition and tell me you're tired too and why. We are both tired for different reasons."

Things have been a little crazy between us as he has been working a lot with teaching a subject and grade he normally doesn't teach. He has been working late into the night and still trying to be with Sookie which I appreciate. I just feel like I have been doing everything and have to do everything because of how much he has to do for work.

"Well *Dean*." I put emphasis on his name to get my frustration across. "I'm not acting like a martyr, whatever that means. I'm trying to make sure this house is clean and safe for Sookie."

He sighs and rubs at his face. His eyes look tired. He doesn't have bags or shadows, but I know him. "I live here too Jackie. Sookie is also my responsibility and I do what I can when I have time."

"But you never have time! You come home and go straight to your office after saying hi. Your job consumes you and it shouldn't. Sookie's first year of life is when all her firsts are. I don't want you missing them because of work."

"I know. It's why I try to take breaks and be with you guys."

"I get that and I see that but you need to find a better job. Your job shouldn't take up your whole life. I'm always so stressed and anxious because I feel like I have to do the cleaning, laundry, and taking care of Sookie. I know you fix things around here and go grocery shopping. I'm not saying you don't do things around the house, I'm saying you do more for your job than here."

He sighs and I shake my head. "Dean, I'm not mad at you. I'm aggravated and annoyed, yes. I hate how you don't hear her but I also want you to sleep. How can I go back to work if all you do is work?"

This has been weighing on my mind a lot. I go back to the preschool near the end of January and it's almost Christmas, which is a week away. That means I start work in a month and I'm worried. I'm worried about everything. Sookie. Dean. Myself. This house. Lance.

"We haven't found a balance and we rarely talk about if going back to my old job is worth it."

"Jackie." He says my name in warning like I've gone too far.

"I don't mean to be rude or cause you stress but we need to talk."

He sighs and seems to accept that we have to talk. "Well, what do you propose we do?"

Normally Dean has more insight as I base what I do off of my feelings. I'm not smart in the heat of a situation and don't always see the bigger picture until I talk with Dean. He helps me see more options.

"I don't know. If I go back, it's an hour drive for both of us. That means my eight-hour work day is a ten-hour day for both of us. I know Sookie adapts easily but that's still long. It also means you can't spend much time with her either and she should know you are around.

"Plus, Sookie still has her appointments and early intervention. If I go back, Sookie won't be able to see her therapist. If she goes to daycare, it's almost two thousand dollars a month. I only make one thousand and eight hundred dollars a month. We would lose money instead of me making money, plus the commute."

"I know. So, look for a daycare closer to home and bring Sookie there."

I sigh in exasperation. It's not what I want. I want to work from home but don't know how I can do that. I would have to work for a multi-level marketing company which I already tried doing and couldn't do it part-time with a full-time job.

"What about a part-time job and I stay home during the day? Your mom told us that's what she did and it worked out for her. You and Jared turned out fine. Well, almost fine." I chuckle as I try to make our conversation lighter.

This is the first time we have really talked about this and I'm glad we're talking. It's much needed and long overdue. I don't want to screw us over financially since we are still getting hospital bills from months ago and haven't seen the open-heart surgery bill.

"You could. Would you want to? Would you be willing to? You aren't a night person and no offense but you shut down once the clock strikes seven."

He is right. I'm like Cinderella. Once it's seven or eight, I just shut down. Shutting down is too harsh. My brain just doesn't work at full capacity and talking to me is futile. I don't remember much and I get agitated quickly. "When it comes to Sookie, I would do anything for her. The only thing I'm worried about is pumping. The preschool knows I pump six times a day. I plan to bring it down to five before I start so I will only need two pumping breaks. But a new job? I don't know the people. If I worked at night, I would only need maybe one pumping break depending on the time and where it is."

"What are some things you would want to do other than preschool?"

"I would want to stay in my field of expertise so daycare, fitness, or health. I know some hospitals need night people as I have been looking occasionally. I just wanted to talk to you because I don't feel like we've been on the same page."

Dean looks at his computer since I came into the office and started talking. He was working and I know he still has a lot to do.

"You know I want you to be happy and will always support what you do."

I interject even though he hates it when I interrupt. "And I want the same for you."

"Jackie." I knew interrupting him would make him impatient with me. "You just need to be bringing money into the house. We can't afford to live on just my salary, especially as I am going to school for my master's."

I try not to tell him he could have started years ago instead of later in life when we wanted kids. I bite my tongue and say, "I know. It's why I stress about money at times."

"I do too. I have a decent amount in my savings but having a baby, especially with a health condition, is expensive."
It seems like our conversation is coming to a close. I know we haven't made any decisions but I feel we are on the right path to figuring things out together. I knew we wouldn't come up with a solution in one night about what I will do for a job but I planted the seed in his head. This has been the one thing stressing me out and even though I have talked with Ellie about my feelings, she can't help us. Ellie has her own fish to fry.

"I know you have work to do but try not to stay up too late. I'm sorry for interrupting."

"Don't be. My door is always open to you Jackie." I turn to leave but he calls to stop me. "Aren't you forgetting something?"

I turn toward him again and see him standing. We hug and kiss. We haven't had sex since after Thanksgiving but our relationship is starting to be what it was after Sookie arrived. I know nothing will ever be "back to normal" but I don't want that. I want us all to be a family. Together.

Chapter 33

It seems like it's any day, but today is Christmas. It's Sookie's first Christmas and I'm so excited. I didn't buy her too many toys but stuck with a music theme. Sookie is taking after Dean and loves musical instruments. I bought her maracas and a book with nursery rhymes that sings. I bought Dean a mandolin and a few other things he needed, plus some cool small gifts for his stocking.

Once I'm done pumping, I bounce upstairs. I'm so giddy about today! Dean's parents and my mom came over yesterday and we all celebrated. Sookie loved all the attention and opened a few gifts herself. She didn't get it as she's only five months old but it was adorable. A few of her gifts she won't be able to use until she's older but they are cute and super thoughtful.

"Dean! Dean!" I try to whisper but I think I'm too loud as I hear Sookie start making raspberries.

I see Dean sit up so I run toward Sookie's room. "Good morning sunshine!" I sing out feeling electrifying.

I get her dressed in our matching pjs for a photo opportunity. It's why I woke Dean so I can get pictures of us together. Yesterday we all wore matching shirts that Rita made for us. Dean was merry about it which made me feel gleeful. If Dean and Sookie are jolly then I am happy.

Once Sookie is all set, I come out of her room and yell, "Dean!"

He comes up the stairs and sees us. "Why good morning, Princess." He kisses Sookie's cheeks and mine.

I smile at him. "Picture, please?" I did my hair after I pumped so it could look less like a rat's nest.
My hair has become its own species. I don't even know what my hair is doing half the time but it rarely looks good unless I straighten it.

Yesterday, my mom gave me a new straightener as my old one barely got hot anymore. I didn't even know straighteners did that.

Dean grabs my phone and his, and starts snapping pictures. I stand there holding Sookie. I didn't realize how much she had grown. My arms start to feel tired which I don't mind as I barely workout as it is.

"Can I see?" I want to make sure I'm looking at the camera and Sookie is at least looking at Dean. "Aw, these look good. Sookie, how come you have to look cuter than Mama?" I beam down at her and she smiles back at me.

Even if today is a bad spit up day for her, it won't ruin my mood. Sookie has been having horrible reflux ever since her surgery and her reflux medicine doesn't even work. I'm starting to think it's another medication making her spit up as some of them cause acidity. I look at Sookie as I walk downstairs and almost trip. This girl might literally be the death of me. I always want to look at her cute face yet these stairs are too narrow for my big feet.

"Santa came!" I exclaim to Sookie.

I want Sookie to be as excited as I am for next year's Christmas. That's the year I plan to go extreme with her. More extreme than the first year of dating Dean. Our first Christmas together I bought him twelve presents and gave him one almost every day. I saved at least two for Christmas day but I was so excited that I couldn't wait. I have always loved giving gifts, but I do love opening presents. The joy on the person's face when they realize what they got excites me the most. I know Sookie doesn't understand Christmas but I will tell her how it's not about the presents, or the quantity of presents, but being together and celebrating the birth of Jesus.

I'm not super religious but I do believe in God and the afterlife. I tell Sookie all the time about spirits roaming the earth and if she sees one not to freak. I remember freaking out when I first saw a ghost, even though the ghost was harmless. I was staying over at

Dean's parents' house and I woke up in the middle of the night. When I looked up, I saw a woman standing at the edge of the bed. I closed my eyes suddenly, terrified that she would do something. The next morning I told Dean about what I saw and he was flabbergasted as he also saw her a few years back. It's a story we love telling people as everyone thinks ghosts aren't real, but they are. Regardless, I want Sookie to appreciate life and love everyone.

I realize I'm getting off track and Dean is saying something that I'm missing. Lately, I have been in my own world and need to snap out of it. Today is special for all of us. Sookie has been moving more and more. She has been rolling to her right side for at least a couple days ever since we have told her to just move. My imaginary bubble wrap for her is gone as I want her to move and progress developmentally.

Sookie is currently sitting up with Dean and I pass him a present and one for Sookie. He opens his present and loves his mandolin. He starts to play with it when I remind him there are other presents to open, especially Sookie's.

Lately we have been calling her Saysay. She loves it especially when I say, "Say something Saysay." Her smile widens from it.

"Sookie! Look at Mama!"

Dean is opening one of Sookie's presents that I got her. It isn't cool like what Grandma bought her, which is an elephant she can walk with that sings. It's the maracas and Dean takes a few for them to play. It's adorable and I can't stop myself from taking multiple pictures. Dean and Sookie look adorable together.

So far, Christmas has been magical. Sookie is on the road to recovery and Dean is on vacation. Dean is always happier during vacation which ultimately makes me happy. I smile as Dean and Sookie play. I do want them to open more presents but I've been learning to live in the moment.

Dean and I had another talk before Christmas Eve and it was nice. I didn't barge into his office like I have been doing lately. I knocked on the door lightly and opened the door. We talked about Sookie's spit-up, a job for me, and me.

It was hard talking about myself as I know I have changed. I have changed into wanting to control everything for Sookie as well as wanting to do everything for, and with, her. It was therapeutic. I have noticed the things Dean mentioned me doing yet I haven't done anything about it. I had tunnel vision, and probably still do, when it comes to Sookie. She is my first and was dealt with a crappy deck of cards to start her life. All I want, and will ever want, is for her to be happy, healthy and safe. With COVID still being high in our area it makes it difficult for me to want to go anywhere. Scratch that. I do want a date night, badly. Yet, when it comes to Sookie, I don't want her getting out unless she absolutely has to. Her bubble wrap may still be on but only due to COVID.

"Mama's turn!"

I snap out of my trance as Dean hands me a present. I open it to reveal slippers. I laugh and thank Dean. I instantly go to the tree to hand him his next gift that "Sookie" bought him. It is also slippers which is why I laughed. Last year, he asked for slippers but never got any. This year I bought them for him so he would have a new pair and his old ones can get tossed. His old ones clank so loudly when he walks it's annoying. If he doesn't throw them out, I will.

"Seems like our minds were thinking alike with that gift." I smile at him.

"I like anything you give me." Dean says this with a sexy grin. He is definitely thinking of something dirty.

I nod my head and mockingly say, "In your dreams. Honey, what's a man's idea of foreplay?" I give a dramatic pause. "A half hour of begging." I'm so proud of myself I start laughing like mad.

Dean laughs with me which makes Sookie crack a smile. Once she starts getting teeth, she is going to be even cuter. She started showing signs of teething recently and even my mother-in-law was saying how she thinks Sookie is teething too. I'm kind of excited to see Sookie's teeth but also know that a teething baby means a night of no sleeping. I'm a woman who only loves a few things in life but one thing I worship is sleep.

I look around me and love everything about it. Winter is magical to me. When it snows magical things happen…except the first year I met Dean. The first year I met Dean and it snowed, he tried to be cool by doing parkour and tore his ACL. The only cool thing about that day was driving my car on our college campus up to the dorms since it wasn't allowed. Our college is extremely small so my tiny Acura barely fit through campus.

Now that it is nearing eight in the morning Dean opens the shades for more light. It is lightly snowing outside and I love it.

"For goodness flake!" Dean exclaims, making Sookie jump a little. I roll my eyes but laugh as it is funny.

Sookie starts rubbing her eyes so I go upstairs to put her down. Her nap time routine is short and sweet. I worked with her to be able to fall asleep by herself and she does a good job. However, when Dean is home, she tries to get away with more. The girl knows how to play her cards. When we are both home, she will cry a few times to get attention. Today she must be too tired for that as she falls asleep within five minutes of me putting her down.

I'm sitting on the couch with a fresh cup of coffee and Dean is picking up the wrapping paper. I have a nice view and I'm enjoying it thoroughly. Dean works hard at his body. He has even told me how some guys are jealous of his butt. I am jealous of his butt. He has a nice one that I love to smack.

I must have sighed as Dean asks, "What? You okay?"

I'm startled by his question. "Yea. Why do you ask?"

"You only sigh when you want something."

This is true but right now I don't want anything. I already have everything I want.

I smile. "This is true but right now I don't. Well...except for a kiss."

Dean grins at me and walks over. I stand up but he leans over me and kisses me hungrily. He has always been passionate with his kisses. I kiss him back and look at him. He certainly wants more.

I pull back. "Dean. I'm fine with just kissing you but I don't want you thinking we will do anything more."

He leans his forehead against mine. "Jackie, I just need something."

We continue to canoodle on the couch. It's not intense, just passionate. I surrender my body to Dean as our bodies become one. No matter how big his muscles get, my body will always meld into his. I nibble on his bottom lip as he tries to pull away. His hands roam down toward my pants when I push his hands away. He kisses me deeper, hoping for more, but I know better.

The last time we had sex I was fully ready for it and freaked out the next day. It wasn't about being pregnant again. Thinking of being pregnant again actually made me smile as I would love to give Sookie a sibling. It freaked me out because I hate how I have a sexually transmitted disease. I felt disgusted with myself and didn't want to do it again. Even though my doctor explained how if I have it then everyone in my household has it, I still don't want Dean touching me that way. I don't like the thought that I gave my family a disease that could be deadly.

Dean also talks about sex so much to me that it turns me off. I'm a girl who when it comes to sex, it's spur of the moment. When we tried for Sookie I did track my period so I could get pregnant, but now I don't want it forced. I want sex to happen when we are both in the mood. I know I haven't been in the mood lately but I've been preoccupied mentally. Hopefully, I can clear my mind of all my negative thoughts about myself and be comfortable in my skin. I'm halfway there so I'm confident it will happen.

My eyes open as Dean's tongue pushes inside my mouth. He is looking at me as he does this. He is testing me to see what I do. Despite thinking quite a bit, I am enjoying this. I deepen the kiss as I taste the coffee on his breath.

I'm a great tease. Always have been, always will be. I pull back with a smile on my lips. I wiggle out from underneath him and stand up. Dean sits up and straightens himself out. I know I turned him on and I'm happy about that.

"I have things to do. Thank you for our makeout session."

I hear Dean scoff as he stands. "Excuse me? Like, what?"

"I have something to do on my laptop." I really don't but I keep a journal on it and it's been helping me cope with my thoughts.

"You must be a keyboard as you're just my type."

"Oh my lanta!" I slap my forehead. "That was so corny."

"Do you like bacon? Wanna strip?"

"Oh my god. Stop."

"Yes, I am a god. Thank you for noticing."

Dean always says that and I should have known better when I told him to stop. I laugh internally as his jokes are funny, just annoying, as he can dish them out like no tomorrow. He has jokes and I have cheesy lines. We were a match made in heaven.

"I love you, but I'm going to go upstairs now. I want to workout while Sookie naps." I was going to journal but I need to move.

"Go. I can watch her so you can workout for as long as you want."

This is why I love Dean. He will always let me take care of myself. I know all I have to do is ask him. It's crazy thinking how before Sookie was born, I never had to ask to workout, or pee, or shower. Life does change when you have a baby but I wouldn't change it for the world.

Epilogue

"How is Sookie doing with the helmet?"

I am talking with Ellie on the phone which is rare. We normally text each other as talking is difficult with our kids' conflicting schedules. Sookie doesn't have much of a schedule at times which I hate. I've been learning to live in the moment which I'm still working on.

"Really good!" It's been a month with her having it and we already see a difference. I never realized how flat her head was all around.

"How are you doing with your HPV? I know how distraught you were when you found out. I hope you know you aren't disgusting and many people get it."

I sigh. I'm still having issues coping with having it. "So-so. I have my days when I forget I have it but other days I remember. Like when Dean wants to have sex, I turn away because I don't want to cause him cancer. I know he probably won't have cancer, but I wouldn't want to be the cause of it, you know?"

"Yea. That's rough. I wish I could help but it's you who has to overcome it."

"That's true. I've been having cranberries lately to help as well as taking B vitamins. I'm hopeful that will work. Sometimes, I feel that I should call my doctor to make sure I don't have warts down there but we are getting all the copay bills from when Sookie and I had appointments. They just keep piling up."

"That's annoying. Why are they sending you the bills seven months later?"

"Who knows? Health insurance is screwed up in this country."
Ellie laughs. "So true. How is work going?"

I started working at the preschool but the commute was too much for me and Sookie. I had to wake her at five in the morning due to her spit up problem. Feeding her was difficult at first as she would pull her head back and stop drinking. Not only that, but she would spit up right before we left, making me almost late to work on too many occasions. It was stressful. We also got home at five since I got out at four but she would be eating right away and going down for the night. I barely spent any time with her.

Now I am working a few nights a week as an assistant soccer coach. I love working with kids and being active. It's great for me. I have to drive a bit and the pay isn't great but I have fun.

"It's going well. I wish I could work from home but that seems far-fetched.."

Ellie was helpful in finding work from home jobs but none of them were the right fit. I applied to a dozen work from home jobs but never got a call back despite reaching out. My qualifications weren't on point but at the moment I'm content.

"That's good! I feel every mom wants to be home with their kids. How are you and Dean doing? Is his master's almost done?"

Sookie is seven months old which means he has two months left of his first course in his master's course. She has had her helmet for a month which was costly. Insurance doesn't cover it even if it's for a medical reason. We can file to dispute it but that appeal can take months. I don't have much fight left in me and just want Sookie's medical needs to be in the past. She is doing amazingly well and I'm hopeful that nothing else will arise.

Beth and Ellie made a GoFundMe page to help with Sookie's medical bills as I kept paying them off with my credit card and the debt kept increasing. I realized if I kept doing that, I would reach the max. Our friends and family supported us so much that we received more than enough for me to pay off our debt and set up a savings account for Sookie.

"We are doing good. We have our disagreements still but I think that's going to happen regardless. We are two different people with different views but with the same end goal. With me being home during the day with Sookie, he tends to listen to what I have to say. When I work Saturdays it's more of a struggle for us. We will get through it, though. His master's course has two more months left and hopefully I will see more of him then. He works too hard and I hate it."

"He always has worked hard. I've never seen him sit still for more than two minutes."

I chuckle. That is an accurate statement about Dean. "So true. Sookie is taking after him too. She rarely is still now. She is either rolling or wanting to stand. She does an army crawl but I haven't seen her on her hands and knees yet."

"Roland is crawling everywhere. He tries to get past the gate we have on our stairs."

Hearing this doesn't cause an ache in my heart like it did during Thanksgiving. I still have my moments when I look at other babies and wish Sookie would do that skill but I know she will get it. Sookie has shown me how determined she is. I have never seen a hard-working baby before her. It warms my heart how much effort she puts in to better herself.

"Yea, Holly is amazing with Sookie during our sessions. I know it's all Sookie but Holly is another encouraging adult whom Sookie loves. It will be sad when Sookie turns three and her session ends. I can't believe how old our babies are getting."

I get nostalgic thinking of how far Sookie has come. She has started talking a lot as well as blowing her raspberries. Also, when I leave the living room, she will be in a different spot when I get back. Before her surgery, she would be in the same spot just looking up at the ceiling.

"You seem happier. Sometimes when we used to text you sounded upset or anxious."

"Yea, I definitely was. I've started finding a balance except when Sookie doesn't nap, and I don't get my me time, but I try to deal. If Dean is home my emotions sometimes get the best of me. I just try to breathe which is hard at times but c'est la vie."

"Yea, I hear you. It's hard for me, too, at times. My emotions get the best of me but I'm almost done breastfeeding. Now I just pump if I need to but I haven't had to yet today. Maybe you should think of stopping, too."

I have thought about it but now I'm pumping three times a day and it's not as bad. When Sookie has her appointments, it can be stressful but I bring my Momcozy if I need to. It doesn't always work though and I end up pumping later than anticipated but it doesn't bother me as much as it used to.

"I have thought about stopping but I don't mind it. I think I'm going to go down to two pumps and stay there for a while. I can see myself doing that for a long time especially if my morning pump stays at five." I've found a rhythm to my schedule. It took me seven month, but I'm finally content with pumping.
"Good for you. I found it to be too stressful since my milk supply was so low."

"Yea, my friend Kristin pumped for a couple months once her boy was born but once three months hit she dried up. She actually was the one who gave me her pumping bra. It's been a lifesaver."

"I bet. I hated pumping. Just being attached to a pump made me feel trapped."

"Yea, I get that. When Sookie spits up while I'm pumping I have to lean over to wipe it up. I know I at least get all my milk out." I laugh. "But I'm doing better with everything. I can't wait to go hiking with Sookie. Dean and I will put the hiking gear that you guys gave us at Christmas for Sookie to good use."

"Yay! I can't wait. We should go hiking together!"

We always say this and we also say how hard it is to travel with a baby. Dean and I are starting with hikes close to home so we don't have to worry too much about bottles. Luckily, Sookie has been using formula since birth. I have always said everything happens for a reason.

Sookie came into my life to not only make it better but to make me a better person. I have certainly had a lot of downs but Dean has been amazingly patient. I am thankful to have him in my life because if I was alone I would be lost. Sookie's Down syndrome doesn't show and she will be seen once a year for her heart after she is a year old, at least for now. I've always been an impatient person which is why I'm waiting for her teeth to show but I'm trying my hardest to go with the flow.

Dean is better at it so I try to match him. No one can match Dean with anything and I mean that in a good way. We still have our quarrels but I love them. It makes us, us. All I care about is him being an excellent father to Sookie which he succeeds at with flying colors. I know Sookie has her whole life ahead of her and there will be so many experiences to enjoy as a family.

Sookie came into this world with a huge performance and she sure knows how to steal the show. I may need to go onto the sidelines and let her be the star that I know she is.

We both have come a far way and I am proud of both of us. I know we aren't perfect, no one is, no family is. I have come to terms with a lot within the past seven months and know there will be more to deal with. Sookie has shown us what she is capable of and I'm interested to see what is in store for our future.

I am enough.

Acknowledgments

I started writing this when my daughter was two months old. It was a way for me to go through all the emotions I was facing. Writing our journey was extremely therapeutic and I hope this story resonates with you.

I wanted to write this for all the new mama's or mama's going through a lot. Being a mother is hard, rewarding work. I wouldn't change being a mom at all. Watching my daughter grow is amazing to see. This story is to let you know that your feelings are validated. A lot of my anxiety stemmed from pumping and here I am. I pumped for eleven months. The emotions we go through due to breastfeeding, is a lot.

I want to thank Ben, my husband. You have always stuck by me and listened to me. I may have been a mess these past eleven months but you stayed as calm as you could for me. The things we have gone through were a lot. We always come out stronger.

Lynn. The insane amount of text messages I have sent you is, well, a lot. You have been such an amazing sister-in-law, and friend, during such a trying time in my life. I will eternally be grateful for you. You truly have been a godsend.

To my family and friends. You have always supported me when it comes to writing. I always second guess myself, yet you always stand by me. You tell me the hard things I have to hear when I don't want to hear it, but I need to hear it. If it wasn't for you, I wouldn't be where I am today.

To my bookstagram friends, especially Brittany and Allie. You two have always cheered me on and were so happy to want to read this. I'm happy I made a book account and met you two. There are so many other people on Instagram that have been supportive through my daughter's surgery. I will forever be grateful for all my friendships with each, and every one, of you.

Lastly, my readers. I write to hopefully have my work resonate with you. I hope this book makes another mom feel less alone in her journey. I hope this book makes a parent know you are doing everything you can. I hope this book makes you know you are an amazing person even when you feel down.

Thank you to everyone who helped me through this journey. This isn't the end for me, or my daughter.

Made in the USA
Monee, IL
09 May 2023

33358981R00162